SECOND CHANCES

CHANCES

a novel by

Greg Coppa

Second Chances. Copyright © 2018 Greg Coppa. Produced and printed by Stillwater River Publications. All rights reserved. Written and produced in the United States of America. This book may not be reproduced or sold in any form without the expressed, written permission of the authors and publisher.

Visit our website at www.StillwaterPress.com for more information.
First Stillwater River Publications Edition

Library of Congress Control Number: 2018939393

ISBN-13: 978-1-946300-52-2
ISBN-10: 1-946300-52-7

1 2 3 4 5 6 7 8 9 10

Written by Greg Coppa
Cover design by Nathanael Vinbury. Book design by Tim Murphy
Published by Stillwater River Publications, Glocester, RI, USA.
This book was set in Bodoni 72 Oldstyle and Minion Pro.

Publisher's Cataloging-In-Publication Data
(Prepared by The Donohue Group, Inc.)

Names: Coppa, Greg.
Title: Second chances : a novel / by Greg Coppa.
Description: First Stillwater River Publications edition. | Glocester, RI,
    USA : Stillwater River Publications, [2018]
Identifiers: ISBN 9781946300522 | ISBN 1946300527
Subjects: LCSH: Boats and boating–Fiction. | Hurricanes–United States
    Virgin Islands–Saint Thomas (Island)–Fiction. | Self-realization–Fic
    tion. | Survival–Fiction. | Saint Thomas (United States Virgin Islands :
    Island)–Fiction. | Narragansett Bay (R.I.)–Fiction. | LCGFT: Sea fiction.
Classification: LCC PS3603.O657 S43 2018 | DDC 813/.6–dc23

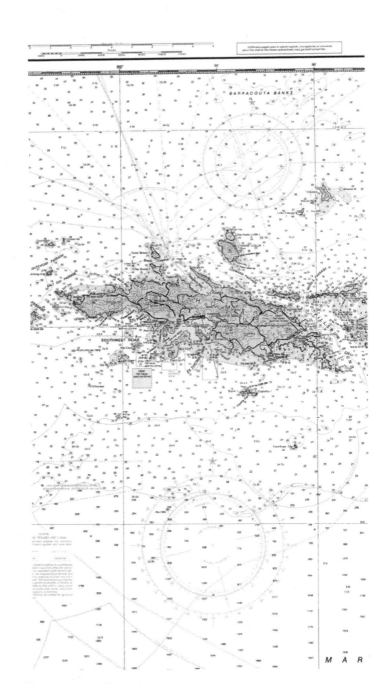

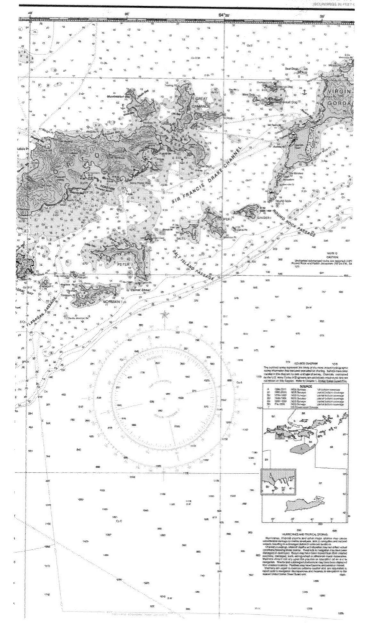

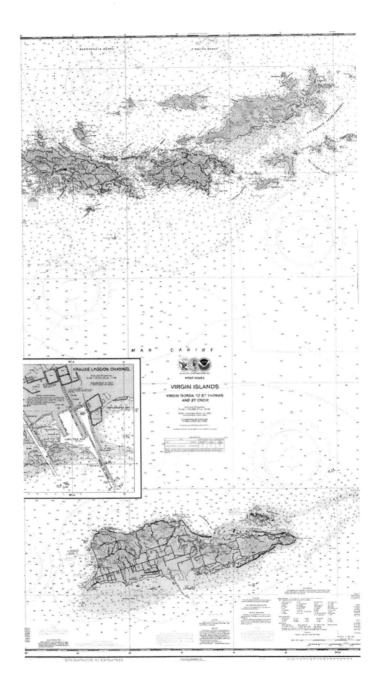

CHAPTER ONE

Constellation Yacht Charter
Basin St. Thomas, USVI
May 4, 2002

JJ HAD JUST FINISHED WORKING ON THE LAST EN-
GINE. THE sweat ran freely down his ebony face as
he came up into the relatively cool air of the cockpit.
The charter boat season in St. Thomas was basically over.
A few boats would be available throughout the summer
months, but most would be cleaned up, serviced like this
one and locked up until the tourist season got underway
again in December.

A couple or three of the luxury yachts would be sent
up to the New England coast for the lucrative summer
cruising season there. They would ply the waters from
Newport to Nantucket and Martha's Vineyard, so that the
rich and famous people who chartered them could meet
and be seen with other rich and famous people.

JJ's goal was to be among the crew selected for one of
the yacht delivery trips. If he stayed in St. Thomas again
during the slow summer season, he would squander most
of his hard earned money and have little to show for it. It
happened to him twice before. Just living on a Caribbean
island was costly enough. But the daily expense for what
most young island men considered bare necessities —

cigarettes, drinks, recreational drugs and restaurant meals, was enough to drain anyone's pocket book. The thought of the amount of money he had wasted made JJ feel guilty that he had not sent more home to his mother and sisters back in Port-de-Paix.

JJ used a rag to wipe a little engine oil off his hands before he touched the freshly dressed, honey colored teak or the recently waxed fiberglass and made more work for himself. He locked up the boat and hopped onto the floating dock. As he walked up the ramp he saw the beat-up company Jeep, with Rick at the wheel, pull into the boatyard and park by the dinghy dock.

All the dinghies had seen better days. They had been salvaged from one place or another and made serviceable in typical island fashion. JJ's little skiff was found off Conch Shell Beach under 10 feet of water. It was pretty encrusted with marine growth when JJ had spotted it while diving with a family that had chartered one of Constellation's yachts. But JJ knew that the crack along the chine, probably responsible for the small boat's sinking, could be easily repaired with a quart of resin and a little fiberglass cloth skimmed from the Constellation Yacht Charters repair shop, part of the Fiddler Crab Cove compound where he worked.

His buddy, Rick "Skip" Thornton, helped him bring the rowboat ashore where they cleaned it up a bit and made a temporary patch with rags before towing it back to the compound. There they did a solid repair job and even put on a nice teak rub rail made from pieces of wood selected from the scrap bin. A couple of used bronze oarlock sockets were installed and JJ cut down one of a pair of mismatched oars to make them almost match. The result was that JJ had a harbor-worthy vessel to get him out to the old Swedish fishing boat moored in Charlotte Amalie that he, Rick and Jimmy called home.

"I finished up *Pleiades*, Rick. Everything is set for next season. And that stuffing box? It just needed tightening... any word yet about going north?" JJ asked Rick about "going north" at least three times a day. "Not yet. Don't worry JJ, we'll get you up there one way or another!" But JJ was worried. He had been on St. Thomas for going on three years, since he had jumped ship off an inter-island rust bucket on which he had been a stowaway. He was in St. Thomas illegally, without papers of any sort, and he was afraid that sooner or later he would be pulled in by the authorities for some minor infraction and his plan would unravel. Then it would be back to Haiti, again. JJ knew that on a small island like St. Thomas, no secret remained a secret forever and every day he worried a little about that.

Jean Jacques Dessalines, aka JJ, was named after a Haitian slave who had helped overthrow the French colonial government and then installed himself as Emperor of the realm. If JJ seemed paranoid about being sent back to Haiti, he could be forgiven. Twice he had left the island with his family and extended family aboard overcrowded fishing boats bound for a new life in Florida; and twice the American Coast Guard had "rescued" the refugees and returned them to their squalor. JJ's father died on the last voyage when the prop of their fishing boat fouled a submerged net only miles off of Key Biscayne. Ramon dove overboard with a knife to attempt to cut away the net. He simply never came to the surface and his body was never recovered.

Day-trippers in cigarette boats blasted past the drifting fishing boat, not even stopping for a moment as they sped off for a day trip to Bimini. But they did hail the Coast Guard and that was that. The Coast Guard cutter brought all the Haitians to shore in Miami to query them before repatriation. Though the Coast Guardsmen saw nothing special about their Miami surroundings, the Haitians looked upon them with awe. What they had only seen before on satellite TV was to them, now, a true representation. The city just oozed wealth. The cars were all new and shiny, the buildings were tall and modern, the streets were neat and clean and the people were dressed casually, but well. A native born American would dispute this rose tinted view of Miami, but of course, all is relative. In any case, the brief view of American affluence was enough to make JJ vow that he would return to America someday and stay.

Five years later JJ jumped from a small coastal freighter one night as it departed St. Thomas. St. Thomas wasn't mainland USA, but it was a towhold for JJ who knew that the opportunity to get on any American soil might not soon come again. At first he swam steadily and confidently back towards the shore lights of Charlotte Amalie. His small nylon backpack provided him some additional buoyancy. It contained all he possessed in zip log plastic bags—a few American dollars, shoes, a shirt, and a pair of shorts.

But JJ had both underestimated the distance to safety and overestimated his strength, a bad combination on the water. Fortunately for him, when he was near total exhaustion and in actual danger of drowning, he literally bumped into the moored *Thor*, which was trailing a couple of dinghies. He latched onto one of the little boats and waited while he caught his breath. At this point, his interest in not drowning took priority over his wish to remain undiscovered as he entered St. Thomas. His breathing was labored and loud and it attracted the attention of Jimmy Fox who was on *Thor's* aft deck having a smoke.

"Who the hell are you and what the hell are you doing down there?"

Between gasps JJ blurted out: "Je m'appelle Jean Jacques..." That was all Jimmy would hear before a large tugboat wake washed over JJ and separated him from his tenuous hand hold on the dinghy. JJ's stomach and lungs filled up with water, as he was still taking in great gulps of air when he was surprised by both Jimmy and the wake. Bobbing to the surface, he spit out some water, vomited, passed out and began to sink, all in rapid succession.

"Oh, shit!! Rick, come up here, now!" Jimmy yelled down *Thor's* open salon hatch. Diving into the clear, but dark water, Jimmy somehow latched on to JJ and brought him to the surface near the stern of the boat where Rick awaited. Rick pull JJ out of the water and rolled him onto *Thor's* swim platform which was attached to the transom. JJ looked pretty dead. Rick was ashamed to admit to himself, even a couple of years later, that he never considered giving JJ mouth-to-mouth resuscitation at the time. But he did roll JJ closer to the transom, so that his body would not fall back into the water and that simple action apparently initiated some more vomiting and a cycle of violent coughing which may have actually saved JJ's life.

Jimmy and Rick cleaned up JJ and brought him aboard *Thor*. He looked pretty pathetic and he began to cry like a baby right there on the deck. He sobbed loudly and didn't look or sound like he was ever going to stop. Though Jimmy and Rick were not particularly sensitive types, they were moved by this abject display of despondency and dejection and they just let it run its course. A few hours later Rick, Jimmy and the newly introduced JJ sat at the table in the main salon drinking coffee heavily laced with rum. In half decent English with a pleasant French accent, JJ related his life story. He and his family had apparently experienced more than their share of poverty, illness, abuse and grief. JJ concluded by tearfully begging them not to turn him in to the "gendarmes." Whether the final decision to let JJ stay aboard *Thor* for awhile was based on altruism or a rum induced clouding of their judgment will never be known. But it can be said that neither Rick, nor Jimmy ever regretted their decision to grant JJ asylum on behalf of the US Government. Rick and Jimmy both had had serious challenges of their own while growing up. Each of them knew of no living relatives and each had experienced a childhood characterized by much more sadness and pain than happiness and fun. On some subconscious level they could identify with JJ and it was easy for them to cut him a little slack.

The three got along very well together from the outset. JJ was bright, outgoing, hardworking, and cheerful. He made Rick and Jimmy laugh and they were touched by his naiveté. From the day after JJ's rescue it had become a joint Rick/Jimmy venture to Americanize JJ. Jimmy suggested that they confine JJ to the boat for a few days for orientation because he would stand out like a sore thumb in his present state. They had JJ watch the local news on TV, listen to the local radio stations and read every old Time, Sail, Playboy and newspaper on board. JJ had a pretty good command of English, but he would never pass for someone who had been on St. Thomas for any length of time. That meant he would be asked questions and that meant he would get himself in trouble. But JJ was literate and smart and that combination allowed him to absorb huge amounts of information each day, even when he was alone aboard Thor and Jimmy and Rick were working ashore. JJ showed his appreciation by bringing Thor to a level of neatness and cleanliness she had not known for years. The old teak decks of the former Scandinavian fishing vessel were sanded and oiled so that they had that beautiful color of nicely tanned women in travel brochure pictures. The brass porthole fixtures were brightly polished. The bronze cleats and hardware were also cleaned up, though they did not shine with the same intensity as brass. JJ even asked Rick to bring "home" some polyurethane from the paint locker at Constellation Yacht Charters so that he could restore the interior and exterior brightwork. As he worked at this and that, JJ would sing along with the golden oldies that he listened to on the radio. He was determined to become an American, through and through.

JJ also turned out to be a good cook. He could prepare exotic French and Creole fare or turn an ordinary grouper filet into something special. At dinner one night Jimmy mentioned that it would be easy for him to get JJ a job as a cook. Jimmy was a bartender and had a lot of connections in the local pubs and restaurants. And Rick said that they always needed people to work at the boat basin to keep the yachts in shape for the tourists. JJ was still a bit insecure, so a job where he drew the least attention was what he wanted and after a week aboard Thor Rick took him ashore to do boat maintenance with him at Constellation.

Constellation Yacht Charters managed a fleet of 17 yachts ranging in length from 32 to 48 feet. Most were sailing vessels, but there were also a couple of luxury trawler designs built in Hong Kong. The boats were actually owned by rich American doctors, lawyers and professionals who used them as tax shelters and who might even sail on them once a year. Expenses could be written off by the investors but the biggest benefit was that they could casually mention at cocktail parties that they owned yachts which they kept in the Caribbean.

If everything went as planned, the notes on the boats held by Constellation would be paid off by those who chartered the vessels. If not, the investors would make up the difference. Constellation also profited handsomely from generous management fees it collected for soliciting charters and maintaining the boats. What a scam! But everybody seemed happy with the scam for the time being.

At first JJ felt like everyone was staring at him and wondering who he was as he rode in Constellation's Jeep or walked through town. But after a few days he realized that nobody cared who he was or suspected that he was anything but a local guy who worked on the boats. JJ settled into a nice routine with Rick who taught him nautical terms and how to do simple engine checks and mechanical adjustments. Rick took him out in the yachts when they had to test a repair or check how a new sail looked; JJ caught on to the basics of motoring and sailing very quickly to the point where Rick used him as a mate for charters. Most of the skippers and other crew members who had worked for Constellation during the winter had moved on to Annapolis and New England already, so JJ had plenty of mate jobs now, though they were quickly declining in frequency.

JJ's pleasant nature and urge to please the paying customers earned JJ nice tips, especially from the occasional French speaking charterers. Rick also paid him in cash, a common practice on the resort islands, which have vast underground economies. It wasn't long after JJ began working with Rick that he had accumulated more money than anyone in Port-de-Paix possessed, though in all honesty that didn't mean much to anyone but JJ.

JJ learned about the Island and neighboring St. John while he sailed and took people to scenic coves for snorkeling or to secluded beaches. He rode with Jimmy and Rick everywhere and learned all the roads, streets and stores. In a surprisingly short time people in Jimmy and Rick's circle were casually saying "Hey JJ!" Then he began making his own contacts at laundromats, drugstores, and bars. Due to the transient nature of the people who worked the service jobs on the Island, JJ was able to assimilate surprisingly quickly, though he was never entirely comfortable with his new identity.

One of the first things JJ asked Jimmy to help him with after his rescue was mailing a letter to his mother, Angelique, and to his younger sisters. They would all be very worried about him. In the letter he related his adventures to a degree, but he changed the story a bit so that it would sound less dangerous than it actually had been. He also made his present situation sound more secure than he felt that it was. There was no point in making his poor mother anxious. She had already known more than her share of anxiety and sadness.

Jimmy showed JJ how to wire money and buy travelers checks to send to Haiti. Though the dollar amounts sent were small, they made a tremendous difference to his family and it made JJ feel good to know that he was a help to them.

JJ had never had an opportunity to make much money in Port-de-Paix. He had done a little fishing, harvested cane, rolled cigars but that was about the extent of his work experience. The lack of opportunity to work was what motivated JJ and so many fellow islanders to take such extreme chances to leave Haiti.

Once Rick took JJ to buy some new clothes in a K-MART. He later told Jimmy how JJ gently felt the fabric of the shirts and pants like he was smoothing the fur of a little lap dog. Then he would look at the price tags and take out his new wallet, awkwardly, like a six year old might, and count the money to make sure he had enough to make the purchase. When he left the store he was smiling. And when JJ smiled or laughed one could not help but notice how handsome he was. He had teeth which a movie star would envy and his skin was smooth with no imperfections. His curly hair was close cropped and, all in all, he looked intelligent, friendly and people who did not know him seem compelled to greet him, even passers-by, as if they did.

The months and seasons, such as they were, rolled right along for the three men on St. Thomas. The daily routine did not vary much. They worked, returned to Thor for a nap and dinner, and then went ashore to meet friends or have a drink. Jimmy and Rick had a more or less unbroken stream of one night stands drawn from the continual parade of women who came to the island aboard cruise ships or who stayed at the resort hotels. Both men were good looking, trim, well-spoken and polite. Jimmy had brown hair and blue eyes and Rick was a sun-bleached blond with hazel-brown eyes. It always worked out that if a woman were not drawn to one of them, she would certainly be drawn to the other. Occasionally, the young ladies ended up aboard Thor which would be a memorable evening for them, for all the usual reasons and for the uniqueness of the setting, too. About these affairs JJ was non-judgmental and during them he was unobtrusive.

JJ, himself, never dated. He was comfortable enough to flirt a bit, but he was afraid perhaps to let down his guard for anyone other than Jimmy or Rick. He enjoyed going out with a group of people, though, to someone's place for a cookout or to a beach party.

In late summer, when work was slow, the three men caught up on *Thor's* maintenance. Jimmy taught JJ a lot about engines at every opportunity, like when they had to rebuild *Thor's* ancient Swedish-built electrical generator. And Rick showed him how to do wooden hull repairs when it was necessary to haul Thor out to replace some rotten planks. *Thor's* hull was about 60 years old and made of some Scandinavian wood that the island ship carpenters had not yet been able to identify. The wood contained a natural resin that largely repelled the usual worms that cause the demise of so many wooden boats in the tropics.

For the hull repairs, which required facilities which were usually cost prohibitive, it was necessary to barter some alcohol and a little marijuana and coke. The latter two items were provided by the resourceful Jimmy, who dabbled in drug sales. He was not personally a big drug user, but occasionally he bought a little extra stuff to defray his expenses, make a little spending money, or play a little *quid pro quo*. Jimmy was a bit of a wheeler-dealer and Rick always said that someday he could make a fortune selling used cars.

Repairing Thor necessitated hauling her out with a heavy-duty lift and blocking her up for a few days. When the yard managers of the island shipyards took time off during the summer to visit the mainland, their facilities naturally became the personal property of those workers they left behind. You never knew what short-term enterprise would spring up at the whim of the cagey caretakers. Boats were hauled for friends or for a little quick cash. Furniture was made in the woodshops. Cars were spray painted with leftover paints in the paint bays meant for boats. Engines for boats and autos were rebuilt. Aluminum towers were welded for fishing boats. And so on. One year a cash strapped friend of Jimmy's even made a half-dozen coffins out of odds and ends of mahogany for a local undertaker. As long as the boatyards basically looked as they did before the managers left and not too much stock appeared to be missing, the widespread entrepreneurship of the hired help was tolerated. Indeed, without the money earned or saved by the island entrepreneurs, many would not be able to afford to stay on the island.

While *Thor* was blocked up for repairs, her hull was pressure washed clean and allowed to dry. After the new planks were fastened and caulked the bottom was given a heavy coat of antifouling paint. The latter was prepared by taking all the partially full cans of antifouling paint that were left over in the paint shed from various bottom paint jobs during the last year and pouring the contents into two five gallon plastic pails. The stirred mixture truly was an ugly color, but it had a good copper content and would convey a good measure of protection to the old wooden hull against barnacles, worms and seaweed.

On the surface, it appeared that Rick, Jimmy and JJ were content. But that was not totally true. There were many aspects to their lifestyles that were agreeable, to be sure. However, all three men were in their early thirties. And while much is made of the ticking of women's biological clocks, men have such clocks, too, although they run at a different pace and toll for different needs.

Although each of the three men had a vague feeling that it was time to move on, to accomplish more, and to "grow up," JJ was the only one actively seeking to permanently leave St. Thomas. But his ability to do so was dependent on the two others. If Jimmy and Rick did a yacht delivery, he would go with them. Once on the mainland he would try to make his way to the small Haitian community in New York City. He had some cousins in New York and they had been in contact with each other by mail and phone. They would help set JJ up with a job, a place to live, and a new identity. If things worked out, perhaps JJ could even someday bring all his family to America, too! If not, he could at least provide them with financial advantages back in Haiti.

After almost two years on St. Thomas, JJ was ready to leave. He now had marine trade skills which were transferable to a variety of other hands-on areas. He had experience to put on a resume and an American residence, of sorts, that he could document. He spoke better English than was spoken by three quarters of New York City residents. And JJ was an excellent conversationalist, having devoured books at the local library and voraciously read any newspapers and magazines he would come across. He even read the *New Yorker*, so convinced he was that he would eventually end up in the Big Apple and so determined he was not to appear too unsophisticated. JJ did not realize how desirable an employee he would be in New York. With his drive, perseverance, honesty and intelligence he would find work quickly and advance rapidly. All he needed was to get to the city! "Let me check the mail, JJ and we'll go out to *Thor* together." Rick unlocked the door to Constellation's offices which were part of the two acre, neat complex which also contained a commissary, showers, changing rooms, storage lockers, a well equipped work shed and two guest cottages.

Just inside was a basket into which fell the mail from a slot in the wall. There was a small pile, mostly junk mail, as usual. Rick did a quick sort, separating out the handful of first class pieces. There was a thank-you note addressed to him from Beverly, a recent "acquaintance." She had included a nice photo of the two of them at Dolphin Cove which Rick rotated slightly to get a better viewing angle. She sure looked fetching in her pink bikini! She mentioned that she hoped to come again to St. Thomas next April. Rick kind of hoped she did, too. Then there were assorted bills. He put them in the "in" box. When the box was full, or at the end of the month, he would pay whatever was in there. This was one of his responsibilities as "assistant manager of operations" while the actual manager was away which was about seven months of the year.

As Rick prepared to lock up he heard a faint "beep." He looked around and saw that it had come from the fax machine. It was out of paper. The one fax page that had been printed out was a cover page indicating that four more pages would follow. Rick grabbed a handful of pieces of paper and inserted them into the paper holder. The fax clicked, blinked and whirred before printing out the remaining messages from memory.

Constellation's home office in Annapolis had sent some instructions, warranty information for a radio and information about two charter parties that would be arriving in early July. "Boy, things are going to be pretty dead around here this summer if that's all we have, so far," thought Rick. The hand written message on the last page affirmed his assessment.

```
Rick
We have decided not to bring any boats up
from St. Thomas in mid-May as we thought
we would. Our clientele has been somewhat
negatively affected by 9/11 and our advance
bookings are not where we had hoped they
would be at this time. Just keep the boats
and facilities maintained. Pete will proba-
bly be down to check on things for the own-
ers next month, but I will give you a heads
up on that. Your job is secure!!! I am sure
business will bounce back for next season.
```

Rick folded Phil's message and put it in his pocket. He would show it to JJ a little later after they had a few drinks on *Thor's* aft deck. Perhaps rum and a nice sunset would soften the blow.

CHAPTER TWO

LTHOUGH RICKY GREW UP IN A RUNDOWN SUBURB
of LA, he never felt that he was a Californian. Mayfield was merely the place that his mother had fled
to when she left Rhode Island and Ricky, being a child,
had no choice but to live there with her. Leah used to say
that Mayfield was just about as far away as you could be
from Rhode Island and still be in the lower 48 states and
that was just fine with her.

But if Ricky's mom didn't miss Rhode Island, Ricky
surely did. He often mused, even as an adult, that his first
nine years of life there were his best; his happiest memories were of sailing with his mother and grandfather in a
sheltered cove close to an old New England seaport town.
He could still clearly see in his mind's eye the Colonial
era church spire that his grandfather, John Wilcox, taught
him to use as a landmark for guiding their little homebuilt
sailboat safely past a sandbar. How Rick loved and missed
that boat and those carefree golden summer days!

There was always something to do with Gramps or
Mom in Rhode Island. Sometimes they would go clam-
ming. At low tide the three of them would row out to a

mud flat with clam rakes and wire baskets. Ricky's job was to throw a stone up high up in the air, which when it landed with a "plop," would startle the clams into shooting up geysers of water about a foot high. Once the clam hideout was detected the three of them would all set upon it with clam rakes and pitch forks. They would dig around the little holes in the mud left by the geysers, so as not to stab or crush any of the clams. After a big hole filled with soupy mud was developed, they would sit on their haunches and use their hands to feel around the edges and bottom of it. The plump clams would be plucked from the sometimes sulfurous smelling mud and would usually register their protest at being caught with a last strong squirt which resembled a stream of pee.

Gramps was Ricky's only male role model. Ricky never knew his father who was killed during a Viet Cong mortar attack on his firebase in the Central Highlands of Vietnam. Gerald Thornton had not been in Vietnam for three whole weeks when he was killed in 1970. Ricky was born six months later.

Rick's mother did not tell him the whole story about his father. This was too bad; because in later life Rick might have thought more kindly of her if he knew the truth. Leah never mentioned that Gerry Thornton had not married her. Nor did she mention that she didn't even find out that she was pregnant until Gerry was about to embark from San Francisco to the Philippines and then to Vietnam. If Gerry received the letter she had sent to him about her pregnant state, Leah never knew. It never came back to her, nor did a reply.

There was no letter from Gerry's commanding officer to Leah explaining the circumstances of Gerry's death, such as a wife would normally have received. And Gerry was so new to his patrol that he probably never told anybody about Leah, so nobody got in touch with her regarding his last days or his final thoughts.

The sad truth, which Leah could never quite bring herself to admit, was that Gerry and she had simply had a very quick fling. There was no memorable romance. There were no deep discussions about a future together. There were no exchanges of tokens of affection. Gerry was merely a high school friend who had graduated with Leah the previous June and who had come home on leave for two weeks prior to reporting for duty in San Francisco. He was in his uniform looking very handsome when they ran into each other outside the drugstore in town. He asked her out miniature golfing one night and to a drive-in theatre another. And that was the entire extent of their relationship.

At Gerry's wake Leah heard from a tearful Kathy Clark, another high school classmate, that she was glad she had seen Gerry when he was home and that they had had a little fun together. They had gone miniature golfing and to a drive-in movie.

Of course, after the baby was born there was nothing for Leah to do but stay home with her single father, her mother having died in a Labor Day automobile accident when Leah was only twelve. Leah earned minimum wage as a drugstore cashier and qualified for no death benefits or insurance. She never told Gerry's parents about their grandson and a couple of years after Gerry's death they moved away to Florida, not being able to deal any longer with memories of their only child which surfaced all too easily for them in the small town. Tragically, but perhaps mercifully, they were killed shortly after arriving in Florida when a tornado picked up their mobile home, along with them, and deposited it in a twisted heap a few hundred feet away.

Leah Wilcox didn't tell John Wilcox who Ricky's father was for a long time. But he knew. Though John truly felt anguish for his daughter he felt anger, too, that she had complicated his life as well as hers. The anger manifested itself as often as the anguish and their relationship after the baby was born could only be termed as fragile.

Nevertheless, after Ricky's birth there were many good times at the Wilcox residence which had been described by some neighbors as an "elegantly shabby" Cape Cod cottage on the water. A baby can soften even a crotchety old man's heart and little Ricky did just that. In a short time John found himself bringing home crib toys; and he actually enjoyed babysitting while Leah worked. In a little shed behind the cottage used as a workshop, John built a sled with a little chair on it for Ricky's first Christmas. Leah would pull the sled with its bent oak runners, into town for grocery shopping before the snow was cleared from the sidewalks. Everybody would stop Leah to tell her what a beautiful boy Ricky was as he peered out from his sled-borne blanket nest. A few old cronies would study his features, rather carefully too, hoping to discern a clue as to who the boy's father might be.

After the sled project was finished, John set about making a little crib and bureau out of cherry wood from a tree that had fallen in the yard a few years before in a storm. John had thought that he might make a grandfather's clock with the wood one day. But when he decided to make the crib it was with the full and sudden realization that he was now a grandfather and Ricky was his grandson. Until that moment he had only thought of Ricky as being his daughter's child.

The strain of being a single mother weighed heavily on Leah. She worked hard, but knew without her father's help she could never make it on her own financially. She was only earning $1.45 an hour and she could not believe how expensive things were. She had never had to care about such matters before and the thought of being responsible for another person's life for the next 18 years frightened her terribly. Part of the problem was that she felt so isolated, especially since her relationship with her father had changed. All her good friends from high school had gone off to college, something that she had once hoped to do, and when they returned she found that they had little in common. Leah wanted to talk about first steps and children's books and they wanted to talk about the guys they met at a war protest rally in Washington, DC.

Life does go on and eventually Leah became more comfortable with herself. She took Ricky to story hour at the library, the playground, the zoo and she networked with a few of the other young mothers. She made some extra money doing day care and she swapped babysitting time so that she could get out a little bit. Although Leah was attractive, intelligent and well spoken she never dated. She actively shied away from men. She was afraid that one thing would lead to another and she had already been down that lane. In any case it wasn't like she was inundated by requests to go out. At that time and in that place there just were not a whole lot of men who wanted to get involved with a situation like hers.

To reduce anxiety, Leah began to drink a little wine. And some nights she resorted to a shot glass of Christian Brothers Brandy, purloined from her father's liquor cabinet, to help her to get to sleep. At the time she simply viewed alcohol as the poor man's all-purpose, non-prescription medicine. But throughout Ricky's early childhood, Leah's anxiety level remained high and her tendency toward sleepless nights increased. The fact was that there was plenty for her to worry about and no easy or immediate solution to her problems on the horizon. Little by little she became alcohol dependent, beginning and ending each day with a drink.

When Ricky's was nearly seven years old, Gramps began building a 12' tender in his shed. He asked Ricky if he would help with the rowboat, which he said that a customer wanted for the following boating season. It was agreed that Ricky would be paid twenty-five cents an hour for his effort when the owner paid Gramps for the finished product. Ricky actually was a big help. He showed a lot of ability with tools even at that young age. To a great degree this was due to Gramps, who had fostered in Ricky an interest in making and fixing things. One of their first joint projects was to construct a wooden toolbox. Ricky was very proud of that first toolbox. When it was finished, Gramps crudely carved on the side of it: "RICKY + GRAMPS 1977."

Gramps helped stock the toolbox with assorted tools. Some of the them were new, but some were better than new-they were old. Gramps gave Ricky rasps, wooden handled screwdrivers, braces and wrenches that were once used by his great grandfather Wilcox. Ricky used the tools alongside Gramps as they set ribs, fastened planks, bunged holes and attached hardware. Not a piece of wood for the boat had been bought, a point that Gramps mentioned to Ricky, no more than a hundred times. Gramps considered himself to be one of Rhode Island's last real "Swamp Yankees," a breed of legendary ingenuity and frugality. As a "Swamper" Gramps couldn't help but pick up promising pieces of driftwood from a beach or drag home the limbs of white oak trees that he came across by the side of the road. Constitutionally, he could no more resist salvaging things than an ant could resist licking a drop of honey it had fortuitously come upon.

Through the fall and winter months the boat slowly took shape with an hour of work put in here and there. Ricky and Gramps steam bent the white oak into a keel and ribs; the mahogany drift-wood was transformed into hull planking and the scrap teak was fashioned into seats. While cutting, drilling and sanding the teak, oak, and mahogany Ricky learned to recognize and savor the pleasant and distinctive scents of each type of wood. They would forever be etched into his sensory memory.

As young as he was, Ricky appreciated being able to see the progress made each day and trying to imagine what the boat would look like with the completion of the next step. With its "wineglass" transom of varnished mahogany and its graceful lines, the finished classic tender was truly a beautiful sight to behold, much classier than the new fiberglass boats, which were quickly displacing the wooden ones at that time.

Finally, one June day, when the glossy white enamel on the topsides was dry to the touch, Leah, Gramps and Ricky gently picked the boat up and settled it down on a small boat trailer. They rolled the trailer outside so that the customer, who as of yet had not made an appearance, could transport it home. In the golden sunlight of early evening the trim craft looked even better to Ricky than it had in the workshop. Ricky liked everything about the boat. Even the faint residual odor of the enamel paint that he could detect as he ran his hands over the smooth varnished rub rails, was agreeable to him.

Ricky was about to ask Gramps if they could maybe just keep the boat or build an identical one that he could keep. But Ricky's train of thought was interrupted. "Time for bed young man," said Leah. "Tomorrow is your 8th birthday!"

It was the best birthday Ricky had ever had. Maybe the best he would ever have! When Ricky came down to the kitchen for breakfast there were blue and white paper streamers hanging from the ceiling light and fancy "Happy Birthday" signs strung in the doorframe and hung on the wall. There were two wrapped packages that were funny shaped and about six feet tall with his name on them. "Go ahead, open them," said Gramps. Ricky still possessed that inability to see the obvious, which God grants to young children to heighten their excitement on Christmas morning and on their birthdays. Until the paper was torn from the odd-looking gift packages, Ricky had no idea that he had been given a pair of oars. And until he saw the big blue ribbon wrapped around the rowboat he had no idea that the oars meant that the boat was his, as well!

What a summer followed! Gramps taught Ricky how to row and it wasn't long before Ricky, wearing a yellow buoyancy vest, was volunteering to row the several hundred yards into town for a loaf of bread, the newspaper, or a gallon of milk. Along with his mother he often rowed to the library, which had its own little dock. Sometimes his mother would ask to take over the oars. Ricky was surprised at how smoothly the boat glided through the water under her control. She laughed when he mentioned that and she told him that Gramps had taught her to row, too, when she was seven years old.

The peninsula on which the Wilcoxes lived was undergoing a transition in the mid-seventies. There were a handful of families, like the Wilcoxes, that had ties to their land going back more than a century. Their ancestors were boat builders, farmers or fishermen. These people were the "permanent" residents of Wampanoag Point, as the neighborhood was known. About fifty other families only came down for the summer. Most of them owned their simple, comfortable, unwinterized cottages, which were stocked with the old set of dishes, chipped mugs, worn silverware, and the saggy couch. A few folks rented, too. Lastly there were perhaps fifteen families which recently converted their summer places into year round houses. That number grew each year.

At the end of June, a family from Providence bought one of the old rental cottages across the street from the Wilcox house. Ricky overheard the real estate man tell Gramps that the newcomers had an eight year old, and that they planned to fix up the somewhat dilapidated place and live there full time. "What luck," thought Ricky. "Now I'll have someone to row with!"

When Ricky found out that the eight-year-old was named "Daisy" he was very disappointed. "THat must mean she's a girl," he told his mother. And, naturally, he was right. Ricky had no use for a girl and as far as he was concerned, it was a waste of a good house that she had to live there, right across the street from him. Daisy's arrival didn't change his sentiment, either. She was a FLaming red haired, freckle-faced, loudmouth. Ricky pointed out, with some truth, that you could always hear her talking, even when she was in her backyard, and she always seemed to be telling somebody to do something rather than asking them to do it. One morning when the water was so calm that the village reflected in it like a mirror, Gramps and Ricky were approaching the Wilcox dock in *Swamp Yankee* after picking up a newspaper. They heard Daisy contradicting her mother over one thing or another. "Someone ought to tell that free spirit that voices carry over water," said John with a chuckle.

Daisy and Ricky studiously avoided each other. Occasionally, when each thought that nobody would see them, they would push a window curtain aside to find out what the other was up to. To his disgust, Ricky saw Daisy place her Labrador retriever pup, wearing a baby's sunbonnet and looking real stupid, in a red wagon and begin pulling it down the street. This confirmed in him the chasm that existed between boys and girls. He merely shook his head as he pushed the curtain back in place. "Another waste," he thought, "of a perfectly good dog."

Daisy wasn't thrilled to be on Wampanoag Point, either. She liked her former house in the city and she liked her friends there, too. The new place looked like a dump and being a redhead she mentioned that fact to her parents quite a few times since they moved in. Her dad promised Daisy that he would have the house fixed up by Christmas and he patiently explained to her that it was better for them to own this house than rent the other one. But what do seven year olds care about matters like that? As for her impression of Ricky? What a geek! Strutting around with that toolbox of his and always doing something to his dumb boat. Who did he think he was? And the way he rowed around the harbor he was going to wear out his arms. It would serve the dope right, too!

In early August, the Bruno family invited a few neighbors from Providence, down for a day at the beach and a cookout. One side of Wampanoag Point faced the sheltered Wickford Harbor and the other side, facing the less sheltered Narragansett Bay had a pretty decent beach with a few low dunes, on which grew white and purple sea roses and wild sweet peas. About an hour before the people were due to arrive, Mrs. Bruno discovered that she had no eggs for a cake she was making and Mr. Bruno had taken their only car to the hardware store and who knew when he would be back? "Daisy, please go over to the Wilcoxes' and see if you can borrow a couple of eggs." Daisy protested, but Mrs. Bruno, a redhead herself, showed that she could raise her voice, too. "Janice Bruno!!! You go over there right now or you will spend the rest of the day in your room!"

Reluctantly, Daisy went over to the Wilcox house and knocked on the screen door. Leah greeted her, mentioning how cute she looked with bows in her hair. Daisy politely relayed her mother's need but unfortunately, Leah had no eggs. Daisy thanked her for looking anyway and began walking back down the front path to the road. "Daisy!" called Leah. "Ricky can row you in to Dunn's Market, if you would like. You'll have to wear a life preserver and get permission from your mom."

Daisy didn't want to go and Ricky didn't want to take her. It was very awkward as they left the dock in the *Swamp Yankee*, especially with the two mothers grinning like a couple of pygmy goats, thought Ricky. Neither Daisy nor Ricky acknowledged each other for half of the short trip. Daisy wore a wide brimmed straw hat to ward off the sun and her demeanor suggested even to the casual observer that Ricky was in her employ.

"When we get to Dunn's dock, throw that fender out so the boat won't get scratched and then hand me that stern line."

"Pleeeeeese."

"Please what?"

"When we get to Dunn's dock, pleeeeeese throw that fender out so the boat won't get scratched and then pleeeeeese hand me that stern line."

It was not a good start. Ricky gave Daisy his best mean look, but she didn't seem at all intimidated. In fact she did this funny thing with her left eyebrow, which made it seem like she was asking him a question.

"Okay, please," he relented.

"Please, what?"

Ricky expertly pulled along side the dock, throwing out the fenders and lines before nimbly hopping out to tie up the boat.

Ricky responded with a degree of exasperation in his voice that surprised Daisy. "Please get off of my boat." Now Daisy gave him her best mean look, about faced, and proceeded up the ramp.

"You ought to take that life preserver off before you go into Dunn's. They frown upon people knocking things over in there."

Daisy looked at the preserver she was wearing and realized that he was right. She unzipped it, slipped it OFF, and threw it right down on the ramp with a flourish. Then she stomped off. With a big smile on his face Ricky walked over and retrieved the preserver. "What a jerk!" he mumbled. He would have been surprised to learn that at that moment Daisy was expressing the same thought about him.

Returning home was even more awkward. Not a word passed between them until they were at the Wilcox dock. "Don't jump out until I tie her up." said Ricky. "I'll jump out when I want to!" replied Daisy. She had had enough of young Captain Ricky's crap for one day.

She almost made it onto the floater, but *Swamp Yankee* was what boaters would call "tender" which means "tippy" to the layman. Ricky had not made the boat fast yet to the cleat, so when Daisy placed one foot on the dock the action pushed *Swamp Yankee* away from the dock. Though she had good balance, Daisy did not yet have a feel for the dynamics of boating and she was further hampered by her death grip on the dozen eggs. The net result was that she fell back into the boat, crashing the carton of eggs on Ricky's head and causing both of them to recoil away from one another in horror. The net effect of that was that the boat turned turtle about three feet away from the dock. Gramps heard the splash and came running. When he saw that neither was hurt he began to laugh a big hearty laugh. "Last time you'll do it that way!" was all he said. Then he laughed some more.

It was just the right thing to do because when Daisy looked at the sputtering Ricky and he looked at her with her slicked down hair with a little rockweed in it, they couldn't help but laugh, too. The ice was broken and a friendship was born. The rest of that summer the two were inseparable. They went to the beach, caught crabs, and rowed every place there was to row within the area enclosed by the breakwater, which protected the town from Northeasters. Daisy easily picked up the knack of rowing and probably had the most calloused hands of any seven-year-old girl around Wickford.

Though in general life was good there on Steamboat Avenue that summer, there was a little tension developing between Leah and Gramps. Ricky heard things but did not quite understand them.

"You have to watch it Leah or you'll get hooked."

"You don't know what you're talking about! I don't have a problem."

"Then just stop for just a week."

"I can stop anytime I want, for as long as I want. I just don't want to do it now."

"Don't say I never warned you!"

"Don't worry!"

Something about the tone of both voices gave Ricky a deep sense of unease.

RICKY AND DAISY WERE IN THE SAME THIRD GRADE class. They actually rowed to school a few times in September since the building was right on the water, but generally they walked, or were given a ride if it were raining. Both liked school a lot. Daisy made some new girl friends and Ricky firmed up his friendships with kids from other parts of the town.

Over the winter Ricky and Gramps brought the *Swamp Yankee* back in the workshop for modifications. A slit was cut in the bottom under the rowing seat and a centerboard box was constructed. And under the seat in the bow they fastened a step for a mast. Lastly, they attached bronze fittings to the transom, so that a rudder could be hung. *Swamp Yankee* was now a sailboat, as well as a rowboat and had that classic look of those open boats, which were sailed by the likes of Capt. Bligh across vast stretches of ocean.

Ricky could not wait for summer, nor could Daisy when she was shown the transformed *Swamp Yankee.* When the warm weather came, Leah and Gramps took turns giving sailing lessons.

Mom was full of surprises. For a girl Ricky thought she knew a lot of things. This was a valid observation. Without any sons, John had made Leah the repository of his considerable knowledge of boats and all mechanical systems.

Under the tutelage of experts Daisy and Ricky learned to beat, reach and run, the points of sailing. Soon they could sail wherever they wanted to go regardless of where the wind was coming from. They perfected the art of tacking and learned to jibe without having their heads sheared off by the boom. Daisy did nearly lose one of her front teeth, however, when she didn't duck beneath a swinging boom quickly enough. Once again she heard: "Last time you'll do it that way!" from Gramps.

With a sailboat, many more areas could be reached and explored. The two crewmembers began visiting some nearby small islands under the watchful eye of Gramps. In other places perhaps children of their age would not be given so much latitude. But in Wickford, Rhode Island, Daisy and Ricky were just doing what was commonly done.

One rainy day the two kids were finishing up a Monopoly game on the screened-in porch when Gramps spread out a well-worn chart out on the table. It depicted lower Narragansett Bay. He asked if either Ricky or Daisy could find where they were right now on the chart. The two raced their fingers around the paper, over features and landmarks, reading them out aloud and hoping to stumble upon one they recognized first. "Whale Rock." "Boiler

Awash." "Sprague Bridge." "Unexploded Depth Charge." "Lone Tree Point." "Abandoned Light House." "Rabbit Island." "Hey, that's near here," said Ricky. Soon they homed in on Wampanoag Point and estimated where the house was. Gramps got out a set of brass dividers and showed them how to record and report their position in true nautical fashion. The consensus was that the Wilcox House was at 41°34.12' North latitude and 71°26.75' West longitude. "Now, if you ever get lost, you can find your way back home!" said Gramps.

A few weeks later Gramps, returning from his chores, drove the old Ford pickup truck on the lawn, parking it by the flagpole. Ricky watched as his grandfather pulled down the tailgate, climbed into the bed, and pushed a small boulder off the edge of the tailgate onto the grass.

"Could you give me a hand, Ricky?" Together they flipped the piece of granite over. Ricky saw that the latitude/ longitude coordinates that they had found for the house had been chiseled on a flat face of the stone. Evidently an undertaker friend of Gramps, who did tombstone carving, owed some money for a custom ash wood tiller that Gramps had made for him and they struck a deal. When the stone was positioned where Gramps wanted it, he challenged Ricky.

"Each time I ask you for the latitude and longitude of our house and you can give it to me perfectly from memory, I will give you a Kennedy half-dollar!" The challenge was extended to Daisy, too. Anytime the ice cream truck was making the rounds of the Point and Gramps was around, Daisy and Ricky would rattle off 41°34.12' North, 71°26.75' West and then chase down the truck for a treat.

The kids, perhaps all Rhode Island kids, lived for summer. While Ricky was in Rhode Island the winters were fairly mild. If you didn't sled or make a snowman the day it snowed, you could not be sure that you would be able to do either the following day. And the ponds were not safe for skating or ice fishing for more than a handful of times each year. Gramps said that it was different when he was a boy...and he said that the snow was whiter too.

Adults seemed different in the winter months. They weren't as much fun to be around as they were in the summer. Daisy noticed that Gramps and Leah seemed to be acting a little weird when she visited the Wilcox house and she asked Ricky several times if everything was ok with them. Gradually Ricky had gotten use to their more frequent spats of anger followed by periods often lasting days, during which the two would ignore each other. At some point that behavior no longer seemed abnormal to him.

If Ricky were a little older he might have noticed the effects that drinking was having on his mother. Leah would often oversleep and be late for work; other times she would be feeling so sick that she would have to stay home for the whole day. She would sometimes forget to comb her hair, or wash her face. Sometimes she wore the same clothing for several days in a row.

But as the warm weather rolled around again, everyone seemed to go back to being the way they should be and wanted to be. Daisy and Rick looked forward to their third year aboard *Swamp Yankee*. For kids they did a very good job painting and varnishing *Swamp Yankee* in preparation for summer. Mrs. Bruno was a little upset when Daisy had ruined a good pair of new jeans while applying a smelly red anti-fouling paint to *Swamp Yankee's* bottom. "Why did you do that?" she asked with some exasperation. "So that grass and barnacles won't grow on it," Daisy replied equally exasperated that her mother didn't know anything about boats. It never occurred to Daisy that her mom simply meant "Why didn't you change into old clothes before going over to the Wilcox's workshop."

The Brunos were amazed at how much their prissy daughter had changed and how much she had learned about boats and Narragansett Bay since they moved to Wickford. It was a good thing, they thought, and the loss of an occasional item of clothing was perhaps a fair price to pay for the transformation.

Daisy and Ricky had been cleared for sailing outside the confines of the breakwater, which meant that they could visit Dutch Island, which was rumored to have caves and underground passages. Gramps said that one day when the wind was right he would sail with them around Beavertail, the southern point of Conanicut island, which was due east of Wickford. That would take them past spectacular stone cliffs and briefly out into the Atlantic Ocean before they headed northeast to Newport. They would stop there for clamcakes and chowder before setting sail for the north end of Conanicut and then west for home. It would be much more than a sailing trip with Gramps on board. By the time they returned to Wickford the kids would have had a good dose of history and enough anecdotes about old coastal forts, shipwrecks, smuggling operations, drownings, German submarines and fishing to last a lifetime.

One thing about summer, when there is so much to do, is that it goes by fast. It seemed that one week you were getting the boat ready and watching spectacular fireworks on the Fourth of July and that in the blink of an eye it was Labor Day and time to get ready for school. Daisy and Rick would often think back to this particular summer, though, because it was perfect. Not only was there the sailing, but the Brunos would often take Leah and Rick with them to the beautiful Rhode Island surf beaches at Scarborough, or Misquamicut where the water was so clear that just before the waves broke you could look through them like you were looking through a window into the sea. The two would build sand castles, body surf, and picnic either at the beach or on the way home at one of the roadside rest areas. One day the Brunos took Rick with them to Block Island, which was about an hour ride by ferry off the Rhode Island coast. There they rented bikes and rode past scenic vistas of the Atlantic and the mainland. The beaches on "The Block," as it was called, were beautiful, too, especially the one near Mohegan Bluffs where legend had it the native Mannisses Indians cast the invading mainland Mohegans off the steep, two hundred foot clay cliffs, right into the sea. Rick was still enough of a boy on that trip that he would stick the end of a five foot long piece of kelp that he would find on the beach into the back of his bathing suit and drag it around like a tail. Daisy was still enough of a tomboy that she would stoop to throwing a small jelly fish at Rick's back for no particular reason.

Rick would always remember the end of the summer of 1979 for two events. To celebrate Labor Day, Gramps decided that it was about time that he should do a big old fashioned, genuine Rhode Island clambake like those he had done for so many years, until his wife was killed. She was the victim of a drunken driver and it did not seem right to John that he should be enjoying himself on the anniversary of her death; he had not done a Labor Day bake since her passing.

He told Leah to invite a bunch of her friends as he passed the word out to his, an interesting cross section of people whom he had met over the years.

The Rhode Island clambake tradition was reputedly modeled on a Narragansett Indian celebration. Basically, a pit was dug in the ground and lined with rocks that were the size of cannon balls. Then a framework of oak firewood was built about four feet tall that was interspersed with more granite stones. The stones would absorb and hold the heat from the hot hardwood fire. When the fire burned down and the coals were raked out, seaweed was placed on the glowing rocks. On top of the seaweed were placed metal open mesh baskets filled with sweet potatoes, white potatoes, corn on the cob, small filets of fish and sausage wrapped in cheesecloth, lobsters and a mixture of clams and mussels. Around the perimeter of the trays were placed pierced cans of brownbread. The whole mound of food was covered with several heavy pieces of canvas which trapped the heated steam, created from the seaweed and the juices of all the ingredients. The steam cooked the bake in a little over an hour, or whenever the "test potato" placed on the coolest side of the mound was done. While the cooking was going on, the participants would drink beer, eat chowder, and talk about other bakes they had been to. Every once in a while someone would walk over to the pit area, put his hand on the canvas, and say something like "Boy, there's a lot of heat in here!" or "Won't be long now!"

It was generally acknowledged that Gramps had been one of the best of the local bakemasters, having apprenticed under his father and uncles for many years before doing his own. People who came early Labor Day morning to help set up, whispered that it was good to see John doing a bake again.

Everyone was assigned a job by the bakemaster. The younger men split wood and built the pit. The older boys went to the beach and picked twenty burlap sacks full of rockweed, a kind of seaweed that had little buoyant air sacks and which imparted a very distinct flavor to the bake, so that it could never be confused with the lobster boils of Cape Cod and Maine. The latter the locals deemed seriously inferior to a genuine Rhode Island Bake.

Perhaps fifty friends, and neighbors of the Wilcoxes were actively engaged in the activity. They rinsed the clams, iced the lobsters, melted butter, wrapped sausage links in fish filets and then in cheese cloth, husked corn, shucked littleneck clams or served chowder.

When the bake was opened the unique seaweed smoke aroma permeated the air; old timers and newcomers like the Brunos stood downwind to catch the scent. The bright red lobsters, golden yellow corn, orange sweet potato, deep blue mussel shells and white clam shells made for quite a colorful plate. It was a wonderful feast with much good cheer and nobody present would ever forget that day.

The other memorable event of that summer Rick wished he could forget. But it was seared into his consciousness and popped into his mind at unexpected times. Twenty years later, Rick could still be thrown into a funk by the recollection.

Gramps and Rick were looking at the sun setting over the harbor on the evening of the autumnal equinox. The water was very still and the air was chilly enough so that they wore sweatshirts. A slight "sea smoke" was forming, extending only a foot or so above the still warm water's surface. Rick had never heard the word "equinox" and Gramps explained what it was and mentioned that the winter constellation, Orion, would be appearing earlier and earlier each evening. Rick went to bed that night, not pleased at the thought of Orion skulking around already.

He was awakened a couple of hours later when he heard Leah and Gramps arguing.

"I don't have to listen to your sermonizing —I'm twenty-seven years old and you treat me like a child!"

"Then you can leave anytime you want," he heard Gramps say angrily.

"I will and I'll never come back," his mom shouted back, loudly.

Ricky had heard this kind of thing before. It was always at night, always while he was in bed. Sometimes it woke him up. Sometimes it kept him from falling asleep. Usually Gramps and Mom didn't talk at all mornings after their blowouts. But little Ricky would pretend that nothing was amiss and continue to talk to both of them. Eventually they would begin to smile and all would be right again for awhile.

Rick fell asleep expecting the usual sequence of events. He got dressed for school and went to the kitchen for some breakfast. Gramps was there, as usual, but he was awfully quiet. He ran his fingers through Ricky's hair and seemed lost in thought.

His mother burst in to the kitchen and told him they were going for a little ride.

"But what about school?"

"I'll call the teacher."

"Is Gramps coming with us?"

"Richard-just get in the car, right now before I change my mind!"

"About what?"

"Get...in...the car," was all she said through clenched teeth. When he got to the car in the driveway and saw that it was packed with clothing, a beat up old Styrofoam cooler and several cardboard boxes, Ricky was pretty sure that they weren't going for a little ride and he knew that Gramps wasn't going to go with them. But he didn't know that he was leaving the only home he had ever known for good.

Ricky never had a chance to say goodbye to his friends at school, his new teacher, Miss Petrucci, whom he really liked, and, especially, Daisy. Ricky cried for days and days as the landscape changed dramatically before him while his mom drove west on Interstate 80. Leah was surprised anyone could cry that long and as determined as she was to leave Wickford, even she was concerned about the fact that Ricky had eaten nothing for several days. Ricky begged and begged his mom to turn around and go back home to Grampa. All Leah would say was that they were going to begin a new life and that they wouldn't be going back to Rhode Island for a long, long time.

Leah would stop now and then at some site like Devil's Tower or Mesa Verde and try to get Ricky to think of something other than Wickford, but it didn't work. For the last four days of the trip not a word left Ricky's lips. He didn't know what was going on, but he knew he wasn't going to like the change.

AFTER SCOPING OUT THE AREA AROUND LA, LEAH settled on Mayfield, the only place she could afford. It was a bit rundown, but not quite what one would call a slum. Leah found a place to live close to an elementary school and found a job at a convenience store nearby.

From the outset Ricky felt like he was a prisoner in Mayfield. Their home, such as it was, was a former two story motel. Two adjacent rooms were joined together and the bathroom in one of the rooms was converted into a kitchenette. The workmanship left much to be desired and Ricky remembered thinking when they first moved in that Gramps would never have done such a sloppy job.

Leah tried mending the fences with Ricky. They went to the neighborhood library, took rides to the beaches, and went to various sporting events. But both knew that they were only going through the motions. Leah would point out the cacti and palm trees and say "They don't have these in Wickford!" Ricky could think of a dozen sarcastic things to say, but in truth, he was so dejected, angry, hurt and tired that he would only stare at Leah, saying nothing at all.

Most of the time after school and on weekends, Ricky sat on a couch Leah had purchased at the Salvation Army and watched TV. Sometimes, when she asked what programs he had watched, he couldn't tell her because he couldn't remember-even when he had watched them only hours before. The happy, busy boy from Rhode Island with the golden brown tan and the big wide smile turned into a pasty white recluse.

Leah let Ricky write postcards to Gramps, Miss Petrucci, and Daisy during the first few months. Ricky told them all that he missed them and sent them his new address. After several weeks of anxious, and fruitless waiting for a reply, Ricky asked: "Why doesn't anybody ever write me back?" He would never find out that his mother never sent any of his cards or letters. She would rip them up and drop them in a trashcan on her way to work. Leah never had the courage to read them before doing this. At some level she knew that what she was doing to Ricky was terribly wrong, but she was too proud and embarrassed to ever go back home to Rhode Island and admit that to anyone.

"Could we visit Gramps sometime?" Ricky asked often.

"Maybe."

"When?"

"We'll see."

But they never did. One day when Ricky was about 12 years old he asked the same questions. This time there was a fight. His mother had been drinking and was in no mood for an argument. But Ricky was becoming Rick and entering that teenage boy phase which under the best of circumstances can be trying to a parent. He wanted an answer and wasn't going to stop until he got it.

"When are we going home? I want an answer!" he said in an angry voice.

"Never," she replied with slurred speech. "This is your home... and your grandfather is dead!"

Ricky was stunned and he was speechless. He cried himself to sleep that night. And Leah did, too.

CHAPTER THREE

WHEN RICK TOLD JJ THAT CONSTELLATION YACHT Charters was sending no boats north due to the weakened state of the economy, JJ took it badly. He swore torrents in French. He repeatedly punched the palm of his left hand with his right fist. He paced the deck. He became drenched in sweat. The tentacles of September 11th had reached and affected even the plans of men in a sleepy harbor in the Caribbean.

Though JJ was crushed by the news, there was nothing that he could do about it, at least for the moment. While JJ appeared to be conversing with Rick and Jimmy in a coherent fashion, his mind was simultaneously engaged on several different levels. On one level he was chastising himself for his stupidity in placing all his eggs in one basket and not having a backup plan for getting to the mainland. On another, he was already considering a number of new escape possibilities. On a third he was apologizing to his mother and sisters for letting them down.

Jimmy Fox had come aboard *Thor* shortly after Rick and JJ. He set out on the round teak deck table a big bowl of jumbo, chilled, pink shrimp along with some seafood cocktail sauce.

"To what do we owe this treat? Make some good tips today, Jimmy?"

"Nothing's too good for my friends!"

Jimmy always paid his share of the bills but he never threw around money. He must have scored on one of the many little deals he always had swirling about him.

After being informed about the trip cancellation Jimmy made JJ take a seat and ordered him to calm down. Jimmy had always liked to play the role of JJ's big brother as he was doing then. The three men picked at the shrimp and drank a pineapple and mango juice punch powered by a 151 proof rum. Jimmy and Rick offered JJ encouragement and tossed around a few ideas. Jimmy even suggested the possibility that if things were going to be that slow during the summer, maybe they should just take one of Constellation's larger boats and sail it and JJ to the mainland for the heck of it. Jimmy mentioned as he had a few weeks ago that he had a few friends in Morehead City, North Carolina that he wanted to see and that they could sail the boat there, and put JJ on a bus to meet his buddies in New York. After a couple of weeks they could sail the boat back to St. Thomas. Nobody at Constellation would have to know they took the trip and, in truth, as long as nothing was damaged, nobody would care.

JJ scanned Rick's face for a sign that this idea had potential and Rick could see that he was doing so. Rick wasn't overly excited about the notion, but it did look like things were going to be slow during the coming summer. And in fact, he had been looking forward to the yacht delivery almost as much as JJ, since he had been slowly developing a case of "Island Fever." Rick dreamed of being able to drive on a highway at 70 miles an hour for three hours without stopping. He needed to see a real city, a red barn, cornfields and trees without fronds. It is hard to explain to off-islanders, but even paradise can get boring if you are in it long enough. A few weeks on the mainland was the only cure; then after experiencing maybe a cold snap, a horrendous traffic jam and assorted other "real world" aggravations, the patient would usually be ready to return to the land of beaches and palm trees until the next bout of fever came along. "You know, that's a possibility," said Rick. "Let me think about it."

After the shrimp was finished they worked on some nachos and a few more glasses of punch. Jimmy was drinking a can of Coke which he almost never did. "What's with the Coke?" asked Rick.

"Bad stomach," was all Jimmy muttered. Rick had noticed that Jimmy hadn't seemed himself the last few days. He had not been eating what JJ had been cooking and he had been smoking more cigarettes and doing more joints, especially late at night on deck.

The three men talked about going ashore later in the evening. The *Reef* was having a big party that night for all the locals who staffed the places frequented by those who came to the island on vacation. Now that the crowds were gone it was time for these people to kick back a little and enjoy some of the money they earned while their customers had been having most of the fun.

JJ decided to stay aboard Thor for the evening to do some serious moping. Jimmy said he would go ashore with Rick, but that he had to be at the *Reef* no later than 9:30, since he had to meet somebody. That was fine with Rick who opted to take a shower and then a short nap.

Thor's shower was rigged up on deck and consisted of a plastic shower curtain within a small closet-sized wooden enclosure, open at the top. The shower water came from a heavy duty black plastic 35 gallon drum which was placed on the aft cabin top, several feet above the shower stall. The drum got a lot of sun exposure, even though the angle of the boat to the sun changed somewhat with wind and current. Suffice it to say that the water was never cold; but at times one might wish that it were. The water from the shower pan was drained into a scupper; frequently JJ made provisions to collect it for watering the small palms, tomato plants and assorted flowers on deck, which depended solely upon him for their life. Fresh water was one of the things that you never had quite enough of aboard salt water boats that were not tied to a dock. After showering, Rick tumbled into his bunk which was on *Thor's* shady side at the moment. A nice breeze came through the twelve inch bronze port hole keeping his small cabin very comfortable; within minutes Rick was asleep.

He was awakened at 9:00 by Jimmy. Throwing on clean shorts and a new shirt which stood out from his sun faded favorites, Rick was ready to go in minutes. The two called out to JJ who didn't reply and who was probably down for the night. Sleep would do JJ more good than moping thought Rick.

There was already quite a crowd at the *Reef* when they arrived there. Rick knew about half of the people by name and most of the rest by sight. The band, *Purple Parrotfish*, was very good and there were already a few knots of women dancing in front of the lead singer. The guys hung around the bar and sat at the tables while drinking and smoking. As Rick asked his friend, Bill the Bartender, for a Red Stripe, another friend passed him a Monte Christo, Number 4. Rick tucked it in his shirt pocket for later. There was no shortage of fine Cuban cigars on the Island. The Brits and Canadians who were free to travel to Habana always brought some back for the "Yankee Imperialists" to enjoy.

It was an eclectic collection of islanders at the *Reef*. Only a few tourists were present, guests of the "natives." Out of the corner of his eye Rick caught some of Dean Gray's boys either selling or dispersing free samples of something illicit. Dean Gray, aka "Mean Dean" was the local drug distributor. He had a pretty good lock on the business due to certain "techniques" hence his nickname.

The free samples were not due to any altruism on Dean's part. It was merely part of his business plan. If people didn't try his products how would they ever become his future addicts and customers?

Between the customers who came to the island on vacation and the local ones, Mean Dean did very well, financially. He had the nice home out on Mangrove Bay, a decent sized yacht, and was granted a degree of deference by most who knew him and all who were smart. Dean was good looking and fit as he approached forty. He had that gangster flair that respectable women find engaging, and that respectable men find an inexplicable aberration in such women. In Dean's younger days he surrounded himself with beautiful women, scantily clad much of the time. Well, Rick certainly could not fault him for that!

Now, Dean was engaged in short-term serial monogamous relationships. The word on St.Thomas was that he actually wanted to settle down and have a family. That probably wasn't going to happen soon, since Dean was one of those people who women found interesting, amusing and fun for about a month. Once they really got to know him they generally ran from him like scared little bunnies.

Rick took the sweating Red Stripe from Bill the Bartender and scanned the room for a table to join. He could see Jimmy with some guys he didn't know. They seemed very involved with some discussion and there was no room at their table. In any case the guys looked a little scruffy. Jimmy sometimes hung out with funny looking people. He would casually talk and drink with almost anybody. That was Jimmy!

As Rick continued looking around the room, Mean Dean and his current trial wife, Sandy, came through the door. They paused for effect and acknowledgment. A hostess scurried up to meet them and lead them to an empty table that had not been empty a moment before. As the two made there way to the table the *Reef 's* patrons nodded to Dean, called out to him, or attempted to slap, if not shake, Dean's hand as he walked by. It was as if Dean and his date were royalty. Dean's bodyguards, a little over-dressed, fanned out as unobtrusively as muscle men packing weapons could, keeping an eye on things for Dean.

Rick noticed that the left side of Sandy's face was ever so slightly misshapen. The left eye was open just a bit less than the right one. Although the makeup job was pretty good, it was obvious to Rick, if not everyone, that Sandy wasn't having or going to have fun tonight. No doubt, if asked about the swelling Sandy would mention how she had carelessly walked into a door sometime during the last few days.

With no place to sit, Rick decided to go out by the *Reef's* floating dock for a smoke. He still had a half decent buzz from the afternoon libations aboard Thor. Instead of the Monte Christo Rick lit up a Marlboro. For five years Rick had been trying to quit smoking, but never seriously. It was on his list of things to do, though, along with losing ten pounds and saving enough money to actually buy a decent CD, that is, a certificate of deposit. Though nobody would accuse Rick of being fat or out of shape, he himself knew that he was slipping some, and a little voice told him to guard his youth for as long as possible. Another, little voice told him that there would be rainy days in his future and that those in their thirties should be preparing for them. Hence the CD.

Rick's thoughts were interrupted by a slammed door. Sandy was stomping down the ramp from the *Reef's* entry way the way only very angry women can stomp. Usually when men witness such footwork they are very thankful that it is not their women who are performing it. Then they usually say very quietly or at least think something like: "Oh my Sweet Lord, please spare me from that shit." Rick was thinking exactly that and reminding himself again why he had not actively sought a permanent relationship.

The door slammed again. "Nobody leaves Dean like that...I mean nobody!"

Dean strode down to Sandy who was only a few feet from Rick and facing towards the water. He grabbed her by a shoulder and spun her around towards him. "Did... you...hear me?" he growled in a menacing voice. When smart women witness such a scene they usually say or think something like: "That girl better dump that guy before she gets killed." As upset as she was, Sandy was not thinking, nor had ever thought, that.

"Get your fancy little ass back in there right now. You're making me look bad."

"You are bad!" she hissed.

"You little tramp... you want to see how bad I can get?" shouted Dean with special emphasis on the word "tramp."

As a general rule Rick avoided interfering in these types of situations. But, being literally in the midst of a potentially dangerous incident, he summoned up as casual a voice as he could, and said to both: "Hey! Why don't you guys cool down for a moment!"

Dean slowly turned towards Rick and purposefully sized him up. "I know you. You're Thornton. If you know what's good for you, Thornton, you'll mind your own damned business."

In an ordinary confrontation Rick would not have hesitated to beat the shit out of Dean at that moment, which would not have been a difficult task. It might even be enjoyable. While Rick was never pugnacious by nature, he was a former Marine and could take care of himself. But Rick knew that Dean would settle the score with him sooner or later in some sneaky way if Rick pushed any of his buttons. But Rick was still not going to let a woman get beat up right in front of him.

"Hey, I was just looking out for you," said Rick evenly.

"You were looking out for me?" sneered Dean incredulously. "Look around, Dean!" said Rick *sotto voce*, while cocking his head twards the door.

Trying to be nonchalant Dean turned slowly to have a look. Indeed, not only by the door, but also in the nearby parking lot and aboard a couple of docked boats, there were people staring at Dean, Rick and Sandy. Even an angry Mean Dean knew it was not good to draw this kind of attention to himself. He turned back towards Rick and Sandy. Looking directly into Sandy's eyes he said: "I'll deal with you, later." With a menacing scowl for Rick, Dean did an about face and walked back into the restaurant.

The silence between Rick and Sandy was awkward. Rick broke it. "You ought to dump that guy before something bad happens!"

"Something bad has already happened."

With that statement Sandy burst into tears. Those who had gathered to watch the blowout between Dean and Sandy went back about their business.

"Can you take me away from here now?" said Sandy in a pleading voice.

Rick hesitated for a moment while he thought of the ramifications.

"Please...can you?"she begged.

"Sure. There is a quiet cove ten minutes from here. You can catch your breath and then I'll drop you off wherever you want."

"That'd be great."

Rick led Sandy to the Jeep. Before turning the key he turned to look at her. "I'm Rick by the way."

"Glad to meet you, Rick. I'm Sandy. Sorry for the trouble."

"Not a problem. Glad to help."

They drove in silence along a road that paralleled the shore. In a short distance they were off the beaten path, heading to the Constellation compound. The compound was empty, as it should be, when they pulled onto its cracked seashell paved lane that was just wide enough for one vehicle. A timer had turned on slightly yellow colored spotlights that were artfully arranged in some of the taller palms on the property. The image of the boats at docks and nearby moorings was reflected in the calm water. With a quarter moon shining above Fiddler Crab Cove it was a pleasant sight.

Rick was always surprised that Constellation did not have a problem with theft or vandalism, what with nobody in residence at the compound except during the charter season. There were two tiny guest cottages which were used by late arriving clients or for the charterers who needed a good night's sleep, or to freshen up before catching a plane back home. The cottages had tin roofs and small, but comfortable verandas complete with wicker rocking chairs. Bougainvillea, cycads, and aloe plants in the landscaping gave the places a cozy tropical look.

Rick parked in front of the closest cottage. "Have a seat," he said as he motioned a hand towards one of the rocking chairs. Sandy opened the door and got out of the Jeep with the barest trace of unsteadiness. "Can I get you anything?"

"Just water with ice if you have it," she replied. Rick returned with two glasses of ice water and passed one to Sandy who now had a trail of a tear beneath one eye. Rick just took a seat in the other chair and waited until she was ready to talk.

It was an all too often heard Island story that she had to tell. Sandy, called so because of her sandy blond hair, was from a small farming town in the Midwest where nothing ever seemed to happen. She had never traveled out of state before taking a cruise with a couple of girlfriends, all in their early twenties. The ship stopped at St. Thomas where she had a lot of fun with the people she had met there. Sandy vowed to return and did so six months later after quitting her job as a waitress in a luncheonette.

Being young and very attractive she easily found work on the island, made friends and had a number or casual relationships which would have been considered scandalous back home. All in all, the Island met her expectations.

One night, about three months before, Sandy caught the eye of Dean Gray. Through his muscle men Mean Dean let it be known to the young men in Sandy's circle of acquaintances that he was interested in her. Suddenly the men were no longer in the circle, but Sandy didn't mind because she was flattered to be the object of Dean's attention. Life became very exciting overnight. There were great parties, trips on the yacht, and servants at Dean's place who doted on her every wish. "If they could see me now," she would often think of the people back home in Indiana.

There was lots of sex too, not as good as with some of her recent lovers, but not bad. Considering the rest of the Dean package it was a more than acceptable arrangement, though.

Occasionally Sandy would fleetingly think that things were moving a bit too fast on St. Thomas for her. She drank a little too much and she started experimenting with various drugs, generously provided by Dean. But then she would have another thought-that she may as well enjoy her liberation now while she could. She could always jump on a plane and go back home if things really got out of hand.

But Sandy soon learned that she would go nowhere unless Dean wanted her to. She and Dean had several confrontations about this, but she was cowed by as many slaps.

Rick listened to what was substantially a soliloquy before he spoke. He told Sandy that she had to leave the island very soon or Dean would destroy her. Sandy said that she couldn't because she had no money-Dean had made her quit her job and told her he would give her whatever she needed. Actually what he did was make her dependent on him, she saw now.

Rick told Sandy that he would buy her a ticket to Chicago and give her some travel money. She could pay him back whenever she could. For the first time that evening there was a smile on Sandy's face. It was the kind of big, open smile that you saw on the pictures of wholesome farm girls who had just won something big at the County Fair.

With her mind made up to go back home, Sandy seemed to be a different person, immediately. It was as if a switch had been thrown. She acted like she and Rick had just met for the first time and she asked him about the boats there at the compound and what sort of work Rick did.

Sandy said that she had never been in a sailboat before. "Do you think we could go out once before I leave?" she asked with wide eyes. Rick chuckled. "I think that can be arranged. But you have to buy your ticket first or you might find that you like sailing and you won't want to go back home!"

Sandy stood and made for the steps off the veranda. She turned towards Rick and tentatively reached for his hand. They walked down the path which ran to the water and strolled along the bulkhead past the neatly docked boats. The only sound was the gentle lapping of water on the hulls and the shore. Continuing past the last dock Sandy and Rick stopped at the little beach that was on the property. The moon was lower in the sky and from the new vantage point it left a silvery path in the water which silhouetted one of the moored sloops. It was a scene right out of a movie thought Sandy. Coconut palms rustled above their heads in the gentle night air that carried a faint but intoxicating scent that she would forever associate with that night.

Sandy squeezed Rick's hand slightly as they gazed out over the water. Turning slightly she placed her head on Rick's chest. "Thank you," was all she said. Rick put his arms around her and they just stood in place for a few minutes.

Rick was about to break the silence and ask Sandy if she was ready to be taken home. It did briefly occur to him that a young, attractive woman was in his arms and that she was probably his for the taking. But trying to be a little more responsible than he had been in his younger days, Rick decided not to take advantage of Sandy in this, her moment of weakness.

But sometimes things don't work out they way you want them to or at least the way that you think that they should. Fate had arranged for all the elements to be in place for a romantic conclusion to the evening. Indeed, how could the night have ended any other way?

Sandy stood up on her toes and kissed Rick, first tenderly and then in a way that made her intentions clear. His hands slowly ran up from her hips to her firm breasts that seemed about to burst. Her nipples were hard and doing their very best to puncture her bra and blouse as she pulled him closer to her. Rick tried to fight off his rising excitement, but it was a losing effort.

"Oh, what the hell!" he said to himself with a smile.

The two reluctantly disengaged. Rick led Sandy to one of the boats that they had passed which he knew had a faulty combination lock to the door of the main cabin. Once inside he opened a couple of the overhead hatches to get a little air flow and then lit a small oil lamp which cast a nice warm glow in the main salon. The stage now being set, they eagerly undressed each other and pleasured one another. Sandy's body had no tan lines which in Rick's experience was unusual. Totally tanned breasts he found quite common. This and other intruding thoughts vanished as Sandy guided him to a bunk and pushed him down onto his back. Straddling him she took him into her and then rocked back into a vertical position. Slowly she moved her body up and down and soon Rick was begging her for release. But that didn't happen for a while and when it did he pretty much thought he had had a stroke. As Sandy collapsed onto his chest, he saw that her experience mirrored his. They embraced, totally spent, emotionally and physically.

Awaking from what can only be compared to a drug induced nap, the two smiled at each other. "I'll always remember this night," said Sandy with complete sincerity.

THE JEEP BOUNCED A BIT ON THE UNPAVED ROADS. Sandy asked Rick to take her to her little apartment which was above a shell and souvenir shop on one of the side streets in the main tourist shopping area. All the roads were empty at that late hour as they made their way to town.

The apartment was reached by steps that ran up the outside of the building. Opening the door and entering the small kitchen a wave of warm air hit them. Sandy had not been back to the apartment for several days. The last time she was there was to pick up some clothes and she had then closed the windows before she left. She opened them and then turned on a fan and the window mounted air conditioner in her bedroom.

Sandy had decided not to go back to Dean's place. If she could avoid him completely before flying out, she would. She had nothing back at his place that was worth the risk of confronting him she decided. She would get her ticket home as soon as she could, say quick good byes to some of the girls she had befriended and maybe have that sail with Rick. Then it would be adios St. Thomas.

"I hope you don't think poorly of me."

"Of course I don't. Why would you say such a thing?"

"You gave me the push I need to go. I was thinking about leaving Dean but didn't know how I would do it. I am so thankful we met."

Rick had given Sandy several hundred dollars that he kept for "emergencies" in a small plastic aspirin bottle hidden under the hood of the Jeep. He told her he would get her more money, if she needed it, and that she should call him tomorrow at Constellation. They kissed by the door as if they had been long time lovers. In the minds of both of them it had been a memorable and pleasurable evening.

IT WAS CLOSE TO 3:30 IN THE MORNING WHEN SANDY stirred in her bed. She had fallen asleep surprisingly quickly given all that had occurred in the previous few hours. No doubt her mind was somewhat at ease now that a decision had been made to leave Dean and escape money had generously been provided by Rick. One of her last thoughts Sandy had before succumbing to Morpheus was that it was too bad she had not met Rick when she first arrived on island. Then maybe she would be returning home with a fiancé.

In a dream Sandy was skinny-dipping in Fiddler Crab Cove with Rick. Dolphins leaped out of the water over the path of the silvery moonlight. The water felt silky smooth on her skin. She wondered if the dolphins would let her ride them.

Suddenly, Sandy felt like she was drowning...and sinking towards the bottom. She struggled to breathe but could not. Why weren't the dolphins coming over to help her? It felt as if someone had his hands around her throat.

Sandy awoke to find that she really could not breathe and someone really did have his hands around her throat! In the dim light of the street lamps coming through the wooden window shutters she could see that it was Dean. "Did you really think you were just going to walk away from me? Did you really think that I would just let you go? You little bitch! You made a fool of me and nobody does that to Dean Gray and doesn't pay!" Dean was straddling Sandy on the bed, his feet spread out in such a way on her blanket that she could hardly move. He removed one hand from her throat and with the other slapped her with the palm, then the back of his hand, three times in rapid succession. There was nothing for Sandy to do but endure the pain. She knew that whatever she said to Dean would just make him angrier, just like the last few times they fought. She would just play possum.

But Dean was in no mood for possum. He wanted a reaction. He grabbed a handful of hair and yanked Sandy's head back and forth, then up and down. When her hair pulled out he slapped her a few more times, even harder than before. Now Sandy was crying in earnest. Dean had never gotten this mad before.

Keeping a hand on her bruised neck Dean removed the blankets and sheets that had covered her. Sandy was wearing a large white T shirt in place of pajamas and nothing else. Dean grabbed the front neckband of the shirt and with one vicious jerk, ripped it completely down the front so that she was naked from head to toe.

Sandy pleaded with him to let her go. She told him she was sorry that she had angered him. She told him she would do whatever he wanted.

"I am going to teach you and anyone else who thinks that they can screw around with me a lesson!" With that he stood up and took off his clothes. Sandy was too scared to move. She hoped that after Dean relieved himself he would just go away. But Dean was a man possessed. He straddled her again. Her eyes were closed tightly. "Look at me!" he yelled. She forced her eyes to stay closed. He became infuriated at this and punched her solidly in the jaw. "When I tell you to look at me-you look at me, bitch." Sandy was now limp. Fortunately, she had been knocked out by his blow. Dean was not pleased at this development, since he had seen no evidence that she was penitent over what she had done. He also wanted her to be scared to death while he screwed her silly. He should throw cold water on her and when she came to he could slap her around a little more so she would take him more seriously in the future. With his legs he spread her legs wide. So intent was he on what he was doing that he did not hear the slowly opening bedroom door, though it made a click clearly audible above the noise of the air conditioner.

The intruder had been following Dean all night. He was surprised when Dean departed through the back door of the *Reef* all alone. He now understood why. Dean didn't want any witnesses to what he was going to do. Or maybe he just didn't want to be embarrassed in front of his boys by a bitch gone ballistic. It was stupid for him to be alone though, with all that money he was carrying. But then again, who could you trust with that amount of cash?

The Pink Conch inhabits the waters of the Bahamas and Caribbean. It's shell always sells well to island tourists.

It is big and hefty with a shiny pinkish interior and a crown full of spiky protrusions. The landlord who ran the shell shop downstairs gave one to the pretty new tenant after she admired it on the counter. Sandy kept the shell in her bedroom where she admired it as only a girl who grew up without an ocean can.

With a gloved hand the intruder reached for the conch shell that rested on the bookcase by the door. He had a 9 mm Beretta pistol in his waistband, but he was afraid to use it. It would make lots of noise and frankly, he did not have much experience with guns. Besides, he had no quarrel with the girl and did not want to hurt her by accident. He slipped his hand into the part of the shell that had been occupied by the marine animal. Gripping it firmly he moved stealthily behind Dean who was about ready to do the act with a knocked out broad. What a sick bastard Dean was!

As Dean prepared to thrust himself forward, the intruder took two large steps toward Dean's naked back. With a powerful side swing he smacked a totally unsuspecting Dean above his right ear. He heard a crack and expected to see one of the spikes broken on the shell. But when he withdrew the shell and looked at it, it was intact.

Dean dropped like a sack of potatoes and was draped over the naked girl who was breathing heavily and making a snoring like sound. With blood dripping from it, her nose looked like it was probably broken. The intruder carefully surveyed the scene for a moment. He was surprisingly cool for someone who had never done anything like that before. In fact, he actually didn't feel like he had done anything wrong. After all, Dean had beaten this girl up pretty viciously. Dean might have even killed her if he had not shown up. The intruder had faults, but girl beating wasn't one of them. Someone should give him a medal for what he had just done. Of course, nobody would, though.

The intruder had read enough detective novels to know a little bit about "doctoring" the crime scene. He was pretty sure that Dean was dead or would be soon. His head literally had a deep dent in it. He had smacked Dean on the right side of the head with his right hand. If the girl had hit him, she would have had to do it with her left hand. With his hands still gloved, the mystery man placed the girl's left hand in the shell and exerted some pressure on it. He hoped that some prints would be made on the shiny part of the shell. He also hoped that she was left- handed. But even if she wasn't, the investigators would probably conclude that a very threatened woman could quickly become ambidextrous and be able to wield the amount of force needed to leave a dent in her assailant's skull.

The woman looked like she needed medical attention. The intruder scanned the room one last time to make sure that he had left nothing behind. He picked up the nondescript medium sized duffel bag that Dean had brought in with him and slung it over his shoulder. On a bedside table there was a phone. He lifted up the receiver and tucked it under the girl's arm. The dial tone seemed unusually loud. The man dialed 911 and quickly walked out of the apartment and into the night.

CHAPTER FOUR

RICK AWOKE AT THE USUAL TIME WHICH SURPRISED him given the time he fell into his bunk and the unscheduled "exercise" that he had had only a few hours before. His first thought was that he hoped his new-found friend would be able to go for a sail with him some-time before she left. But deep down he knew that Sandy really should get "out of Dodge" as quickly as possible.

Rick took a moment to stare at himself in the mirror in the tiny head until *Thor* stopped rocking. He had cut himself enough times with the razor for failing to do so, and he had finally learned to be patient. He turned on the portable radio and adjusted the dial while the boat motion subsided. It was a little past 8 and it appeared that he had just missed the news. "...and we'll interrupt programming with any late breaking developments."

"Wonder what that's about?" he thought. The boat was stable enough for Rich to finish shaving. He didn't rinse off his face though, deciding to take a cool shower instead. Shutting off the radio he grabbed a towel and a new bottle of shampoo and proceeded to go up on the main deck.

JJ was already up there. Before going ashore each morning JJ liked to tend to his plants and have a smoke under the awning.

"Hey, Boss!"

"Hey, JJ. How you feeling?"

"Not bad. Better than Mean Dean."

"Better than Mean Dean... What does that mean?"

"*Sacre bleu*! Listen to the radio. Everybody is talking about it." "About what?"

"On the news this morning they said that Mean Dean and his girlfriend were killed last night!"

"Holy crap! You're kidding! I saw them both at the *Reef* last night and... and they looked fine." It was a stupid statement. But it prevented Rick from saying anything that he might regret later.

JJ went on. "The police are questioning everyone who was at the *Reef* last night. If you're in town you should stop and talk to them." JJ was a few steps ahead of Rick at the moment. What JJ meant was that if Rick did not go to the station, the officers would come to *Thor* or to Constellation. And if the officers saw JJ they would question him as a matter of course and that would not be good for JJ.

"Yeah, I'll do that," said Rick without any conviction. His legs were already jellied and the sweat was dripping under his armpits. His vision actually was blurred. He needed to think. He went to the shower and lathered up while his mind became mired in turmoil. "What the hell happened?" he said softly several times to himself while shaking his head.

Rinsing off he went back to his cabin and put the radio on. While he dressed he caught the full news report. Dean was definitely dead. But the girl, "whose identity is being withheld at this time" was not dead; however, she was not expected to live. Police were asking that anyone possessing any information about the crime call the crime tip hotline.

Life was turning into a nightmare for Rick very quickly. He fought to avoid panicking, but everything told him that in a matter of time, and probably not all that much time, he was going to be a prime suspect in a murder or two. Maybe a rape. He was seen with Dean and Sandy outside the *Reef* and he was certain that the severely injured girl was Sandy. He was probably seen driving off with her in the Jeep. And, "Oh my God!" he suddenly realized, his semen was probably still in her, too. No doubt, a forensic examination would find that out! A quick run through the several obvious police scenarios produced no favorable results. Rick knew that he would have to lay low. Real low. Lower than a beer can run over by a Mack truck. Because if no other good suspects were found by the police, they would have enough stuff on Rick to put him away for a long, long time.

Rick went back up on deck with some coffee that JJ had made and sat under the awning to ponder. He lit a cig-arette and had to admit that for something he knew was bad for him, that first drag really felt good.

As he looked over the harbor he noticed that the Old-port launch was coming towards *Thor*. In his new paranoid state he reached for the deck binoculars, always available to check out babes, and he trained them on the launch. He expected to find police aboard but was relieved to see that Jimmy was the only occupant. He waved to Paula, the skipper of the water taxi, as she dropped Jimmy off.

"Hey guys! Any coffee left?"

It was not that unusual for Jimmy to stay ashore for the night. It usually meant that he scored with a sweet young thing. He returned with a mug of coffee which gave off the distinct odor of rum. Rick looked at the mug with a smirk but was thinking that a little coffee laced with rum might actually be a good idea. "A bit early for the rum Jimmy Boy, isn't it?"

"Rough night!"

"Must have been. Where is your dinghy?"

Jimmy hesitated for a moment. "Have you heard the news?"

The three of them talked about it for a few minutes, but Jimmy had nothing new to share except that when he went to get his dinghy which he also kept at the Constellation dinghy dock there was a police car sitting in the parking lot. "Really?" said Rick, thoughtfully. Jimmy said that he ducked into the bushes near the dock and watched as the single patrolman drove off. Then he took his moped back into town and grabbed the launch. Jimmy didn't have to explain why he avoided a direct run in with police.

Jimmy's minor drug dealing could still land him in jail. So, the less contact he had with law enforcement, the better. Jimmy offered the observation that the police would be like hornets for the foreseeable future. The story of Dean's murder would probably make national news and every facet of the tourist town and perhaps even the police department itself would be placed on a microscope stage. Who knew what would be revealed? It would be bad for island tourism and it could be bad for people like Jimmy, as well. Rick didn't share with Jimmy the fact that, now, he too, had good reason to be afraid of being stung by the hornets.

JJ made another pot of coffee and brought it up on deck...with a bottle of rum. They all filled their cups and talked small talk; none was in a hurry to go ashore. But each mind was engaged in deep thought and each man would be very surprised at what the other two were thinking. Rick analyzed the situation carefully now that his nervousness had abated. On the positive side was the fact that Dean had made a large number of enemies over the years and there were more than enough suspects for the police to quickly round up and question for the moment. The cops would be occupied for a while. But Rick still knew that he would be on their suspect list somewhere and that at some point the island's finest would want to talk directly to him.

Looking at JJ he said as casually as he could, "Still want to take a trip to the States?" JJ's smile was answer enough. "That might not be a bad idea" Jimmy chimed in. "Things won't be cool here for awhile."

"Where would we go?"

It had to be someplace where the boat owners would not find out about the unauthorized trip. That meant that Annapolis and north were out. Florida was out, too, because there was a certain amount of coastal scrutiny to which JJ could attest. That pretty much left the Carolinas since Georgia was a yachting wasteland.

Jimmy again mentioned Morehead City, North Carolina, and his suggestion made sense. He did have friends there and that was always a help when you landed somewhere and needed supplies or had to get things fixed. And Morehead was relatively close to St. Thomas because of the way that part of Carolina projected out from the rest of the mainland.

With the port of entry decided the next decision was which boat to take. The trawlers were out. They didn't have the range, about 1300 nautical miles, as Rick recalled, and the three of them could not afford the fuel, even if they did. It would have to be a journey by sail in one of the larger ketches. That meant an almost two week open ocean trek. "Which Pearson do you think is in the best shape, JJ?" JJ did not hesitate a second with his answer. "*Pleiades* is like new. And the engine is new, we replaced it last October, remember?"

Rick was familiar with all the company boats and *Pleiades* was his first choice, too. It would take a couple of days to get her ready and provisioned without attracting attention. The three discussed what would have to be gathered together and what minutia had to be taken care of on shore. What occurred to all of them was how little was holding them there on the island at the moment. "How pathetic!" thought Rick to himself.

It was agreed that they would leave St. Thomas in two days, after sunset. Each man had assigned duties as well as their personal responsibilities. Rick wanted to remind his friends to keep their mouths shut. But that would sound strange coming from him. He had to just trust that they would not spill the beans about the trip. With a little luck, when *Pleiades* returned to the island in several weeks, everything would be back to normal. The real murder culprits would be in jail and Sandy would be fully healed. This last thought brought on another: if Sandy got better, there would be no reason for her to leave. Now that was something to look forward to!

THE TWO DAYS PASSED VERY QUICKLY. THE ONLY diffi-cult thing for Rick was getting someone to look after the boats, mail, and answering machine. No charterers were due for over a month. Rick reluctantly decided that he had to call one of his friends who ran a similar charter service on the other side of the island to watch the yard and fleet. He had covered for the guy once, taking care of his business, when he had an appendectomy. He told Carl that he was going to take some vacation time and fly back home. Carl didn't know him well enough to know that there was no "back home" to fly to. Carl asked why JJ could not take care of the place. Rick told him that JJ had quit a couple of weeks previously.

Although *Pleiades* would slip out on a Monday evening, Carl was told that Rick would depart the following Sunday. That would throw off any investigators should they snoop around and eventually get to Carl. The Constellation yard would just have to take care of itself for a few days.

Rick didn't like what he was doing. He was already having to lie and make up stories. Moreover, he knew that he would be doing a lot more of the same for the foreseeable future. He also did not want to forsake his responsibilities vis-à-vis Constellation. But at the moment he had no other good options. He had not yet been charged with anything and he was still free to do whatever he wanted, including leaving the island. However, if the police got a hold of him all that would surely change. The bottom line was that he had to go ASAP and hope for the best.

JJ and Jimmy did a great job of provisioning the boat. They would eat and drink well on their journey. One problem that Rick was concerned about was the low fuel capacity of the boat-only forty gallons. That was fine for the inter-island charter business, but that was not nearly enough diesel fuel to do any significant powering if they hit the usual calm spots that were out there at that time of the year. JJ cleaned out two 35 gallon blue poly paint solvent drums he found in the paint shed and they filled them with diesel oil. That would be good insurance. At 4 miles per gallon, they would still have to do a lot of sailing, but at least they would be able to power when they had to without worry.

THE DEPARTURE TIME WAS SET FOR 22:00. THEY ARRIVED at the boat at staggered intervals with no luggage. Everything they needed had already been unobtrusively loaded aboard. They even sat in the cockpit for a little while and drank beer. If anyone had been watching them it would have looked like a few guys just taking a little night sail to cool off.

Rick backed *Pleiades* out of her slip and slowly turned it around to the opening of the cove. There was no sense of urgency in the departure, at all. A cloud bank kept the moon hidden from view as they motored out of the cove; suddenly there was the patter of large raindrops on the deck. It took the three by surprise. Rick was quick to realize, though, that this was a good thing. It would obscure their departure visually and dampen any sounds of the engine for the few minutes when it would matter. Rick told Jimmy to shut off the running lights while he quickly established a NW heading. He brought the engine up to maximum cruising speed. If they could maintain that speed and course heading for only half an hour they would be out of range of prying eyes. The only thing they would have to watch out for was a Coast Guard patrol.

Jimmy was assigned the job of bow lookout. If any boat approached, which was unlikely given their course, they would have to turn on the running lights and play stupid.

But there were no vessels in the area. At midnight they shut down the engine, set all sails and turned the running lights back on. The breeze was comfortable, and steady. They were broad reaching on a port tack and moving at a good six knots over the ground according to the Garmin GPS. Rick set up the autopilot and once he was convinced of its effectiveness he told his crew that he would take the first three hour watch. His adrenaline level was high and staying awake was not a problem. Concentration, though, was a problem since there were so many thoughts running through his head. He had many questions, but no way of getting answers to any of them. That reminded him that he should bring up a portable radio into the cockpit. The St. Thomas FM radio station signals would be fading out soon and by tomorrow the AM ones would be gone as well. He would try to pick up the news during the next few hours and see if there were new developments to the murder case.

The boat seemed to be handling well. The sails were drawing nicely and the engine proved to be very smooth running for a diesel. Despite the turmoil in his mind, sailing a boat was already having the effect that it always had had on Rick. It calmed him. The mind can only contemplate so much. Being engaged in constant evaluation of sky, sea, wind, course heading, weather, and sail trim simply supplanted other thoughts.

Scanning the radio stations on the hour and half hour for Dean- related news provided the same facts except for one: Dean's funeral would be in a couple of days. Rick felt nothing but anger for Dean. He wished the bastard had died a month before. Rick had no dealings with the man, ever, and now he had to flee the island because of a chance crossing of their paths. There was no fairness in this! But if there was one thing Rick understood having never known his father, having lost the one grandparent he had known, and having at 19 years of age had to bury his alcoholic mother who had died of liver failure, it was that life could be very, very unfair.

Before he knew it Rick was a half hour into Jimmy's watch. They had agreed to a three hours on, six off rotation. He still wasn't sleepy and Jimmy obviously was. Rick decided to keep the helm for a while more. Then both Jimmy and JJ came up on deck together. JJ brought up coffee and Jimmy took orders for breakfast. As the sun popped out of the ocean on an incredibly beautiful morning, a very pleasant smell of bacon and eggs flowed from the galley into the cockpit. Suddenly, all was right with the world. The three men ate with ravenous appetites at the cockpit table while "Otto" steered the boat. "Otto" was the name that they gave to the self-steering device. While gazing at the sun rising, somewhat behind them they saw flying fish leap out of the water and glide inches above the surface. Then two dolphins really leaped out of the water and took up position about a hundred feet off the starboard side of *Pleiades*, matching both the boat's speed and course.

By midafternoon, the men had everything stowed and they had all claimed bunks. The music system on deck was up and running though they only had a handful of CDs to play. The radio stations that they were familiar with back in St. Thomas were history, and the only ones that were coming in strongly seemed to be in Spanish, probably from Puerto Rico.

Jimmy was showing JJ how to enter waypoints or latitude/longitude positions into the GPS. He told JJ about the network of circling satellites that allowed them to determine their correct position within 23 feet at that moment. He showed them that they were directly on course for Morehead and that they had gone precisely 89.56 nautical miles since leaving the island.

By the fourth day the crew of *Pleiades* was actually in a comfortable seagoing routine. They took turns cooking and smoothly traded off watches. JJ was ahead in the 1st annual *Pleiades* chess tournament having amassed four convincing victories and having had no defeats. The CD selection was getting old already but it was still entertaining to watch Jimmy dance and do karaoke on the lightly moving foredeck. He could have been on stage at the *Reef* on any Thursday night!

There was something very incongruous about the scene. There were no boats on the horizon which was clearly visible for 360° and perhaps there were none in any direction for 200 miles. The only sign, since the journey began, that they were not the only ones left on earth, was a well lit container ship, which cut across their bow perhaps 10 miles away, the night before.

JJ was preparing a special dinner for the evening. They would have the last of the lettuce and fresh salad fixings, a good French Bordeaux, and for the main course, dolphin, the fish not the mammal, would be featured. Rick had found some fishing gear and set up a trolling rig with a beat up old blue plastic lure with very rusty hooks. The way he figured it, it didn't cost anything to try to catch a fish. So what if the lure was dragged for 132 miles before it snagged the very iridescent dolphin with the high, distinctive forehead?

The mahi-mahi, as dolphin was sometimes called, was excellent and the men felt very content as they had coffee and watched the sunset. JJ was starting to get excited, and worried too, about the landfall. Jimmy told him to just act normally when they docked. His friends could care less who JJ was or where he was from. After they spent a few days in the Carolinas and JJ made contact with his amigos in New York, they would decide how JJ would get up there. Hell, it was even possible, according to Rick, that they would just rent a car and drive straight up route I 95.

Rick wished he could find out how things were going at Constellation and how the investigation was proceeding, but there was no way to do so. They were out of cellphone range, and out of the range even of the marine operator who can sometimes be reached via the 25 watt VHF radio. The boat was really rigged for coastal cruising, though it was easily capable of completing the journey it had undertaken. Rick would just have to wait until they got to the mainland. Then he could call a few friends back on the island and catch up on the news.

JJ WAS THE ONE WHO HEARD ABOUT "*ABBY*" FIRST. He was roaming the radio bands while on watch and picked up a fading Bermuda AM station around sunrise, as the ionosphere shifted. JJ didn't understand the significance of a name beginning with the first letter of the alphabet. He then promptly forgot about *Abby*, as he tried to find another station.

Two days later, Jimmy was listening to a powerful New Orleans station which mentioned that "*Abby*," the first tropical storm of the season, was gathering surprising strength. Her latitude and longitude were given which Jimmy didn't exactly remember, but he did remember to mention the storm system to Rick.

Rick, the only real blue water sailor of the bunch, immediately started to scan the radio constantly for word of the storm. He found that it packed winds of 45 miles per hour, a number only impressive to people in small boats at sea. He did not hear her coordinates, but did hear that "she posed no threat to any land at this time."

Rick was not particularly nervous about the storm. It was like someone in Boston worrying about the DC weather. But he would listen carefully to her position updates and plot them on the charts. She would probably impact their weather at some point, but at this time of year there was not quite enough energy stored in the nearby ocean water to sustain the growth of a tropical storm. This thought he conveyed to his two crew members. He also reminded them to give him any weather info they came across while surfing the airwaves.

They proceeded on towards Morehead City, still over 580 miles away. The sailing was perfect and the air temperature was very comfortable. During his night shifts Rick marveled over the beauty of the stars and planets. He could see how the ancient star-gazers could attribute their fate to the motions of the heavens. On the ocean, without the polluting lights of the land, the stars, moon and planets were truly a spectacular sight. So spectacular, that ironically they seemed artificial! Many times Rick shut down the running lights and told the guys to witness how the ocean and sky had appeared to Columbus, Magellan and Cook.

Strangely, the stars made Rick think about life's big issues. Despite his superficial, happy go lucky style, Rick carried lots of scars. Each night, when JJ and Jimmy were asleep, he would think about how messed up his life had been for the most part. Sure, he had been thrown some curve balls, but he also felt he could have done more with his life. He should have gone to college when he got out of the Marine Corps. Who knows what he might be now? He might be a successful businessman. Maybe a lawyer. Maybe he would have been a professor or an accountant with a nice wife and a couple of young kids. He wished that there had been somebody to guide and mentor him when he was growing up in California. What a difference a Scoutmaster, coach, or teacher might have made. But there never was anybody like that for him.

Perhaps this flight to the mainland was a good thing. Maybe he should stay on the mainland after the Dean thing blew over. He could return the boat, maybe hookup with Sandy. He could still go to college, too. He could get a decent job that would give him the time and money to do so. Rick had a lot to think about and sort out.

Tropical Storm *Abby* had not dissipated and had actually intensified slightly. She was suddenly about 310 miles away from *Pleiades*.

"How the hell did that happen?" mused Rick aloud. His face did not betray the fact that he was now concerned. It would not do to have his two inexperienced crew members become scared and even less useful than they were going to be anyway.

There was no place to run. Rick knew that they would not make Morehead City before Abby overtook them, if she maintained her present track. And he knew that they could not get *Pleiades* into any Bahama port without even more serious risks. There were too many banks and shoals in the Bahamas which would present an even more dangerous situation in a storm, especially if *Pleiades* were caught outside of a safe harbor.

They could only hope for a radical track change for Abby or conditions that would cause the storm to fall apart. But the plots and computer models, which they now heard about clearly and frequently on the closer mainland radio stations, indicated that neither of these possibilities was likely to occur.

CHAPTER FIVE

TROPICAL STORMS AND HURRICANES ARE SOLAR-powered wind machines and it has been estimated that despite their sometimes fearsome fury, they typically convert less than 3 percent of the energy available to them into damaging waves and wind.

For a tropical storm to be born, the ocean water temperature needs to be about 80°F and not just at the surface alone or the storm would be very short lived. Warm, moist air first rises spontaneously from the ocean's surface by convection into the troposphere, the lowest level of the atmosphere. At some point it condenses into raindrops in the relatively cooler upper atmosphere and releases its heat energy into that atmosphere. Then the newly warmed and consequently less dense atmospheric air continues to rise higher still. This upward motion of gas requires that more air must rush in at the base of the birthing storm from all directions. The direction of this inwardly moving air is turned slightly by the rotating earth, an effect of a phenomenon known to scientists as the Coriolis Force. That explains why tropical storms have spiraling winds.

It was first recorded that hurricanes, called cyclones in the Pacific and Indian oceans, might be cyclonic in 1821. A saddle maker from Connecticut named William Redfield noticed after a particularly severe storm that sometimes a forest full of trees and a field of corn stalks were blown down by winds coming from different directions. The evidence was, of course, the downed trees and stalks pointing, like so many little arrows in the direction from which the wind had come. Putting together observations from elsewhere in New England, Redfield concluded that only a whirlwind could produce such results.

If the winds of a tropically born storm exceed 74 miles an hour, the storm is classified as a Category 1 Hurricane. Fortunately, only on rare occasions will a Category 5 Hurricane form with sustained winds of more than 155 miles per hour. Such a storm can generate monstrous 50-foot waves.

Some hurricanes may be only 100 miles in diameter and others as many as five hundred miles across. When hurricanes hit an island in the open ocean they may do so with a storm surge of only a few feet. But when extensive land blocks the flow of wind driven water, such as it did in 1969 when Hurricane *Camille* hit Pass Christian, Mississippi, the "tidal wave" was 24 feet high. Hurricanes usually are accompanied by a lot of rain. The '38 Hurricane dumped 17 inches on parts of New England, causing massive flooding and damage almost beyond belief.

The good news is that tropical "disturbances" can now be tracked easily and their projected paths predicted within reason. Still, hurricanes have been known to stall, dart forward at 70 MPH as did the Hurricane of '38, or loop back on their former path such as Elena did in '85. Like the humans they are named for, hurricanes are never entirely predictable.

It is unlikely that hurricanes will ever again kill the numbers of people they once did. In 1900 about 6000 people perished when Galveston was surprised by a furious storm. Today, with our guardian angel satellites up above us constantly monitoring tropical disturbances, you would have to be either stupid or very unlucky to be killed by a storm.

Rick, JJ and Jimmy were unlucky. They knew they were in for some weather and they also knew that there was no way they could escape it. With the edge of *Abby* some 96 miles away and a sea swell that was quickly building, Rick, JJ and Jimmy had to think about weathering this statistically too early in the season tropical storm, which had already sneaked up on the West Indies and now them from its spawning ground off the coast of West Africa.

By early afternoon the sky behind *Pleiades* had darkened ominously. It is a trite description, but there simply is none better. As they watched the gathering storm, the hearts of all three men beat faster, their mouths went dry, their knees felt weak and their stomachs grew sour. Their replies to one another were clipped. Sometimes they would stop talking in the middle of a question. Sometimes they would stop talking in the middle of giving an answer. They were all scared and their minds were preoccupied with fear of the unknown. Unvoiced were many thoughts. JJ thought that leaving Haiti may have been a mistake. Rick thought that the possibility of being jailed in St. Thomas was a better prospect than the certainty of being caught in a storm at sea. Jimmy wondered why he had left the god-damned island in the first place.

In hours, at most, the three men were going to be severely tested and they had better be ready because the alternatives resulting from failure were not good. Rick de-cided to power the boat northward. They would not avoid the storm, but maybe its duration would be shorter given the projected path. Also, they would be giving the batteries a good charge which they needed.

While they began their dash to the north Rick gave directions for converting a heavy wool blanket into a sea anchor, basically a parachute designed to slow the backward motion of a boat attached to it through the water. Four lines of equal length were tied securely to the corners of the blanket and then the opposite ends were spliced together. Several holes the size of a fist, were cut into the blanket to let water flow through and keep the sea anchor from oscillating. A five-gallon pail was attached to the center of the blanket on the side opposite the lines to create a little more drag. Rick wanted to have the rig ready to deploy if the boat became uncontrollable. It would keep the nose of *Pleiades* pointed into the wind, so that it would present the angle of least resistance to water and wind.

The hatches were sturdy and could be secured from the inside. The hull was in good shape. Still, Rick had heard other people's stories of being caught offshore in fierce storms. Windows, portholes, hatch covers, hatch doors could easily be stove in by waves. Water weighs 64 pounds per cubic foot. Wave propelled water can break just about anything if it hits it long enough or from the right angle.

They didn't have many good pieces of wood to screw across all the points of weakness. They would have to hope for the best and have a drill, screws, and screwdriver handy, if the need arose, to install the several pieces of wood used as covers for the food storage compartments under the bunks.

The sails were removed and placed in the sail locker. If a sail got loose in a strong wind it would shred, whip the crew to death, or both. The spinnaker pole was removed from its holder and placed in the V berth. Extra lines were neatly coiled and placed below decks and in the rope lockers where they could be quickly reached. You never knew what you might need the lines to secure during the course of a storm. Another line was tied to a large fender and was set to drag off the stern. This was the man overboard line, a last chance for anybody ejected from the boat.

Lastly, the best PFDs, what the Coast Guard called Personal Flotation Devices and the rest of the world called life preservers, were selected. "Life preservers" seemed like a better name for them to Rick at the moment. Strangely, though those PFDs always looked good enough to Rick for the charterers, they seemed a bit ratty looking and frayed with the storm approaching. Rick told the others that it was almost time to put them on and keep them on while on deck until he said otherwise.

Though none of them felt hungry, Rick told JJ to heat up some canned beef stew. They were going to be in for many hours of pummeling and they would need all their strength. They also would not be able to cook anything once the storm got underway. Jimmy was the first to voice what they all were asking in their minds.

"We going to be all right, Skip?"

"We'll be fine. We've got a good boat and the storm is not as bad as it could be. The winds are topping out at 55 according to the last report. It will be rough, but we should not be in for more than 6 hours of crap unless she stalls and she hasn't stalled since we've heard about her. We've done everything we can. Let's just try to rest and get some food down."

But the tension made it impossible to really rest. JJ was the first to actually see the approaching storm. Against the intense blackness of the clouds and in the faint remaining light of early evening, the horizon to the SE turned snow white. Rick knew that this was a wildly driven rainsquall that would be impossible to see through and which would contain small bits of hail that would sting their exposed flesh and force their eyelids shut when it overcame them. He turned the boat immediately in the direction of the coming rain and ordered the sea anchor to be run out. JJ and Jimmy did it expertly, like they had done it a hundred times before. Rick backed the boat down to "set" the anchor and just as he did the white squall hit with a vengeance. It was so loud! It roared and the men could not hear each other, even while shouting, though only a few feet separated them. Rick locked the wheel brake so that the rudder would not bang back and forth and then joined his soaked companions in the main cabin. They toweled off and set about making themselves as comfortable as they could. The rigging was singing eerily to the accompaniment of a vibrating mast slapped by oscillating halyards. Soon the boat moved with a different motion, actually several different motions, since there were no sails to prevent the boat from swinging from side to side. A queasiness quickly set in for all three men. Soon it was very difficult to stand, even when holding on to handholds and countertops. Waves crashed into the boat, from all directions, and began to wreak their havoc. Closed doors began to fly open and disgorge the contents of their cabinets. Soon the cabin sole, or floor, was littered with just about everything and no purpose was served by trying to put things back, because nothing was going to stay in place for long, anyway.

Rick turned on the spreader flood lights which were about two thirds up the mast and he looked out the ports and transparent overhead hatch covers. The visibility was five feet at most. The opaque view was of wind driven rain and spray. Turning on the VHF radio, Rick tuned in channel 16, the hailing and distress channel, setting the power button to the maximum 25 watts.

"Any vessel, any vessel, any vessel, this is the sailing vessel, *Pleiades*, over."

Rick repeated this message 20 times, but there was no reply. The signal probably would not radiate out more than 50 miles and the likelihood was that there was nobody in a 50 mile radius to hear them. Rick left the radio on in case somebody moved into range or atmospheric conditions somehow improved to allow for better radio transmission and reception.

It was amazing how things had changed so quickly. The previous day it was sunny and the ocean was that beautiful sapphire blue color. Looking around, the three men could believe that all the weather reports they had heard were in error as they contentedly playing a few games of High, Low, Jack in the cockpit. Now they sat in fear for their very lives. Severe nausea was beginning to set in. The men sat on the cabin floor on bunk cushions in a dazed state. They began to yawn, a sure sign of sea-sickness. Jimmy suddenly sat up and fumbled in his pockets. Pulling out a plastic bag he withdrew a previously rolled joint and dangled it from his mouth. Then he carefully wrapped the remaining joints back in the baggy and put it back in his pocket. He then took out a Zippo lighter from another pocket another pocket and lit up.

"Just what the hell are you doing?!"

"Just what the hell does it look like I am doing?

"We're in the middle of a goddamned hurricane!"

"Oh! I thought it was just a tropical storm."

Rick gave Jimmy an exasperated look.

"What's the problem? Are we going anywhere or doing anything for the next few hours"

Jimmy had a point. They weren't doing anything or going anywhere for the next few hours.

"Besides, I heard that marijuana is used to fight nausea during chemotherapy. It might work for seasickness, too."

Rick had heard the same thing. He reached for the proffered joint and took a couple of hits. He then turned to pass it to JJ but he was already comatose from fear.

The marijuana actually did seem to cause the nausea to abate. Rick looked around the cabin illuminated by a single light and let himself nod off. Soon all three men were breathing heavily with eyes closed. But their half sleep state was hardly restful. They were sweaty and had to be awake enough to use hand and leg muscles to brace themselves from being thrown around the cabin. JJ gave in to a total hypnotic trance first. He actually appeared to be dead and was flopping around like a life size sock monkey in the back of a pickup truck going down a bumpy unpaved road.

Though they did not know it, more than two hours passed by while they dozed and they were in the strongest part of the storm. Had they been awake there would have been nothing to see in the maelstrom raging outside the confines of the hull. It was pitch black out there and though there was an occasional roll of thunder, the lightning never seemed to illuminate anything. The lack of visual reference was good. If there were any visibility at all, the crew of *Pleiades* would have been even more terrified than they were, because the sea was truly in a hellish state. A bad storm at sea is one of God's best recruiting tools.

The boat was gyrating wildly. Nevertheless, the sea anchor was working surprisingly well, keeping the bow basically pointed in the direction of the wind.

Rick was the first to hear a different sound and react to it. There was a low roar that grew steadily in intensity. A very large wave was breaking somewhere up ahead of them. The bow of the boat began to lift and incredibly continued lifting until it was up at a 45° angle. Jimmy and JJ woke with eyes wide open as they slid backwards on their cushions. In a few seconds the hissing and pounding wave was upon them and *Pleiades* was entirely under water, spinning out of control like it was a toy boat in the water at a surf beach. Water was pouring through cracks in the hatch doors and from somewhere else, too. The cabin floor was suddenly a couple of inches below sloshing water and then the dome lights flickered on and off adding to the dramatic effect.

Nothing gets your attention quite like water in your boat in the middle of a storm. With adrenaline surging the three swearing men sprang up and grabbed pots and waste baskets for bailing. Nobody had to suggest the course of action. Rick removed the companionway door slats so that they could bail from the cabin directly into the cock-pit which drained through scuppers. To his surprise the cockpit was a swimming pool and the stern of the boat was dangerously low in the water, illuminated by the white stern running light which also flickered on and off.

Reaching for one of the spare lines in the cabin, Rick tied a loop around his waist and told Jimmy to tie the other end around the mast, which came through the deck to be stepped directly and solidly on the keel. He then slid back the hatch cover and jumped into the cockpit to start bailing with the plastic waste basket. Suddenly he vomited, but he didn't stop bailing. The water level in the cockpit did not go down at all with the torrential rain and the constant spray. Something was wrong. Water should be draining through the scuppers. If it didn't pretty soon Rick knew that it was going to start coming UP through the scuppers, a pretty good sign they were going to visit Davy Jones' Locker. Reaching down in the cockpit for the drains Rick found the problem. One drain was blocked by a small rag used for cleaning; the other by cellophane from a package of cigarettes. "Jesus, smoking really can kill you!" Rick thought.

With the scuppers clear the water did drain, albeit slowly. But already the boat was riding better. Jimmy, and JJ were bailing into the cockpit like wild men and Rick would have to keep checking the scuppers since in the water they were throwing out of the cabin there was a lot of stuff like napkins, sponges and pencil stubs that could again prevent the water from draining.

Rick was absolutely exhausted by the activity. His chest was heaving and he just could not seem to breathe in enough air. Once again the men could hear a roaring wave up ahead. Rick tumbled into the cabin and Jimmy and JJ quickly secured the hatch and companionway slats. Once again they were effectively a submarine vessel and the water that they had bailed out had been replaced by a similar amount. "We're going to die," was the unspoken but identical thought they had simultaneously.

After the wave passed they again removed the slats. The cabin and running lights flickered, almost like strobes, adding to their agitation. Jimmy noticed a long strand of rubbery kelp caught across the steering wheel pedestal.

And he noticed that the water was not draining again from the cockpit. Grabbing the bucket he went out to do what Rick did before. Sure enough bits of seaweed from who knows where were caught in the strainers of the drains.

Without warning a wave broached the cockpit from the starboard side. Jimmy actually floated upward for a moment and then out of the cockpit. Fortunately he was able to grab the stainless steel stern rail and hold on. Rick and JJ were unaware of his dilemma. The same wave had poured at least a hundred gallons of water into the open companionway. They actually bailed for several minutes before they realized that Jimmy was not with them and not in the cockpit. "Jesus Christ! JJ! Jimmy's gone!"

Rick sprang into the cockpit. Jimmy had been flung off the rails but had managed to grasp the trailing line and fender. Rick did not see or hear him at first but caught a glimpse of him when the stern running light came on. Jimmy was holding on for dear life and he had the wild, scared look on his face of a man who was about to die and knew it.

Rick grasped the line and tried to pull it in. It didn't budge at all. Rick could not figure out why, when they were sea anchored, it looked like Jimmy was being pulled forward. But the fact was that the stream of water that Jimmy was caught in was moving away from the boat with enough force to create the effect that the boat was pulling him forward.

"Hold on, Jimmy!" cried Rick again. "We're going to have to winch you in."

Rick explained to JJ that they would take a spare line and wrap one end around a deck winch. The other line they would tie to Jimmy's line and then they would use the winch to pull Jimmy close enough to the transom to grab. JJ nodded, but had no idea what Rick was talking about.

Rick tied the lines together while he kept yelling to Jimmy to hold on. He knew Jimmy was terrified. They all were terrified! Jimmy, yelled back what sounded like "I'm sorry."

Looking over the stern rail Rick told Jimmy to hold on tightly because JJ was going to begin winching him in. Now Rick could hear Jimmy, somewhat more clearly. He was saying: "I'm sorry...I'm sorry guys...I'm sorry."

With everything set up all JJ had to do was use the ratchet action of the winch to bring Jimmy aboard. Rick told JJ to begin cranking. Going back to the rail while the sea still raged about them Rick yelled: "You'll be aboard in a minute Jimmy, just hold on for one more minute." JJ hauled Jimmy towards the boat easily. He was only a few feet from the transom but he didn't seem to know it. In the irregular flickering light Jimmy seemed as catatonic as JJ had been earlier. Rick wiggled his body through the safety rails keeping his right hand on the line to guide it and Jimmy in. Unexpectedly a small wave broached the cockpit and Rick closed his eyes while it passed. Suddenly he tumbled back into the cockpit. There was no resistance on the line that he was holding. When he got up and looked back he could see that Jimmy was gone. And in that instant Rick knew with certainty that Jimmy would never be seen again.

FOR YOUNG MEN, RICK AND JJ HAD ALREADY EXPERIENCED some pretty bad nights. But in their remaining lives this night would be their worst. They knew that Jimmy could not be recovered and though they knew they could not be expected to do anything more, they felt guilty and angry at themselves. But fear was still their overriding emotion because the storm raged on and three more waves surged over *Pleiades*. The two men did everything they could to keep the boat, which was by then in total darkness, afloat. But finally they collapsed on the cabin sole and couldn't get up. They had reached that point where they were beyond caring about what would become of them. Their bodies could not respond with any physical action; their minds could not cope with any more thoughts.

The storm weakened slightly, but JJ and Rick were unaware that it had. *Pleiades* would just have to take care of herself now... and them.

CHAPTER SIX

Rick awoke on his back on the teak and hol-ly cabin sole. Brilliant shafts of sunlight streamed through the ports and hatch covers and by the way the patterns of light danced haphazardly around the cabin, Rick knew that the sea was still very confused. The stench in the sealed cabin was overwhelming- a mixture of vomit, sweat, diesel fuel, seeping sewage from the holding tank and odors which could not be identified but which were as unpleasant as all the rest. JJ was still asleep on the cab-in sole folded into a bunk cushion which was wedged be-tween the bottom of a bunk and the base of the table in the main salon. His breathing was heavy and an oily sheen covered his face. There was no point in trying to rouse him yet thought Rick.

Removing the companionway slats Rick drank in the fresh air like the submariners in the old WWII movies who had been underwater too long after being depth charged by pursuing destroyers. He stumbled into the cockpit, which was amazingly clean and bright in the sunshine.

Indeed as he looked forward the whole boat reminded him of a car coming out of a carwash. The wind driven rain and sea had scoured the fiberglass surfaces. The dodger which protected the cockpit from sun and spray was gone. All the screws had pulled out surprisingly neatly, the result of the force of the monstrous waves which had swept the deck from bow to stern. The GPS screen, apparent wind indicator, and engine gauges which were mounted on the steering pedestal for the helmsman to use had also disappeared. But other than that, the boat looked fine as it was lifted up by the still giant rollers and then gently settled into the deep troughs. The sea anchor was intact and functioning; there was no need to adjust anything for the time being.

Jimmy. What a way to go! If he had only put on a life vest he would have had a chance at survival. Rick could only hope that he drowned quickly without enduring the terror of a night alone in the darkness, lashed by waves, pelted by rain with only an occasional lightening flash to give vision to the horror of a fully deployed tropical storm which as far as Rick was concerned was a hurricane. Rick thought again about what Jimmy meant when he shouted: "I'm sorry." Sorry for what? Abandoning ship in a time of need? Rick was the one who was sorry.

Jimmy had often said that he was the last of his breed. Rick remembered feeling a bond with him. Both were alone in the world, at least as far as blood relatives were concerned. There was nobody to notify of Jim's loss. Even the other boat rats that passed as friends at the St. Thomas bars would be little affected by his death. "Poor bastard!" and a raising of a glass would be about the extent of the eulogy and memorial service for him, if they ever learned how he died.

Returning to the cabin Rick flipped the instrument panel switch. There was no beep of the radio and no initialization of the old backup LORAN at the nav station. More switches were thrown, but nothing came alive. There was absolutely no electrical power flowing through any of the circuits. Inspecting the battery bank it was easy for Rick to see why that was. The batteries and power distribution panels had been doused with water from assorted leaks and a sloshing bilge. Electricity had leaked out all night long until nothing was left. A quick check showed that the battery fluid levels were fine. Rick disconnected the main battery cables to prevent further power drainage and would wipe down all connections later on.

JJ groaned and stretched as much as it was possible to stretch in his cramped position. Coming fully awake, he stood to look out the salon ports. The sight did not please him. He was a rum punch, cruise around the island type crewman. The ocean sailing shit did not agree with him at all. He was still feeling quite queasy and plopped himself on the bunk.

"Mon, this be the last trip I ever take with you," he said with mock anger.

Their eyes locked and they both began laughing until they nearly choked to death. Then they did the same thing again.

When they stopped laughing the second time they both grew still and quiet. After a moment JJ shook his head back and forth and murmured: "Poor Jimmy, poor Jimmy. poor, poor Jimmy."

Rick had the same feeling but was already again in captain mode. He was thinking about the difficulty of two men, one of them not a real sailor, bringing this boat to a safe harbor still several hundred miles away. Suppose he was incapacitated? Could JJ function at a level sufficient to avoid catastrophe? JJ was going to have to be educated in the ways of boats and the sea very, very quickly. He then wondered fleetingly about their ability to weather another storm, even a much less severe one. He thought about not having charts of the nearest coast and how difficult it could be to make a shore approach with no GPS coordinates to plug in. There were ways to do it, of course, but it would take some thought and planning. Luck would help. Like seeing a ship departing from or arriving at the channel entry point they themselves would have to take.

If captains voiced every thought that popped into their heads, nobody would ever ship with them. Everyone who had not ever been fully responsible for any vessel sailing offshore would think that they suffered from paranoia. Rick's last thought before he passed out in the storm was that there must be places in the hull of the Pearson where only a half an inch of glass fiber reinforced plastic separated him from a raging sea. Supposing the boat struck some floating debris or supposing a whale struck them while surfacing for air? Whales still needed to breath air in a hurricane, didn't they?

Rick decided that a little paranoia was an acceptable trait in a captain as long as it didn't get out of hand. And before his current episode did get out of hand and his fears were transferred to JJ, he decided that they better do something to take their minds off things they just couldn't do anything about.

"JJ! You hungry?"

"I'm starved but I don't think I can keep anything down yet." "How about a cold Coke? You are probably pretty dehydrated from puking. Sip it slowly while we check out the boat and inventory things."

They began in the forward cabin and straightened things out as they went along. Everything was wet. Later on they would have to bring cushions and bedding up on deck to dry, if it were calm enough to do so. They paused frequently as the motion of the boat pushed them one way or another or gave them a bad case of butterflies. They came across the portable radio which now had a cracked case. The D cells had been ejected from it, but once they were replaced there was the reassuring sound of static and a distant radio station. Playing with the AM tuner, for they were still too far to receive FM signals, they picked up a station from Savannah. There was traffic news and the usual morning radio announcer banter, but no mention of a storm. Later they would hear that what nearly killed them referred to as an: "unusually early, but now minor tropical disturbance heading for Bermuda."

Rick explained about the boat's batteries as he prepared to make coffee using the gimbaled LNG stove.

"Fire up the generator JJ."

JJ disappeared for a few minutes while Rick got the LP stove lit. When JJ returned he did not look happy.

" Mon...we got a problem. There is no generator."

"Shit, fuck and goddamn! What do you mean, no generator?"

Rick was exceptionally aggravated that there was in fact no auxiliary generator on board. Even a primitive one with a pull cord would provide enough power to recharge the batteries, start the engine and provide all the comforts of home. As luck would have it *Pleiades'* generator had been sent out for off-season servicing and had not been picked up before they left the island.

The immediate problem of having no electricity was that the bilge pump could not operate, the engine would not start, the radio was useless, the old LORAN, and even the hand-held GPS were dead; and there would be no lights later on in the evening unless they could scrape up candles and an oil lamp. Basically, JJ and Rick would be operating a vessel in the manner of the early 19th century.

Rick wondered what other surprises there would be. He didn't have to wait long. He poured two mugs of black coffee and passed one to JJ. They cradled the warm, comforting mugs in their hands for a moment and then drank simultaneously and deeply. Both swallowed the coffee before they could spit it out.

"Sonofabitch!"

"Yuck!"

The water that was used to make coffee was contaminated with seawater. How this scourge could still happen in this day and age was still a mystery. The tanks were one-piece fiberglass and the fill fittings were tightly sealed. The only thing that Rick could figure was that the overfill vent had been submerged and ocean water siphoned back into the main tank. One hundred gallons of freshwater was now useless.

Fortunately, Jimmy had been fond of beer. There was enough on board to keep two people hydrated for at least several weeks. But Rick and JJ would not be drinking coffee any time soon.

The seas had calmed down surprisingly quickly. Still, a boat riding at sea anchor is not a comfortable place. *Pleiades* pitched and yawed and there is only so much of this that anyone could take, even Rick with his stomach of cast iron. He decided that by sailing with reefed sails or a small storm jib and a small jigger rigged off the mizzen mast they would be more comfortable. Jib and jigger won out and he explained to JJ his reasoning for getting underway before he set about to retrieve the sea anchor and set sail. He also explained that they would have to take turns hand steering *Pleiades* since there was no electricity to run the autopilot. This could become very tiring very quickly, especially in their weakened state. But if they really became physically and emotionally drained they could always deploy the sea anchor again and put up with the uncomfortable motion.

Rick located the needed sails and sheets in the lazarette. He made sure to secure the sails well-the jib on deck and the small aft sail to the boom- with short lengths of line so that they would not catch any wind until they were ready to be set. Quickly he pulled aboard the sea anchor and gathered it up to his chest, so it would not fill with wind and act like a parachute. If it did, Rick could be pulled overboard. He stuffed the sea anchor into the anchor locker recessed into the foredeck and yelled to JJ to turn the wheel hard to port to fall off the wind slightly. Untying the hold downs and pulling up the jib halyard were done with smooth motions. Quickly the halyard was made fast and the jib sheet was trimmed. Immediately *Pleiades* stabilized and with the draw of even such a small storm jib she began to overcome her inertia and perceptibly move forward.

Moving aft, Rick set the small mizzen sail and the yawl seemed to be well balanced with the combination very quickly. This would be enough sail power for the time being. JJ could manage the vessel rigged this way in his still queasy state and it would keep his mind occupied.

"Where should I head?" called JJ. Wishing to keep it simple, Rick told him to head northeast. That would bring them generally in the right direction until they got a good electronic fix.

Rick made his way back to the cockpit to join JJ.

"We going to be OK, Skip?"

"We'll be fine. It will be tiring, but we've got plenty of food and plenty of beer. The storm was a fluke and we'll have smooth sailing the rest of the way. It will be a milk run."

"What's a 'milk run'?"

Rick explained the meaning of the expression and laughed. The laugh was important because it conveyed to JJ that the skipper felt that they were really going to be okay. The "fluke" bit was pure speculation on Rick's part at best. Actually it was an outright lie. But what was the point in allowing JJ worry about something that they had no control over?

"With your sailing ability and my navigation skill we'll be on *terra firma* in a few days!"

"What's 'terra firma'?" Again Rick took a moment to explain. "You're going to be one smart Haitian by the time you get ashore!"

Now it was JJ's turn to smile and laugh for the first time in days.

"The important thing is that we are not boarded or seen. Technically we are in a stolen boat and you have no papers." Rick didn't see the need to also bring up the possibility that he was wanted for murder. When it really calms down we're going to have to get rid of the name on the transom and our VI registration numbers on the bow. We can wet sand them off. Let's start thinking about a new name for the boat."

JJ nodded and Rick then stood up and took a slow and thorough 360° survey. Visibility was clear to the horizon and there was nothing out there but water. The atmosphere seemed particularly well scrubbed by the storm and there would be even more stars to be seen that night than usual in the open ocean and that meant a lot.

"I'm going below to look for charts and guide books." Actually he would be pretty satisfied with a AAA road map of the southeastern states.

Rick rummaged around the main salon, opening drawers and cabinets. The cabin still stunk and was damp. Making his way up to the bow cabin he opened up all the hatches a couple of inches. There was no danger of any water sweeping in any longer and the fresh, cool air was welcome. On the V berth Jimmy's duffel bags caught his eye. One was an OD US Army bag held closed by a carabiner and the other one was an unzipped, faded brown canvas duffel which was open and showing a pair of boxer shorts, a shaving kit, a worn khaki shirt and Jimmy's more worn and much valued New York Yankees baseball cap. Not much of a legacy. Rick was reminded of a passage he read in a book about one of the last of the original tall ships sailing around Cape Horn in the late Twenties. It had embarked from Germany bound for Chile where it would pick up nitrates and drop off manufactured goods. Two men were washed overboard in a storm. The officers quickly went down to their bunks and gathered up all the gear of the lost men, so that when the rest of the seamen returned from their watch, they would not gaze upon it and think dark thoughts.

Perhaps that was a smart thing to do. At this point JJ was certainly prone to dark thinking. JJ had more than his share of thrills in his short life. Perhaps "danger" was a better word than "thrills." He was still shaken by the storm experience and Rick would not be surprised if he never again set foot on a boat after they reached land. And JJ was going to miss Jimmy, his best friend since beginning a new life in St. Thomas. Rick knew Jimmy for a few years before JJ's arrival and he remembered how he was surprised at the interest Jimmy took in JJ and the genuine concern he seemed to have for him. Jimmy was not the sort of person anyone would have described as having a "sensitive nature." Yet he always had taken good care of JJ. Once, when JJ was having a lot of trouble with his wisdom teeth, Jimmy took him to a dentist and paid for them to be yanked. Rick laughed as he remembered that JJ very well may have been as scared then, as he was during the storm. He had never been to a dentist before, or for that matter, known anyone back in Port-de-Paix who had.

When things settled down, JJ and Rick would go through Jimmy's things. It would be nice for JJ to have a memento of his friend. But for now it would be best to stow Jimmy's bags out of sight in the space under the V-berths. Rick removed the access covers to the stowage compartment. Then he zipped up the duffel bag with the personal gear in it and stuffed it in the space as far forward as he could. He then grabbed the other bag which was practically bursting from whatever was stuffed into it. "God this is heavy," thought Rick. "What the hell is in there?"

Whatever it was, it did not compress well and the bag was not going to go through the access port. Rick put the bag back on the bunk and unzipped it, intending to remove some of the contents, so that the bag could be stowed.

What he saw in the partially opened bag, he could not believe. There were dozens of neat bundles of cash, each perhaps, two inches thick. Most of the bundles seemed to be in hundred dollar bills, but he could see bundles of 50s and 20s, too. As he spilled the contents out onto the bunks he found a 9mm Beretta automatic pistol and a few loose rounds in a clear plastic zip lock bag. There were also two other zip lock bags of fine white powder. Rick was pretty sure it wasn't sugar.

"Jimmy, Jimmy, Jimmy... just what have you been up to?" said Rick softly to himself.

Rick was in shock. There had to be several hundred thousand dollars on the bunk. Maybe more. He picked up a few packs of the money and thumbed through them. The bills were used and real. For some reason he sniffed them; they even smelled like money.

Satisfied that he was neither hallucinating, nor dreaming, Rick decided to put the money in the stowage space under the berths. He had to put some of the stash into small plastic garbage bags, so that it would all fit. Then he covered the loot, gun and drugs with the extra blankets and sheets which were originally under the bunks. Closing up the compartments and replacing the bunk cushions he stumbled back into the galley. His head hurt. His brain actually seemed to ache. This new development was going to require some thought. He reached for a couple of beers that were still cool and made his way back up to the cockpit.

CHAPTER SEVEN

EAN'S DEATH RAPIDLY BECAME OLD NEWS ON ST. Thomas. People were concerned with more pressing issues like rebuilding homes and businesses, getting back electricity or phone service, or applying for relief from one source or another. Tropical storm *Abby* had ravaged the island. Nobody would be paying good money to visit St. Thomas for a good while. The goal of the business community was simply to buckle down and try to get things in shape for the season beginning January 1. It was going to be tough, though. Getting building supplies is problematic even under normal circumstances on an island. Getting them in the quantities needed after an Act of God would require another Act of God. For a tropical storm *Abby* had done some serious damage. She hit the island dead on and the problem was that no place was spared damage since at one time or another during the approach and recession of the storm the wind had slammed the coast from literally every direction.

Some places were unrecognizable. Beaches had disappeared and reappeared in other locations. The remains of one hotel, which many locals claimed that building officials should never have certified for construction in the first place, were now effectively on an island. The hotel developers paid off the zoning board people to build on what was essentially a sandbar and insurance company lawyers who got wind of this fact were now having a field day as they attempted to eliminate a potentially big liability because of fraudulent practices.

Of course Dean's distribution territory was cut up and quickly absorbed by his former competitors, some of whom actually attended his wake and memorial service. They were probably there as much to make sure that Dean was really a stiff, as to pay him any sincere last respects. Apparently a large sum of money, rumored to be in the neighborhood of $200,000, disappeared about the time Dean expired. Some snitches reported to the police that it had been voiced by a few of Dean's business associates that Dean may have actually staged his own death and run off with a load of cash. Such a possibility had to be at least checked out by those with naturally suspicious minds. The criminal elements always had such active imaginations didn't they?

A tribute to the laws of supply and demand was the fact that the island's illicit drug supply was never interrupted by either Dean's demise or the storm. Corporate America seldom engineered such a smooth transition of leadership. Business was business, after all, and would go on in spite of the damage caused by *Abby* or the very temporary vacuum caused by Dean's passing. There were even some advantages to the new situation. The heat from the authorities would be off the dealers and suppliers for the foreseeable future. There were too many other things for them to worry about.

For those who cared about Sandy there was some favorable news. Evidently she was not going to die anytime soon. The question was how she would live. After being stabilized by her doctors and surviving a hospital environment plagued by power outages and shortages of medical supplies, she had been airlifted to the mainland aboard a specially outfitted Air National Guard C-130 which evacuated many island patients to better equipped and less taxed facilities. Her family quickly got Sandy into a private clinic that dealt solely with the victims of head trauma.

At first the doctors in St. Thomas thought that only Sandy's jaw had been broken. But when she didn't come to, an MRI showed that her brain was filling with fluid. A shunt was immediately installed to prevent her from becoming hydrocephalic, but she still never regained consciousness. The doctors gently explained to Sandy's parents that Sandy might be in a coma for hours or forever. And if she did regain consciousness, there was no telling to what degree she would remember things or be able to function. They said sincerely that she was in "God's hands."

With the usual post-disaster looting and other matters to deal with the police pushed the Dean/Sandy matter to the back burner. From their point of view a bad guy had gone to his eternal reward. It was clear to them that the raped victim, Sandy, gave him a well-deserved and permanent headache. The ME didn't even bother having the semen sample that was taken from her analyzed. After all, what else did the police really need to know? Case closed.

There was no Constellation Yacht Charters any more. Well the bulkheads were still there, but that was about it. The sheds and bungalows were surprisingly heavily damaged. They actually looked like they were hit by a tornado rather than a tropical storm and, in fact, meteorologists were seriously examining that possibility. Several masts protruded up from the waters of Fiddler Crab Cove and the beach was strewn with wreckage which could not be identified as coming from any particular boat. One of the Constellation vessels had been salvaged 40 miles offshore by a private firm, three days after the storm. The sloop had parted its mooring line and somehow drifted away unscathed. The sea could be very strange sometimes. Other vessels, which could no longer be recognized, blew up on offshore reefs and broke up. In several cases the only thing left of them was an engine block or two nestled in the coral while they bled beads of oil or gas that created a rainbow effect on the water surface above them.

The island really was in turmoil. Those who could, simply left. Why not? They had damaged living quarters, no jobs, no money and maybe some debt. All in all, it was a good time to move on. The local authorities noted that there were only three confirmed storm related fatalities. Lot's of people seemed to be missing, but the official explanation was that they had jumped a plane or ferry before their departure could be properly documented.

Rick, Jimmy and JJ could have never have planned for their tracks to be covered so well. Unfortunately, Rick and JJ were unaware that their getaway was such a perfect one.

CHAPTER EIGHT

RICK AND JJ FINISHED THE COOL BEERS AND CHAT-
TED about nothing in particular. They were both far
from their normal selves and were both burdened
with their own deep and personal thoughts.

"I'll take the helm JJ. Why don't you go below and get
some rest?" suggested Rick.

"Can I just rest up here, Skip? I don't think I can go
below again just yet."

Rick offered to bring up some blankets, cockpit cushions and pillows. JJ accepted the offer and curled up in a
corner where he made a nest for himself. It was early afternoon and the sky was clear and the air warm. There was no
dodger to block wind and spray, but no great need for one,
either. It seemed to Rick like JJ was breathing deeply, then
snoring in only two minutes. Fear and anxiety had that
effect on some. Before nodding off, JJ probably hoped that
he would wake up and find that this was all a bad dream,
or that if it wasn't, Rick had miraculously solved a number
of their problems while he had been cutting Zs.

Rick's first urge had been to immediately tell JJ about his discovery of the money. But he held his tongue. His street knowledge was evident in his reasoning: He could always tell JJ later about the money, but he couldn't un-tell him. Until he figured out what was going on, the best thing would be to keep quiet. A possibility that jumped into his mind was that maybe JJ already knew about the money! That would be complicating. He would have to ex-plore that possibility real soon.

Everybody dreamed of finding a pile of money some day to solve all of life's problems. But Rick could now un-derstand why many people said that money "can cause a lot of trouble." If *Pleiades* were stopped now by the Coast Guard, INS, or US Customs and anyone found the small fortune in cash aboard, what would they think? He could tell the truth, but the way the minds of law enforcement people worked, they would definitely think that he was ly-ing. They might even think that he took the money and killed Dean on St. Thomas and Jimmy to boot.

"Damn it, Jimmy. What the heck were you up to?" he thought to himself.

Nobody carried around honestly earned cash in an old US Army duffel bag. How Jimmy came to be in its possession must be an interesting story. He didn't just find the money, that was certain. He must have taken it. Maybe from Dean and his associates. The gun and drugs hinted at that. And taking money from the kind of people who deal in cash could only mean that some drug dealer was very pissed off. He even might be looking for Jimmy right now. And if the drug dealer had good intelligence, he could also be looking for JJ and Rick, too. That was not good.

Rick's emotional state was not good, either. A week ago he was reasonably happy and stable. Relatively speaking, he had been extremely content with his life. Sailing, cavorting with beautiful women, drinking. Lot's of people wouldn't mind being him! Now, he was wanted for questioning in a murder he did not commit; he was meandering around in the Atlantic Ocean after barely surviving a storm which was as close to a hurricane as he ever wanted to get; and he was possibly the prey of an unknown drug lord.

"Shit, hell and goddamn!"

But Rick was nothing if not practical. Neither the police, nor the other bad guys would get him out here on God's blue ocean. As he approached land, though, that could change, of course. For the time being another storm, or the wide variety of unpredictable offshore marine mishaps were of much more immediate concern. While JJ slept and he sailed along his mind was busy. The most important thing would be to get electricity in the next few days. Electricity meant the engine could be started, more electricity could be generated, they could communicate by radio, they could navigate with space age accuracy. They could drink cold beer.

The voltmeter showed that the battery bank voltage was less than 12V, hence the batteries were useless for the moment. The small PV (photovoltaic) panel on board, which measured one foot by two, was meant to be nothing more than a trickle charger for the batteries. The silicon wafers which were the working part of the panel directly converted sunlight into electricity. The device was supposed to keep the battery bank topped off during long periods of boat inactivity, but it was not meant to quickly charge up significantly discharged batteries. The batteries would recover a bit on their own, but not enough to spin the starter. The plan would be to get one battery charged up enough to start the diesel engine and then take it from there. That plan would get priority attention the following day.

JJ was still sound asleep and looked like a little kid. Rick sailed along and continued to turn over idea after idea in his head. Before he knew it the sun was low on the horizon. He had been in a semi-hypnotized state for hours! But it looked like the boat was still on course and the sails were properly trimmed. Rick made a decision: tonight he and JJ would eat well, relax, plan a few things and sleep. They were only making good a couple of miles an hour under reduced sail and it was not worth the expenditure of their energy. In a couple of days they should have all the electricity they needed. They would then have the autopilot to give them a hand when they had other tasks to do, or when they wanted to rest at night. With a little luck they might be able to use the GPS the following afternoon. It drew hardly any current but needed the full 12V to function properly. They would get a quick position fix and then be able to set a proper course to a proper destination.

Rick gently woke up JJ who stretched, yawned, sat up, and looked about. JJ looked and said he felt a lot better. Rick spelled out the plan to him. The two then dropped and furled the sails, set the sea anchor, and went below as the last glow of the sun disappeared from the horizon. The stars were soon as bright as Rick predicted that they would be and he made a mental note to check them out a little bit later. For the next few hours Rick and JJ would concentrate on gathering their strength and regaining their senses.

JJ and Rick feasted on a nice hot meal that was a culinary clash if ever there was one. Chef Boy-R-Dee spaghetti was served first, which was followed by La Choy Chicken Chow Mein and Chinese vegetables. Completing the evening's menu was canned brown bread, pan-fried in butter, along with a bottle of beer for each of them. The dinner was filling, and probably reasonably nutritious, too.

A bulkhead mounted, brass oil lamp on gimbals filled the cabin with a pleasant yellow glow which along with the oiled teak woodwork somehow made for a comfortable setting. It was hard to believe that they were on the same ocean that nearly killed them only a day ago.

JJ and Rick settled into the bunks on opposite sides of the main salon, separated by the drop leaf table.

"So how are we really doing, Skip? I know you been thinking a lot.

"We're doing fine and we'll be doing a lot better by tomorrow afternoon."

Rick ran through the things again that he wanted to get done the following day in more detail.

"Are we still going to this Moohead City?"

Rick laughed. "It's pronounced 'more head....' Why not?"

"We don't know nobody in Morehead."

JJ was right. Neither of them had any contacts there. In fact Rick either had forgotten, or had never been told, the names of Jimmy's friends. He thought for a moment. Did JJ have a motive here? If he knew about the money, it was possible that he knew other things. Maybe he, Jimmy and the shore contacts were all in on some sort of scam together. Maybe they were supposed to split the money in Morehead City. And maybe, too, that is where the police would be expecting them all to arrive. Hell, the drug kingpin's men might be there waiting, too. Scratch Morehead.

"I guess we don't have to pull in there, do we? Where should we go."

"You the man, Skip. We can go anywhere. I don't care where we go as long as I can get to the 'Big Apple' and meet my cousin, Napoleon."

Rick noticed that JJ seemed to be regressing in his speech patterns, sounding less and less almost American and more and more like he did when they first met. Rick wrote it off to nervousness. Given his situation as a wanted man, and JJ's situation as an unwanted alien, it didn't matter where they went and it was better off if nobody knew them wherever that was. Having said that, it occurred to him that they probably would attract less attention in New York than anywhere else on the coast.

"How about NYC?"

"The Big Apple?"

"The same!"

"Can we do it?"

"Don't see why we can't!"

"Then let's do it," said JJ excitedly. He even clapped like a child who just got the present that he had always wished for. Rick could see at that moment, that JJ was completely without guile. Rick was absolutely certain that JJ had no connection or knowledge of whatever Jimmy was involved in.

"Let's get a good night's sleep. Dream of the Statue of Liberty. I promise you.. you'll see her in a few days!"

JJ got his blankets all together and made his bunk. He set up the bunk restraints so he wouldn't slip out of the berth and onto the floor. Meanwhile Rick went on deck to check out the sea anchor and see if there were any threats on the horizon, literally or figuratively. But all was as it should have been. He grabbed a handhold and sat on the dog-house for a moment looking up at the sky. The North Star, or Polaris, was definitely a bit higher in the sky than it was in St. Thomas. He could see it and still see the line of the horizon clearly. He knew that he could go get the sextant that he knew was on board somewhere, do a simple measurement of the angular height of Polaris and he would have his latitude. Instead he went below and tumbled into his bunk. His mind went blank and he fell instantly to sleep.

BOTH RICK AND JJ WOKE UP QUITE REFRESHED. AFTER a breakfast of dry sweetened cereal and a small can of tomato juice, each, they went on deck to begin their projects. Rick directed JJ to begin wet sanding off the name, *Pleiades*. There was plenty of 400 grit wet or dry sandpaper in the lazarette as well as a small plastic bucket with a short line attached. JJ threw the bucket, mouth facing downward, into the water off the transom and expertly hauled it up full to the brim. He soaked the sandpaper and then poured water over the boat's name and home port so it would be somewhat lubricated when he used the fine abrasive to remove them. Bracing his legs around a convenient winch, he hung over the stern and began wet sanding. Bluish paint mixed with the water and dripped down the wet hull into the ocean where it spread like milk does when it is poured into water. JJ took care to sand as much of the blue and as little as the white as possible, so he would not have too much buffing to do later on to remove any of the dullness caused by the sanding.

Rick set about to rig up the solar charger. He unstrapped one of the heavy lead batteries and brought it up into the cockpit, securing it to the steering pedestal with a short length of line. It would not be good for this battery to shift around. It was heavy enough to punch through the cockpit fiberglass if the boat took a good roll, or it could spill out sulfuric acid.

The solar panel had 10' connecting wires terminating in pinch clips. Rick found a spot on the deck for the panel at the right angle to the sun, about 35°, to maximize electricity production. He used duct tape to keep the panel in place. Taking the voltmeter he made sure that the PV array was functioning. At the terminals he was reading about 15 volts. The lead starting battery was still reading under ten volts by itself and about 13.5 volts with the PV attached. That was good. He would have to keep an eye on the panel during the day and make sure that no shadows fell across it, decreasing its efficiency. Then it was just a matter of waiting. The amps would trickle in and at some point there would be enough electrons stored up in the battery to spin the starter motor and get the diesel going. He was sure that it would take a couple or three days to reach that point. But he could actually hook up the inexpensive backup hand-held Garmin GPS system in a few minutes. He went below to retrieve it and the auxiliary cable for a direct battery connection.

The GPS came alive immediately. The LCD screen showed that it was acquiring a half-dozen satellites and that the estimated position error was only 17 feet! What Columbus would not have given for this gadget, thought

Rick. He yelled out to JJ that now they knew exactly where on God's ocean they were. Rick dashed below to retrieve a pencil and notebook and recorded the time and the position: 27° 58.36 N, 69° 02.15 W. Without a chart he did not know where this was relative to where they wanted to go, but using another GPS screen and zooming out on the crude black and white LCD "map;" it seemed like they were basically in the middle of nowhere. He and JJ would have to rummage around the boat looking for some sort of map or chart. He thought he remembered some placemats stowed aboard somewhere that were reprints of charts. Vaguely he recalled viewing locations such as Bermuda, St. Thomas, and Chesapeake Bay as he ate dinners when the placemats were used. These dinners would have been served to the paying customers on a "captained" charters. The help never bothered with such niceties for themselves.

Of course they could always go due west, encounter land, and then run north up the coast. That would be much more time consuming, though. It was too bad that there was not a single mainland waypoint entered into the hand held GPS. Jimmy, who did most of the navigating, would have entered one into the main cockpit GPS system, but that was now history. But perhaps there were some useful destinations entered into the memory of the backup Raytheon LORAN at the nav station. He would have to scope that out later.

Suddenly he smiled and hit the "GOTO" button of the GPS and began entering the following coordinates: 41°34.12 N, 71°26.75 W. When Rick was a boy, his grandfather in Rhode Island told him to memorize these numbers. They represented the latitude and longitude of Wickford, where they lived. Gramps used to say that if he remembered those numbers he could always find his way back to their seaside home. Whenever Rick wanted an ice cream all he had to do was correctly utter the latitude and longitude coordinates; Gramps would laugh and then give him some ice cream money. Briefly, Rick wondered if the stone, on which the numbers were once carved, was still at that precise location.

Rhode Island was not New York, but at this distance it was close enough. The course/distance screen of the GPS reported that Wickford, Rhode Island was 823 nautical miles away at a bearing of 06° Magnetic. For now they could head 0° and that would be fine until they got New York's coordinates. If Rick really had to, he could probably estimate some reasonably good numbers, since he knew that NYC was about a 100 miles west of Wickford as the crow flies. A fleeting thought was that maybe he should sail to Wickford. Gramps would smile from his grave if he did.

Rick looked up and watched JJ wriggle back up from his awkward position.

"All set, Skip. The transom looks white and shiny like it did when the boat was pulled from the mold. It's all set for a new name."

Rick filled JJ in on the details of their position.

"How long before we get to New York?"

"Depends on a lot of things, but once we get the autopilot up and running we can conservatively figure on making good a hundred miles a day, so we are about eight days away. Figure on ten."

Rick then asked JJ to peel off the boat's plastic registration numbers and wipe the area down with acetone to remove any glue. Documented vessels, which were registered with the Coast Guard, did not need to display local registration numbers. The boat name and home port on the transom was sufficient. They would have to get to the name painted on soon for if they came upon another boat, or a search plane came upon them and saw neither numbers nor a name, that would be a suspicious sign.

After lunch they set all sails in a nice fresh wind and steered due north. Rick repositioned the PV panel and he and JJ decided to see how a four hour watch worked out. It would get tiring if they had to do it for more than a couple days. The danger was that if some problem, like a storm, came up, even a small one, neither man would be at full strength. That was something to worry about when you were shorthanded as they were. With a little luck, though, Otto, the autopilot would be working soon.

JJ took the first shift beginning about noon, and Rick went below to check out the engine. He changed the fuel filter and emptied the water separator, finding no water but only clear diesel oil. He then began searching the bookcases and cabinets yet again for anything that looked like a chart. He didn't find one but he came across the plastic sextant. It was a toy, really, made for super novices, and left aboard *Pleiades* by a charterer who must have been a student of celestial navigation. If the sextant were dropped overboard you probably would only be out twenty dollars! It had a very abbreviated instruction sheet and truncated celestial tables taken from the navigators bible called "The Bowditch."

Something that old Gramps used to often repeat to him popped into his head: "Better to have it and not need it, then need it and not have it." This statement was nowhere truer than on a boat at sea. If something happened to the electronics, this sextant could be a critical backup piece of equipment. Though he understood the fundamentals of celestial navigation, he would have to learn how to use the sextant properly and he promised himself that he would, given that he had plenty of free time and no place to go.

He remembered an old navigator's trick that could also be helpful. The portable radio could be tuned to a NYC AM radio station. These portable radios all had directional antennas. If the width of the small internal radio antenna was rotated and at some point was aimed directly at the radio station broadcasting antenna, the signal would come in poorly. You would hardly hear anything. In the old days this was referred to as a "null" signal. That meant that the length of the radio antenna was aimed directly at the radio tower on shore or directly away from it. This rudimentary radio direction finding system (RDF) could be used to home in on a port.

Rick suddenly felt better about the navigational aspects of the trip ahead. They had three methods to find the Big Apple. One would get them there, though he was going to use all three to be certain.

While Rick continued looking for something that would be of value in making a safe and easy NYC landing, he was tempted to go forward to just peek at the money. But he thought that would be a bad habit to get into. It was ironic that for all the money over which he had suddenly come into control, it was of no immediate value to him whatsoever. A good chart was worth at least a portion of the fortune at the moment.

Sorting through a pile of fairly recent magazines he came across a paperback book with a yellow-or-ange cover. "Holy shit," he yelled. The title read: "El-dridge Tide and Pilot Book, 1985, One Hundred and Eleventh Year." "This could be it," he said aloud. "Hey, JJ! I think we just got lucky!" Rick brought the book up to the cockpit and JJ gave him a dubious look after reading the cover. The table of contents was printed on it and it included headings for the "Daily High and Low Water at Boston" and the "Current Table, THE RACE."

"Skip, it's 2002! What be the good of that?" Rick ignored the question and started frantically flipping through the pages. The "Eldridge" as the book was called, was a collection of tide, current and astronomical information interspersed with nautical advice. It was first published in 1870 by Capt. George Eldridge and sold on the Vineyard Haven docks by his son of the same name. The Eldridge had little tidbits of information like how far you could see for each foot your eyes were above sea level, how to use a barometer to predict the weather, and how to find the "magic spot" on a boat where the compass was un-affected by magnetic interference and read as it was sup-posed to. Rick had seen other editions of the publication before when he had done yacht deliveries to or from the Northeast, but he did not know this copy was aboard until he found it.

Rick stopped thumbing through the frayed pages. On page 257 was advice for sailing in a hurricane. He pointed it out to JJ with his finger.

"Where was this when we needed it?" he muttered. Then he continued turning pages and scanning them quickly.

He scared the daylights out of JJ with a long drawn out rebel yell. "Eureka!" There on page 100 it read: "Current Table, The Narrows, N.Y. Harbor, Mid-Channel 40°36' 36" N X 74° 02' 48" W. Then on page 110 he found a crude, but more than adequate current chart that showed the approach to New York Harbor with Sandy Hook, NJ off to port and Coney Island to Starboard. "JJ, there is a God!"

A more leisurely perusal showed that the Eldridge held a wealth of information about navigation aids and other potential ports of entry should they have to change destination for some reason. Now all they had to do was concentrate on their sailing and plan what they would do when they reached shore.

For two days after finding the Eldridge, *Pleiades* sailed along on a northerly track without incident. Rick and JJ got into a routine and the four hour watch system worked fine. They were a little tired, but it was not a serious problem, yet. They listened to the radio in the morning at 8:00 a.m., at noon and at midnight for five minutes only, to conserve the battery. Most of the news was superfluous. News about the weather was not. They had to piece together the weather reports, though, since they were receiving them from such diverse places as Bermuda, Boston, Charleston, and Philadelphia. The AM signals were bounced off the ionosphere and the earth several times before they received them, so the reception was always weak with static, fading in and out. But basically they seemed to be in a big high-pressure system and that was good.

After several cockpit discussions, it was agreed to rename the boat *Spray*. *Spray* was a good name for several reasons. First, it was a common name like *Teacher's Pet*

or *Irish Mist* and a boat with this name could hail from
any port north of Mexico. Second, it was short and would not
take much time to prepare a decent looking stencil for it and
apply the new name to the transom. The last reason was
personal. Other kids grew up reading the Golden Books of
this or that. Rick's mother and grandfather read and
encouraged him to read books by Robin Lee Graham, Sir
Francis Chichester, and Joshua Slocum. Each had sailed
alone around the world and their stories of adventure
made an impression on the mind of the young Rick
Thornton. Joshua Slocum's story was still one of Rick's
favorites. *Spray* was Joshua Slocum's 37 foot boat which was
the first to carry a solo voyager around the world in the late
1890s. Slocum found her sitting abandoned in a pasture
and refurbished her with his own hands. *Spray* was so well
designed and built that Slocum was able to merely lash the
helm, trim the sails, and she would sail herself for hundreds of
miles at a time.

While JJ sailed along in seas which became very gentle,
Rick sketched several full size stylized versions of the name,
Spray, on sheets of newspaper. None looked quite right. JJ
tried his hand at the sketches while off duty and on his first try
came up with something which looked like it was done by a
professional sign painter. Using the scissors on his Swiss Army
knife Rick fashioned a stencil out of JJ's sketch, leaving paper
in strategic places to hold the image together. It was a delicate
piece of work, but it only had to survive a half hour, or so,
taped to the transom while the paint dried.

The new name looked incredibly good on the boat. The
size of the letters was just right and the centering was perfect. JJ had used a piece of sponge dipped into some blue
boot stripe touchup paint found in a small can in the lazarette and applied it sparingly, so it would not run. It dried
quickly since the sun fell directly on the transom which
as luck would have it was facing south. Three light coats
produced a nice, solid color and the overall job looked as

good as anything that would have been done on shore, though JJ completed it using moves that would be a credit to a contortionist. They also made a stencil and painted on the homeport of Dover, Del. Thousands of boats had the same homeport though most had never even visited Delaware. But small corporations often were the actual owners of yachts and the corporations were registered in Delaware for tax purposes.

At the end of the third day an important experiment was scheduled for sunset. Rick and JJ were going to try to start the engine. The voltage had been holding steady above 12 even when they checked it in the morning and the battery had been sitting all night. Rick had taken a probe wire from the multimeter and attached one end to the positive terminal and then brushed the other end past the negative one. There was a satisfying crackle and snap of electricity and he was tempted to witness the phenomena again but decided that they needed the services of every last electron to heat up those glow plugs and turn over the engine. JJ had sanded the lead battery terminals so they shined like silver and then sanded the copper terminals of the battery cables so they shined like gold. They were taking no chances. If this attempt to start the engine failed, the effort would drain the batteries of all juice and they would have to start solar charging all over again.

Rick brought the battery down to its compartment, hooked it up and then strapped it into place. He checked the water level in the battery once again out of insecurity. If it was full this morning, of course it was still going to be full now. At noon he similarly had put the measuring stick into the fuel tank three times, to be sure that it really held about 50 gallons of diesel. Rick noticed that his palms and underarms were sweating. He thought once more about what he was about to do to make sure nothing was overlooked. He decided after much deliberation not to use the glow plugs to make the fuel vaporize easier. To do so would use current that would be better used in turning over the high compression engine. Rick judged that the air and engine temperatures were warm enough for the fuel. He set the Guest battery switch to draw from the battery that had received the solar charge and then he took the ignition key off its hook in the galley.

JJ was at the helm holding a steady course when Rick put the key in the ignition. "Say a little prayer, JJ!" They both actually lowered their heads and prayed for a moment. Rick hadn't said a prayer in 20 years, but today he prayed like an altarboy at a Christmas Eve Midnight Mass. JJ prayed to Dieu, a number of saints, and to cover the bases he made a promise to sacrifice a chicken to a voodoo spirit at the first convenient opportunity.

"Here we go!" The key was inserted and turned. They heard nothing from the engine compartment at first. Then slowly, the flywheel began to spin. Suddenly it spun more quickly, like it had broken something that was trying to hold it back and then it definitely chugged to life. Beautiful black smoke belched from the exhaust as the engine settled into a comfortable rhythm.

In all likelihood there were no other humans within a hundred miles of Spray's location to hear the whoops, yells and laughter. The engine was allowed to warm up for five minutes and then was thrown into gear. Boat speed perceptibly increased immediately. The wind was almost behind them at that moment and so the boat was probably making a good seven or eight knots in the right direction. Perhaps more with a slight Gulf Stream assist! Rick ran below and got one of the bottles of beer and was back on deck in a flash. JJ thought the beer was for a toast, but Rick took the bottle and moved smoothly towards the bow. Looking back at JJ he raised the bottle in the air. "I christen thee, *Spray.*" And with that pronouncement he brought the bottle down hard on the short stainless steel bowsprit.

CHAPTER NINE

ONCE SPRAY'S ENGINE WAS STARTED THE MOOD
aboard her was instantly good. For three hours
the engine powered an alternator which in turn
brought the battery bank up to full charge. Psychologically, JJ and Rick felt like they had re-entered the 21st
century and that as a result they would be protected and
assisted by all the technological marvels a modern vessel
had on board.

Each day for the rest of the journey the engine was
only run for an hour, essentially as one big battery charger.
Any additional distance the boat made good during this
charging period was seen as a fringe benefit. The fuel had
to be conserved, of course, for emergencies and to enter
the harbor. There was simply nowhere near enough fuel
to power all the way to the Big Apple. The plan was to sail
as close to the Verrazano-Narrows bridge as possible and
then motor up the Hudson from there.

Rick decided against siphoning the fuel in the remaining plastic barrel into the main tank. He knew it was unco-

ntaminated with water and was not sure about the main tank. He would keep it in reserve just in case. Rick tested all three batteries several times a day with a multimeter to make sure that they held the electrical charge since he was still not positive that the batteries were not permanently damaged by salt water immersion. Two batteries were connected to the alternator. One was used just for starting the engine and the other supplied electricity for the instruments, lights and to Otto, the name they had given to the autopilot. The third battery was charged up but not connected to anything. It was their insurance battery.

One instrument that did not work was the backup LORAN. The LORAN (LOng Range Aid to Navigation) system was an older, but still reliable, electronic navigation method that utilized ground station signals rather than satellites. It apparently could not acquire signals and a little checking turned up the reason: its five foot antenna, also, had been cleanly washed away sometime during the storm.

Since the engine started, the sailing was uneventful, even boring. There was not a lot to see: just sea and sky. Not a single vessel came into view which was surprising since they had traveled about six hundred miles and were only a couple of hundred miles from New York. There were no birds, no dolphins, no turtles. There was a possible Portuguese man-of-war sighting, though JJ insisted that it was in reality a partially inflated sandwich bag with algae growth trailing from it. One night they heard the spouting of whales, but could not actually see them. JJ didn't like that. They were probably migrating fins or humps heading up to Stellwagen Bank off Provincetown to hang out and eat sand eels for the summer.

Rick was pretty sure one curious whale approached close to the boat. He saw a large trail of phosphorescence in the water about 15 feet down which had to be made by either a whale or a large fish. It was an awesome sight but one which would not be appreciated at the moment by his shipmate.

In the days after the storm the men concentrated on sailing and navigating. Rick was getting half decent at obtaining celestial position fixes with the sextant and tables that he was able to confirm with the GPS. And the AM signal from WCBS in New York was right on the nose according to the radio direction finder that he had rigged up. Finding the entrance to New York Harbor should be a piece of cake.

For a couple days the wind was right on *Spray's* nose and the going was slow and sloppy. Rick was tempted to power through but ultimately decided to exercise some patience and sail as close to the wind as he could. He told JJ of a story he had heard about a master of an old time sailing vessel spending a month trying to go into the wind around Cape Horn at the tip of South America. At the end of the month the Cape was right where it had been at the beginning. Ultimately, the master decided to turn the ship around and sail almost completely around the world with, rather than against, the prevailing winds. "Life was hard then," said Rick. "Life is still hard," thought JJ.

JJ was able to collect about six gallons of nice fresh water. They ran through several rain showers of short duration as they made their way north, all which occurred at night. JJ waited until the rain washed off the salt from the sails. He would let water from the sails run into his mouth. When it no longer tasted salty he would let it run into assorted plastic jugs, wine bottles and jars. The rainwater was chilled in the functioning fridge and to JJ it tasted like the best beverage he had ever drunk. Rick used the water for coffee. He had really missed his coffee for a few days and with it he felt like his life was almost normal.

With Otto doing all the tedious work of steering *Spray* there was plenty of time while sitting in the cockpit to talk and plan their approach to New York and JJ's ultimate "insertion" into Manhattan.

"JJ, are you sure that you feel comfortable doing this?" Rick asked one last time.

JJ paused before answering. "For me and my family I must do this. Otherwise Papa will have died in vain. Papa always said that the Dessalines would forever be poor unless we cast our lot with your country. Even if I am the only one who makes it to America I can work hard and send lots of money back to Port-de-Paix. It can buy doctors and medicine and food and maybe even a better house with two bedrooms for my mother and my sisters. I have so much to gain for my family and so little to lose. I must take this big chance or I will always regret that I didn't."

IT IS A FALLACY FOSTERED BY THE INS THAT IT IS EVEN remotely difficult for aliens to enter the United States. The border between Mexico and the U.S. is reasonably well patrolled, but the truth is that the one between the U.S. and Canada is pretty porous and the coastlines, particularly along the Atlantic and Gulf of Mexico, are incredibly easy to broach. The only way that vessels smuggling illegals are caught by American authorities is by dumb luck or a tip from a jealous competitor. Vessels, especially those coming up from the Bahamas or Caribbean in the summer with aliens aboard, would have to be tracked every minute of their voyage if there is to be any chance of any government agency capturing them. Even when that occurs, they often give the Coast Guard the slip. Sophisticated smugglers closely mingle with participants in offshore sailing races, yacht club and power squadron cruises and fishing fleets, performing the radar version of the shell game.

Once close to land, the boats, identical to those that routinely cruise the coast from June through September, can calmly choose any small harbor for a landing. As long as the passengers don't look too scruffy, wear American style clothing, have American dollars, and can speak fluent English, they have almost nothing to fear. Hours after landing in Annapolis, Nantucket or Newport the new immigrants can be in Washington, Boston or New York. If they have contacts in those places they can be working the very next day; if not, it might take a week to find a job.

Rick, of course, knew all of this. He had only once taken the time to contact customs when he delivered yachts between mainland USA and the Islands, and the experience was so time consuming and aggravating, he never thought about doing it again.

His plan for JJ was simple, yet elegant. *Spray* would sail up along the Jersey Shore, then under the Verrazano-Narrows Bridge and up the Hudson right past the Statue of Liberty. The Lady would properly greet JJ as she had so many others in the past. Then they would continue motoring to the Jersey side of the Hudson just west of lower Manhattan. Rick knew from another trip years before that there were still little indentations on that shore where you could anchor or tie up. Once they got their bearings, so to speak, and scoped things out, they could even pull into one of the marinas near Liberty State Park. They would stay there for several days while JJ called his friends and got acclimated to his new surroundings.

Some plans work as they are supposed to or even better. Rick chose to actually sail, rather than power, right into one of the world's greatest harbors. He did it, purposely, so that someday JJ could tell his children and grandchildren a more romantic and true story of coming to America and approaching the Statue of Liberty on a beautiful June morning aboard a vessel under full sail. JJ was mesmerized by the Manhattan skyline which was visible from many miles in a light morning fog which hugged the water. The buildings seemed to him like they were built on clouds. The absence of the World Trade Towers made not as much of an impression on JJ as it did on Rick, who was awed by the fact that something so monumental and symbolic of his country could be literally wiped off the face of the earth. There was some sort of a life lesson in that observation which Rick would ponder later on.

Soon JJ could pick out Lady Liberty with binoculars, then he could see the torch with the naked eye. The Lady and the skyscrapers grew larger and larger by the moment and soon JJ could not take his eyes off the former. As Rick prepared to give the order to luff up and take down the sails only a few hundred yards off Liberty Island he noticed the tears streaming down JJ's jet black face and dripping onto his T-shirt. Before he knew it tears were streaming down his face, so he angled *Spray* off towards Manhattan to give them both time to regain their composure.

Sails down and furled, *Spray* nosed into one of those little indentations which once were bordered by shipping docks on the Jersey shore. The spot was very seedy. An old tug and a couple of dilapidated fishing draggers were tied up to half rotted pilings. The water had a film of oil on it and as Rick surveyed it he saw what he hoped was a deflated balloon but was pretty sure was a used prophylactic.

The water was about 16 feet deep according to the depth sounder. There was space at the docks but Rick decided to bow and stern anchor rather than come in contact with the shore. He wanted to be far enough away from the docks to prevent rats, both the four and two legged varieties, from being able to hop aboard. Once the anchors were deployed Rick and JJ high fived and congratulated themselves on their arrival and gave thanks to the Almighty.

Rick went below and surfaced with two cold beers. The two made themselves comfortable in the unshaded cockpit. Rick opened the bottles and proposed a toast: "To Jimmy, wherever you may be!"

Adrenaline was starting to flow in both men's veins. There is a rush that comes after completing an ocean voyage, especially an eventful one such as theirs. JJ said what Rick was thinking: "Can't wait to get my feet on *terra firma*!" And they both laughed as they pulled out, unwrapped and inflated the dinghy. After lowering it over the side JJ jumped down to put the now somewhat more dented and venerable British Seagull outboard on the transom.

A marina was just up the Hudson from where they were anchored on the Jersey side. They would probably move *Spray* there at some point but Rick wanted to check it out first, though why that was he didn't know. Perhaps a sea paranoia vacuum had to be filled by a land paranoia one.

The Seagull came to life after two pulls of the starter cord and the two men putted over to the boatyard, tying up at the dinghy dock. There was a snack bar, showers and marine store housed in an old lightship that had been converted into excellent facilities for visiting boaters. Rick and JJ ordered hamburger platters, beers, and picked up a newspaper. Sitting out on deck at a little table surrounded by planters filled with brightly colored flowers it appeared to any onlooker that a couple of local working guys were just enjoying one of the first warm days of summer. To the men the experience felt strange but they would get over it quickly. In fact, later that afternoon they jumped aboard the little commuter ferry at Liberty State Park which brought them down by Wall Street. Being in Manhattan after what they had been through over the last few weeks was a real trip. JJ's head was twisting all around to see everything but he was absolutely ecstatic.

They made their way up to Canal Street and picked up some little things from sidewalk vendors like a $12 fake Rolex, an NYFD baseball cap and an "I Love New York" T-shirt. It was all cheap tourist stuff but it somehow made JJ feel more "American" and that was just fine by Rick. The time went by quickly and after a filling dinner in Chinatown they scooted back across the Hudson to *Spray*. Both men were exhausted and turned in early, sleeping exceptionally well since they did not have to be concerned about waking up for a four hour watch, or worry about the routine dangers of a boat at sea.

The next day Rick and JJ moved *Spray* to the marina and began to explore the area and make contacts. Rick used his real name when he registered at the marina and regretted doing so the moment he did. But since he paid his bill in cash and the boat name was different from what it had been, he did not think it would create a problem. But he was not going to be able to use his credit card anymore if he wanted to keep his whereabouts unknown.

JJ tried calling his cousin, Napoleon, but nobody answered the phone. The two men decided to try to make contact with Napoleon later in the day and again roam the city a bit. First priority was for JJ to get some evidence of having a New York "history." He had a fake driver's license that he had bought in St. Thomas, which didn't expire for another six months. It was probably more useful in the States where nobody was exactly sure just what a St. Thomas license should look like. Using his cousin's address and the license, JJ applied for and got a New York City Public Library card. Then he got a photo ID type membership card to a big discount store. And when they stopped at a pharmacy which was part of a national chain for some toothpaste, JJ picked up one of their discount cards. Though none of these pieces of plastic were IDs in the real sense, JJ felt that they somehow linked him to his new surroundings.

Rick and JJ crisscrossed Manhattan getting the lay of the land as they consulted a free souvenir tourist map. Rick thought it would be a good idea to walk, take subways, buses, and cabs to acclimate JJ to this very unfamiliar environment and JJ enjoyed every minute of it. JJ was surprised at how he felt being in the city. He had seen it on TV and in the movies and, of course, read about it a million times. But there was an energy and pulse to New York that he felt everywhere which was so hard to describe. It was at the same time both exciting and frightening.

While walking through Central Park, Rick was thinking about things, too. He decided that he could assume Jimmy's identity, if he had to, though he did not mention this to JJ. It was a bit risky, he knew, because Rick didn't know all of Jimmy's life history. Jimmy's cash stash a case in point. But at that moment there were probably no police bulletins out for James Fox, though by that time St. Thomas' finest probably had linked Richard Thornton with Sandy and by extension Mean Dean. Rick had thought over the situation and was still convinced that unless Dean's real murderer was identified and apprehended he would be the main suspect with no good alibi.

But James Fox was a fairly common name and Jimmy's billfold had a license, laminated social security card, and a few other pieces of paper including a low balance credit card bill with convenient change of address form that would make becoming Jimmy relatively easy. To use the license he would have to let his hair darken to its natural color, cut it short, and pray that either nobody asked for it, or looked too closely at it if they did. With luck he would not need to use the new identity, or use it for long. But who knew?

Late in the afternoon JJ got a hold of cousin Napoleon using a streetside pay phone and he chatted excitedly with him in French. Rick only caught drifts of the animated conversation but it seemed like the news was good. JJ asked for a pen and scribbled down several names, telephone numbers and addresses on the back of the map. When he hung up he had that great big smile on his face that Rick was going to miss.

Napoleon had to work that night, but the plan was for JJ to get his gear together, what little of it there was, and meet Napoleon at the entrance to the Staten Island Ferry Terminal near Battery Park the following morning. Napoleon and his wife would have a car parked nearby to take them to their apartment in the Flatbush section of Brooklyn. JJ told Rick that Napoleon was working three jobs and that there was an unexpected opening for a night cashier in the convenience store where Napoleon cashiered afternoons. Rick marveled to himself. There were native Americans who were unemployed for months, yet JJ no sooner got through the gates then he had a firm job prospect. What a country! JJ was going to do just fine in America.

In the New York metro area there were an estimated quarter to half million Haitians, a good number of them living in Napoleon's neighborhood near Church and Nostrand streets. Many of these were "undocumented," if not most, but as long as an "undoc" had no brushes with the police, he or she could live a pretty good life in America without a hassle. Certainly better than the life left behind in the Caribbean. And despite strident calls by xenophobics and politically motivated legislators to "send back all foreigners," most people in New York didn't really want to. A majority of the population was foreign or remembered when their parents or grandparents were. Most of the remainder didn't want to lose good customers or workers. More than one over-zealous INS cub was told to curb his enthusiasm for enforcing the immigration laws or risk a variety of impediments to career advancement. Sure, the law was the law; but vigorous enforcement could only have troublesome and unpredictable consequences. Cooler heads understood this and as a result the immigrant communities in New York flourished.

Rick and JJ, like close brothers who knew that they may not see one another again for a long while, were glad to be able to spend a little more time together before saying goodbye the following day. The two men walked down Fifth Avenue. JJ could not believe his eyes as he looked into the windows of stores which catered to the wealthy. JJ knew that if there were enough people with money to support shops like these, there had to be many ways for him to make money in this city. And he was right. All he needed was a start and he knew he would be on his way to becoming another American success story.

"Take a right at the corner, JJ."

"Where we going, Skip?"

"It's a surprise."

And it was a surprise, too. The lights and billboards of Times Square caused JJ's mouth to drop, almost theatrically. But JJ was not acting-he was simply amazed. They spent a half hour just circling around, reading the news tickers, watching people and taking part in the show called New York City.

"Hungry?" Rick asked, realizing that neither had eaten anything all day.

Rick had been to New York several times in recent years as a guest of "friends" he had made in St. Thomas. As a result of taking personalized tours conducted by strikingly beautiful women on their own turf, he knew the city surprisingly well.

"I can eat a cow."

"You may just do that," Rick laughed.

They stopped by the Carnegie Deli where Rick offered to treat JJ to lunch. JJ made the mistake of ordering a large corned beef sandwich. Seeing this Rick only ordered a beer. When the sandwich arrived JJ saw why-and they still had a piece wrapped to bring back to the boat with them.

Taking to the sidewalks again the two survivors slowly made their way back towards the ferry. Suddenly JJ blurted out what had been on his mind for a long time.

"I owe you my life, Skip. You have saved me from the sea twice and every day from people who would have sent me back to Haiti. You risked going to jail by giving me a home in St. Thomas and then bringing me here. You have taught me so much and given me so much and I have given you so little. May God someday allow me to repay you." There were tears in JJ's eyes and a tremor in his voice. And Rick was deeply touched. He was silent for a moment.

"JJ, you've been a great friend. You owe me absolutely nothing and I am going to miss you and your cooking!. But we will stay in touch and we can always visit each other."

JJ asked Rick how he would sail the boat back to St. Thomas for he still assumed that Rick could return there; as far as he knew the sea voyage was for Rick and Jimmy to "stretch their legs" a bit and to get him to the States. He would not know the full and complicated truth until years later, when the two men would meet again at the Carnegie

Deli. Rick vaguely replied that after a short stateside stay he would pick up some sail bums at a local yacht club, and either take *Pleiades* back to her home port, or to Annapolis, where he would "report in" and pick up a crew for a return trip at the end of the summer. More than that he didn't want to say. It was too much effort to lie to JJ; he didn't want to complicate or compromise JJ's future by telling him the truth.

JJ's last night aboard *Pleiades/Spray* was bittersweet. He knew he would miss Rick and he was still depressed over the loss of Jimmy. At the same time he was looking forward to getting his start in New York and fulfilling the dream his father had shared with him.

Early the next morning they joined the Manhattan commuters on the ferry from Liberty State Park. They made their way down to the Battery dodging the foot traffic which seemed to be paying more attention to cellphone conversations and drinking coffee than they were to where they were going.

As they approached the ferry terminal JJ suddenly started running ahead. At the same time a tall, well-built, bald, black man began running towards him. They came together with a big hug and started chattering away in an animated French interspersed with Creole. After a couple of minutes they stopped and were embarrassed to see the stares that they had drawn by the onlookers. Stepping back, introductions were made. Simone, Napoleon's wife, was strikingly beautiful with her flawless skin, the color of JJ's, and her high cheekbones. She had the proud air of an African princess, thought Rick.

There was an awkwardness when it was time to part. The two men who had shared so much together looked into each others eyes and exchanged more than they could with words. They hugged briefly.

"*Au revoir, mon ami.*"

"Take care of yourself, JJ. I'll contact you through Napoleon and I promise we'll get together after you get settled in."

With that Rick turned over his beat up nylon back-pack and told JJ there were a few mementoes in it that he wanted him to have. The little group said their goodbyes again and Rick walked off alone with a last wave to JJ.

Returning to New Jersey aboard the little ferry Rick looked back at Manhattan and wondered what JJ would think when he found the $20,000 in cash wrapped in a brown paper bag. Rick put a note in with it explaining where it had come from and giving advice to hide most of it and put the rest in his new bank account. With $20K he should be able to use Napoleon's contacts to get a new identity and decent papers to support it. With luck and hard work he hoped that JJ would quickly blend in to his new surroundings and begin to live the American dream.

CHAPTER TEN

THE TWO-DAY SAIL UP LONG ISLAND SOUND WAS uneventful. Rick missed JJ's company, though, and hoped that things would work out well for him in New York.

"Otto the Auto" made the trip an easy one. Of course, Rick could not sleep while sailing the waters relatively crowded with barges, commercial fishing boats and assorted recreational craft, but he could go below for a sandwich or to check the charts and cruising guide he had purchased in Jersey. His first night alone aboard *Spray* was spent in the lee of one of Connecticut's Thimble Islands. Rick thought the rocky shores looked awfully red at sunset because of the red sun. But he read in the guidebook later that evening that the stone there was actually pink and some was even quarried for the pedestal of the Statue of Liberty.

The following morning Rick weighed anchor early to take advantage of the substantial advantage of a favorable Long Island current which propelled him towards Fishers

Island and Rhode Island Sound. The coast changed dramatically as *Spray* sailed smoothly past Watch Hill. The rocky shores and outcroppings of the Sound gave way to white sandy beaches with quite a few sunbathers on them. Rick noticed that nobody was yet swimming and reaching his hand down through the lifelines and slapping a wave it was evident why. The ocean water temperature felt like it was still in the fifties!

After rounding Pt. Judith, Rick sailed almost due north, past Scarborough Beach awash in surf which he recalled being at as a boy, past the dark granite cliffs of Bonnet Point, past the abandoned white brick lighthouse of Dutch Island and into that island's lee. Narragansett Bay was as beautiful as Rick remembered it. The vegetation of late spring was that special color of green that contrasted with the bright blue sky and cobalt blue water.

Rick headed *Spray* up into the wind and coasted up to within a few hundred feet of the north end of the island before dropping anchor. This was a good place to rest and straighten out the boat, he thought. He waited for the anchor line to pull taut and then he made his way back to the cockpit. A slight shift in the air brought him the incredibly fragrant scent of the red and white beach roses that he could now see covered the shore almost up to the water's edge. He had forgotten about this sensual delight and it triggered a flood of early childhood memories. He recalled cradling hard, transparent jellyfish in his hands and counting horseshoe crabs on the beach. At this time of year the Bay would be host to large numbers of both. The horseshoe crabs would swarm up onto the warm sand to lay eggs during a full moon tide, looking much like turtles doing the same thing. Often the male crab would be tightly mounted on the back of the female. Rick laughed as he remembered his mother smiling when he told her that the big crab was giving the little crab a ride. Talk about innocence!

Going below to the galley, Rick grabbed a beer from the icebox. He was about to open it when he put it back and took a can of iced tea instead. He figured that he may as well drop some of his bad habits and pick up some better ones. He probably would not quit drinking altogether, but he had been gradually weaned of cigarettes since leaving St. Thomas and now he didn't miss them at all. The voyage and storm in some way constituted the beginning of a new phase to his life. What it would bring he couldn't know, but he hoped that life would become more meaningful and less frivolous.

Returning to the cockpit, Rick watched the afternoon sun begin setting over the mainland to the west. A few boats were sailing up the Bay and an offshore dragger was proceeding in the opposite direction. It was suddenly very peaceful here at anchor and he was getting a bit lethargic. It would not take him long to fall asleep after he made himself something for dinner.

In the waning light Rick thought about the last few weeks. Who could have predicted such a course of events as he and the boys had just experienced? JJ's longstanding wish came true, Jimmy was fish food, and his own future was very, very uncertain, at best. Not that his future in St. Thomas was particularly promising. Were it not for his ill fated, alcohol induced dalliance with Sandy he would probably be roaming the bars of St. Thomas right at this very moment one hand around a glass of rum and the other arm around a tanned beauty. And there was a pretty good chance that he would have been a denizen of St. Thomas for many more years to come. The odds also were that he would someday be stabbed in a fight or come down with cirrhosis of the liver or some really bad sexually transmitted disease. Rick normally tried to look on the bright side of things. But it was far too early to believe that there was a silver lining to this current twist of fate.

After checking the anchor, wind, sky and current Rick went below and lit one of the brass oil lamps. He settled into a bunk in the main salon and felt surprisingly confident as he looked around the cabin illuminated by the warm, golden lamp glow. There were many worse places to call home; he had already lived in a few of them. The next few days would not be easy, for sure. But with a little planning he thought all would work out just fine.

Thinking of his return to his boyhood home, Rick wondered if he would be recognized. Not likely. There was probably nobody in Wickford now who was there when he was a kid. And in any case, he bore absolutely no resemblance to the scrawny ten year old who left twenty years ago. But he had decided while making his way to Narragansett Bay that he would need that new identity. Assuming Jimmy's made sense. If in the future he needed to renew the driver's license, open a bank account or get another credit card, he would reevaluate what was the best course of action.

Rick decided that he could keep the nickname "Skip" when he introduced himself. That way he would respond naturally when people addressed him. And anyway, it was a common enough name around the water and would draw no suspicion. "Rick Thornton," however, would have to go for the time being and he would have to get used to being "James 'Skip' Fox." If he didn't like being "James Fox" he could always pick out another name when he went to another place.

Having found an identity he could live with, Skip fell peacefully asleep. Nature called at 3:30 and he went on deck to urinate over the side. He did not know why he just didn't use the head in situations like this, but he never did, and he never knew anyone else who did, either. Perhaps it was some sort of genetically engineered way that nature used to make sure that the boat, campfire or whatever needed checking was checked during the night. Dutifully, Skip went forward to make sure assorted rigging lines were still fast and that the anchor was holding. Reassured, he made his way back to the bunk and did not awaken till the sun was well above the horizon when *Spray* rolled in the wake of a nearby lobster boat that came to check traps by the island.

After a breakfast of coffee and canned corned beef hash, Skip got to work organizing his finances. The good thing about the cash was that there were plenty of used twenty and fifty dollar bills. The remaining tender was in the $100 denomination. Big bills took up less space but attracted more attention. Skip, himself, had only used $100 bills a few times in his life and always felt self-conscious when he did.

The money was bulky; it would have to be hidden away in separate locations. If the boat was boarded by any law enforcement officer who saw lots of money lying around, Skip surely would have a problem. His fingerprints would be run and they would match the ones filed away somewhere by Uncle Sam when he joined the Marines. They would also match the ones of the chief suspect in a St. Thomas murder and boat theft investigation.

Some money had to be easily accessible. Skip would keep funds for day-to-day expenses in a zip lock bag behind a fuse panel that was easy to lift up. That could be replenished from a larger stash temporarily tucked under the engine. Finally, $110,000 would be split and fiberglassed into the bilge. Upon examination Skip found a couple of locations where interior hull lines could be continued and voids created into which could be stuffed neat stacks of money.

The work only took a couple of hours. On board was a hull repair kit complete with acetone, polyester resin, catalyst, brushes and almost a square yard of heavy-duty fiberglass mat. The finished job was quite opaque and completely matched the interior hull except that it was new and clean. That Skip would take care of later, after the resin cured, by roughing up the surface with a wire brush and dousing it several times with bilge water. In a couple of days after the resin smell dissipated, there would be no hint at all of any new construction.

Skip felt the need for land under his feet again. He unrolled the inflatable dinghy on the foredeck, and then slightly under inflated the three separate compartments with a foot pump knowing that the warm sunlight would firm them up in a short time. The shore was close by, so he would not bother mounting the small outboard engine on the transom, choosing instead to row. He loaded the dinghy up with the small amount of trash he had accumulated since New York, including the left over fiberglass cloth and hardened resin and brush which were in an old coffee can.

Dutch Island was a coastal artillery fort at one time but it had probably been abandoned for half a century. Today it was part of a state park system having about a dozen well-separated campsites all a stone's throw from the water. Skip was the only person on the island and walked to the closest site. He threw the trash in a fire ring and set a match to it. In a few minutes all was ashes and a burnt out can due to the intense, resin-fueled flames. Skip scraped together damp soil and covered the fire pit. He then walked back to the shore.

The wind was slight and the water sparkled in the sunlight. It was going to be one of those perfect early June days. The tide was out quite a distance and there were thick masses of mussels on the exposed rocks. Skip, picked up a half buried plastic mesh bag on the shore, the kind in which onions or oranges are shipped and which shell fishermen use for their catches. He walked to the mussel-clad rocks and pried off a few clumps of the blue-shelled mollusks, which he then placed in the bag. He would have mussels for lunch or dinner. Maybe both.

Getting back on board *Spray* he set out to make himself look presentable. Skip new the value of good impressions and again he reminded himself of the need not to attract attention. And a scruffy skipper of a fairly expensive yacht would definitely attract attention. In the aft cabin's lavette he shaved; then he rinsed himself off in the cockpit using a solar shower hung from the main boom. The latter looked like a big plastic IV bag that was clear on one side and black on the other. It held a few gallons of water that heated up amazingly well in a short period of time. Showering on deck kept the area below deck clean and ship shape the way he liked it. Skip toweled dry, then went into the aft cabin to change. He felt ready to meet the world.

Using the electric winch Skip weighed anchor and then slowly powered away from the shore. The wind was still too weak for sailing, especially with the tide running out from the direction in which he had to travel. Looking at the chart it should not take much more than an hour to reach Wickford Harbor.

Approaching the breakwater protecting the outer harbor, Skip felt that he had been transported back to his youth. Absolutely nothing looked different from the way he remembered it! He slowed *Spray* down a bit to flatten out the wake and proceeded up into the inner harbor, past the mooring field of sailboats, past old colonial homes, past large and small commercial fishing boats and past boatyards filled with pleasure craft. He could swear that some of the same boats were at the same slips but that had to be his imagination.

The water was perfectly calm and mirrored all that was adjacent to it. Shifting into neutral, he let *Spray* coast up to the little bight where his grandfather had had a small dock and old railway for hauling out boats to be repaired. Surprisingly, that looked the same too. There was even an old lobster boat hauled up there for repairs. A new owner must have taken over the business, as well as the property. Shifting into reverse Skip brought the boat to a complete stop and let the memories wash over him for a moment. This spot was where he learned to row with his mom. The library was a few hundred yards away and had its own dock back then. They used to row over to it for story hour and sometimes after dinner they would row into town for ice cream. He smiled to himself as he remembered when he and his friend Daisy capsized at the dock the day they met.

Just a hundred yards away was where the two had capsized again when they were learning to sail. The skipper of the cabin cruiser cussed them from the flying bridge for being in the channel. Then Grampa, who had been trailing behind the novices in a skiff while shouting out sailing tips, cussed the stinkpotter.

"Leave them alone or I'll break your god-damned head," he fumed. "They're just kids having fun," he yelled up to the surprised powerboater.

That was the only time Skip could ever recall that grandpa swore. Skip and Daisy laughed so hard that they almost drowned, as the big powerboat backed off and disappeared. Skip had laughed a lot back then! Those were golden days and golden times. But it had been pretty much down hill for him since then.

HIS REVERIES WERE BROKEN BY A SHOUT FROM SOMEONE at the end of the dock which displayed a small sign: "Dockage 1$/ft." "Can I help you? It's too shallow in here at the floater for you on a moon tide, but I have a couple of pilings behind you where you can tie up if you don't need power. It's cheaper, too. You can pull up to the dock for water or a washdown when you need to."

Skip hesitated for a moment before answering.

"Sounds good," he yelled back. "I'll tie up and square away with you in a few minutes."

Skip's knees were shaking violently and he instantly felt nauseous. He thought he might actually pass out right there in the cockpit. He could feel the veins in his temples pulsing.

Skip took off his sunglasses, watching with disbelief as Gramps walked slowly back towards the house. Then he put the glasses back on so that if anyone were looking they would not see the tears falling from his eyes.

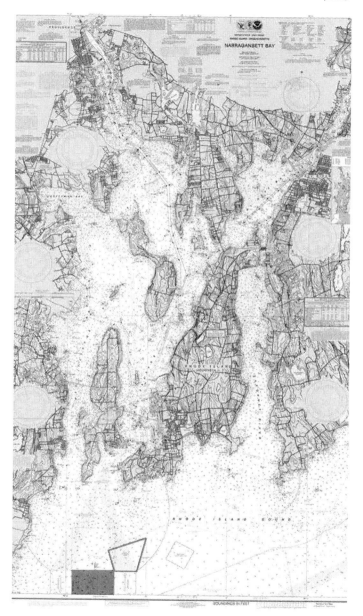

CHAPTER ELEVEN

L EAVING ENOUGH SLACK IN THE LINES FOR THE three-foot-plus tidal variation which he knew existed in Wickford, Skip Fox tied off *Spray* between two pilings, about 150 feet away from his grandfather's dock. Despite his recent resolution to modify some of his bad habits, he went below to mix himself a good stiff rum and Coke. He took it up to the cockpit where he made himself as comfortable as one could be under the circumstances.

"Why did mom lie to me? Why did I believe her?" he asked himself.

The answer to the second question was that he was still just a kid when he was told the big lie and he still entirely trusted adults. There would never be a definitive answer to the first question.

The enormous magnitude of Skip's loss of the love and guidance of his beloved Gramps for almost two decades washed over him. He wanted to scream out like a raving lunatic, punch a wall or cry.

And then it hit him. Fate had dealt him another bad hand. He had found his grandfather alive and apparently well at the moment when he could not reveal that he was his grandson. Truly Skip felt cursed! What could be more unfair?

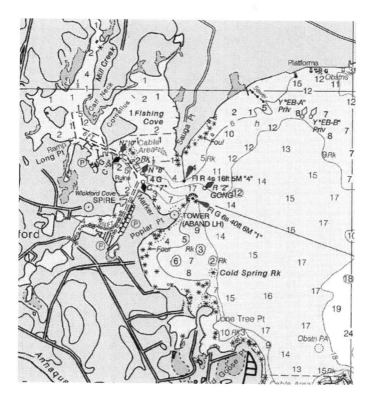

"Hey Gramps! I'm your long-lost, grandson, Ricky. I am visiting you in my stolen boat loaded with what is probably ill got drug money. I'm not really a bad guy, though, but you can't tell anyone about me because I am wanted for a murder back in St. Thomas that is all just a big mistake."

Skip gulped the rest of his drink down and thought about going ashore. He didn't know if he could stand the tension. He wanted to go but he didn't want to go. Finally, with a bit of a buzz on, he pulled the inflatable dinghy along side the Pearson, stepped in, and rowed to the Wilcox dock.

Nobody was around, so he tied off the dinghy on the backside of the dock where it would not be in the way, as he had been taught to do at that very spot so long ago. He walked up to the house, past a sizeable wooden skeleton of what looked like a lobster boat, which was being built on the old railway used for the hauling and launching of large boats. Again, he marveled as he looked around the yard, at how little the place had changed since he had been a ten year old.

Continuing up to the back door he heard a snatch of a conversation coming from what he knew to be the kitchen.

"...there's nothing wrong with the septic system and you know it! You already flushed the dye through it twice and did you see any evidence of it along the shore?"

"Mr. Wilcox, we are only trying to protect our harbor and......"

"Protect my ass! I know exactly what you and your buddy are trying to do and you can tell him that I'll donate this here land and house to a church or children's hospital before he'll ever get his hands on it."

"Now, Mr. Wilcox, besmirching the reputations of honest public servants and businessmen can have serious legal consequences. You should be more careful of what you say," replied the man in a calm, somewhat pedantic and slightly threatening manner.

"I'll call a spade a spade. And you ought to start thinking about spending less time aboard Mr. Stilwell's yacht sipping Manhattans and entertaining half-dressed tramps in Newport harbor at 2 o'clock in the morning. Some people in Town Hall might be interested in what Stilwell's trained monkey is up to."

The relation of this fact seemed to end the conversation rather abruptly and Skip had to step back quickly from the door as an obviously exasperated man of about his own age burst through it.

Gramps stepped out and was surprised to see Skip standing there.

"How you doing, young fella? What can I do for you? I'm John Wilcox." Skip fought the tendency to say "I know."

Gramps extended his hand and Skip felt a surprisingly firm grasp.

"I'm Skip Fox. Hi there! I just wanted to ask how much I owed you for dockage."

"Well the sign out there says 1$/ft. You look smart enough to do the math and I'll trust you on the length. How long you stayin? If you stay for more'n a few days we can work out a better rate."

"I'm just passing through. But I'll be here for at least three days."

With that Skip peeled off $140 from the wad in his pocket. It was kind of a nice feeling to do so, he had to admit. He had never had a wad of cash like that in his pocket before.

"And with tax what does it come to?"

Gramps stared him right in the eye for a moment. "What the governor don't know won't hurt him. I won't tell if you won't."

"Sounds good to me!" Rick laughed. If you need anything you can get it in town. We've got a good little market, hardware store, and diner. Ever been here before?"

"I don't think so. Maybe when I was a kid, but I don't remember it for sure."

The part about not remembering the town definitely was not true. Skip remembered Wickford perfectly. He could see in his mind the houses on the back streets, the churches and library, the old school with its interior of glazed honey-colored brick and marble toilet stalls, as if he had seen them yesterday. He had dreamed so much about this place while in California that it was seared into his brain.

"You can get into the village by boat and tie up at the town dock, or you can borrow one of these here old bikes and ride there in about five minutes."

Skip looked at the bikes that Gramps gestured to and was pretty sure that they were the same bikes that were in the very same spot twenty years ago. Swamp Yankees don't throw anything away that works or might work sometime with a little tinkering.

"I think I will go in a bit later."

"Well you might want to go in now if you need anything. Wickford closes tight as a drum by seven."

"Thanks, but I'm pretty well set for supplies."

Both men walked towards the back yard and John stopped to look at his 38 foot boat-building project. Gramps bent down to pick up a piece of scrap wood and handed it to Skip. Though it looked like teak, it didn't smell like teak or feel waxy like teak. Rick asked about it.

"You won't see much of this around. It's Angelique. Comes from the tropics. It was delivered here last winter as one big tree trunk. The rest is still over there if we need it." He gestured at what was now a third of a tree trunk cut longitudinally.

Gramps related how the tree was harvested in some Brazilian jungle, then floated down a river by natives who guided it from their dugout canoes to the sea. Arrangements had been made for a rendezvous with a coastal trading freighter that lowered a sling over the side and then hoisted up several thirty foot sections of tree trunk which were then secured on deck. Eventually those pieces were trucked to Wickford and sawn up by a portable sawmill rig. Gramps recut and milled some of the stock and he had a stack rough boards, separated by one-inch scrap to improve air circulation, curing under some clear poly along the south side of the old garage. Skip noted that the end grain was painted white so the wood wouldn't dry too quickly and split. At one time it used to be his job to paint the end grain white.

"Tomorrow we begin bending the planks to the ribs and pretty quickly she'll begin looking like a real boat rather than the skeleton of a whale.

The owner wanted Yellowheart for the ribs. Usually I like to use good Rhode Island white oak for that. Below the waterline we'll use Angelique and above we'll probably use some Wana. Of course the decks will be teak. You can guess that this isn't going to be no lobster boat. It will be one of them fancy 'picnic boats' made to look like a lobster boat."

Gramps went on to explain that the man who commissioned the boat had deep pockets and wanted things done right.

"You know, there aren't a lot of people left who could still build a wooden boat like this."

"Looks like they picked the right man!" said Skip knowingly. "See you, later."

With that Skip went down to the dock and took the dinghy back out to *Spray*. He had had enough for one day. Even the innocent exchange with Gramps of the previous half hour had taken its toll on him psychologically. He was afraid that if it had continued he would have slipped and said something stupid or revealing.

Deciding it was best to get his mind off things for awhile, Skip tuned in a local radio station which played easy listening tunes and started to rustle up some burgers with the last of the ground beef he had bought in New York. He brought them up to the cockpit along with some chips and rum laced coffee. Again he thought about his "resolution" but he felt he really needed a drink to calm down. And he did calm down. But whether it was due to the rum or the tranquil setting of a waterfront colonial town he didn't know.

The surface of the harbor was like a mirror, reflecting images of church steeples, boats, and seaside homes. Though it was well after 8 pm there was still plenty of light that colored whispy clouds, low in the western sky, a nice hue of pink and purple. There was even a thin, thin sliver of a new moon to watch.

As had happened several times during the days at sea, Skip entered some sort of hypnotic state, coming out of it to notice that the moon had followed the sun below the horizon. Skip wondered what he looked like during these moments. He was able to hold a course while at sea during these spells and he didn't topple over or drool over himself while in the cockpit... but it was a bit disconcerting. He knew he had some deep seated issues to resolve in the near future. Skip went below to his berth and in a moment was fast asleep. But it was not a restful one.

THE FOLLOWING MORNING WAS GORGEOUS. THE MORNing air in Rhode Island at that time of the year had a freshness and softness about it that he had never experienced in the tropics. The ubiquitous purple, white and pink sea roses which crowded right to the water's edge, added their perfume to the barest hint of the offshore breeze, even there in the inner harbor.

Skip poked his head up the main salon's hatch to survey a scene he had not witnessed in decades. Near the Wilcox homestead, behind the sea roses, was a discontinuous swath of Black Eyed Susans. He had had a hand in their planting! With his mom he used to pick the daisies that had gone past, shredding the seed filled centers with his fingers as he walked along the shore. The result was the naturalized belt of yellow and green before him.

After cleaning himself up, Skip went ashore. Gramps was already by his project, sighting down a plank that he was holding by one end. It passed inspection and was placed in a pile of others that had done the same. Off by the garage a man was running a board along the fence of a table saw, probably because it didn't pass inspection. Instinctively Skip stepped to the front of the saw to catch and guide the board, which was sagging downward, so that it would not "chatter," resulting in a rough cut. The man shut the saw off as the blade came to a stop.

"Thanks!" he said.

"Ed Northup, that's Skip."

"Good to meet you." they replied to each other in unison. "Northup" was a venerable Rhode Island name like Dodge, Hazard, Jencks, Almy or Greene.

Ed appeared to be a few years older than Skip and wore his hair pulled back in a ponytail.

"Mind catching a few more boards? It won't take long."

"No problem," replied Skip as he moved in front of the deck of the heavy old Craftsman table saw. He noticed that the saw's General Electric motor had been jury rigged a bit to fit in place and he was pretty sure that it had come from a discarded washing machine. That would be about Gramp's style he thought with a grin.

Skip and Ed wordlessly carried the newly cut boards to the pile for inspection. Instead of looking them over Gramps sat on a weathered old mule back chair and poured a cup of coffee for himself out of a battered stainless steel thermos bottle. He topped off Ed's heavy ceramic cup on which was scrawled "Ed's Cup" in magic marker.

"Coffee?"

"Sure."

Gramps looked into several styrofoam coffee cups up on a nearby scaffold and found one that was either unused or hardly used and poured coffee in it for Skip. He didn't ask whether Skip wanted sugar to go with it because there wasn't any sugar out there in the yard, anyway.

Neither man seemed particularly curious about where Skip was from or who he was. It wasn't that they were being rude-they just didn't seem to care. Instead they talked about boats, weather and fishing.

It turned out that Ed was a lobsterman and he was working off some of his repair bill by helping Gramps out. The fishing grounds were apparently closed for some reason and Ed used the time to have a sprung plank refastened and a bent bronze propeller replaced by Gramps.

When he had finished his coffee, Skip asked Gramps if he could borrow one of the bikes so that he could go into Wickford.

"Sure. Check the tires, though. There is a hand air pump over there somewhere if you need it."

Skip selected the best bike of the bunch, walking it down the driveway to the street. He noticed the flagpole in the front yard; though he could not see the granite stone on which the latitude and longitude of the house was inscribed, he knew it had to be there.

As he rode down Wampanoag Point's main street it was evident that not all had stayed the same. There were no summer cottages left at all on the Point. The houses were pretty upscale from what he could see. In fact it was pretty plain that Gramp's house, though not a shack, was at the low end of the housing spectrum.

Riding on towards the village he passed the Town Hall. It looked exactly has he remembered it and probably exactly like it did when it was built in 1888. The statue of a Civil War soldier was still standing guard in front of the building, as he was the day when Skip and his mother had left for California.

Crossing over the old concrete arched Hussey Bridge he looked right at the inner harbor. He could see the steeple of St. Paul's church that he had once attended and where he had made his first communion, reflected in the water.

All of Main Street was in a time warp. The same stores were in the same places and probably run by the same people. Again it crossed Skip's mind that he might be recognized in the village, especially if he went into the candy store. He decided that if anyone said anything like: "Don't I know you?" he would just say: "Not likely. I'm from California and I have never been here before!" He definitely didn't have a New England accent anymore, so that would probably be the end of the conversation.

Strolling down by the village dock area he found that it had been gentrified. The parking lot used to go right up to the granite retaining wall of the dock. Now there was a nicely landscaped swath of green along the wall and a cobblestone walkway with a quaint rope fence. Teak benches placed here and there provided a restful place to watch harbor activity.

A couple of what looked to be Dutch canal boats were tied up along an adjacent expanse of wall. On deck were canvas covers that he knew were protecting racks of life preservers from salt and sun. His experience told him immediately that these were day charter boats. As he approached the boats he could see a sign in the rigging listing sailing times and prices.

Feeling the need for another coffee, Skip made his way to a shiny aluminum food cart parked by the curb on another little bridge which spanned a stream leading to a tidal pond behind the village. He was totally unprepared for what happened next.

"What can I get you, Skip?" the vendor said nonchalantly.

Skip's heart pounded and his knees actually weakened for the second time in as many days. How did this guy know him? Looking into the vendor's eye for a clue he found none, so he just asked for a coffee and lemon Danish pastry and tried to pretend that he had not heard his name and that his fingers weren't shaking.

Paying for his order he made his way to the nearby concrete bridge railing which several others seemed to be using as a table as they either talked to one another or looked out over the harbor. As Skip sipped his coffee, the vendor's voice again caught his attention.

"Good morning, Cap. What can I get you?"

Turning quickly he saw a grizzled old man place his order. To his relief Skip realized that "Skip" and "Cap" were just part of common local greetings. Relaxing, he turned his attention to a pretty young mother and her son who were throwing pieces of stale bread off an adjacent stone wall to a collection of frantically feeding mallards, white ducks, swans and geese.

For the second time in minutes Skip's heart started to pound. It was as if he was looking at himself and his mother who used to do the same thing at that very same spot. His eyes became moist. It then occurred to Skip that coming to Rhode Island may not have been such a good idea after all and that perhaps he should leave right away rather than subject himself to the series of psychological land mines which he knew were waiting for him there.

Finishing up the last of the coffee and pastry, Skip briskly rode the bike back to the Point. While he was gone Ed and Gramps had made progress in getting several planks into place, held temporarily by C clamps. As Skip watched, the two men used portable drills, side by side, without a word passing between them. Gramps drilled a hole through the Angelique plank and the Yellowheart rib to which it would be fastened. Then Ed used another drill and bit to make a hole for the wooden bung which would hide the head of the bolt. He then pulled a bronze bolt from the pocket of his carpenter's apron and inserted it in the hole.

When all the bolts were in place they stopped. Gramps then got into what would become the inside of the hull and appeared to place a nut on the protruding bolt end. Then Ed held what looked like a lead window sash weight up against the bolt head from the outside while Gramps hammered away. Skip realized as he watched, that nuts and bolts were not going to hold this boat together. It would be riveted, probably with copper rather than bronze. Somebody wanted to own a real classic vessel!

It might seem strange to some, but Skip just had an urge to pick up a tool and join in. A boat being built, though, has that effect on many men.

When the planks were fastened, Ed removed the clamps and Gramps disappeared into the house. Ed then went to the pile of boards and selected another few for placement. Awkwardly, he lifted one into position to join another that was already riveted, while he reached for a C clamp to act as a third hand. Skip handed it to him and took a second clamp which he slid over another rib further down the plank. Ed seemed not to take notice and Skip knew that this was surely another Swamper who would just as soon drop a heavy board on his naked big toe, as ask for help so he wouldn't. The two men positioned several more planks.

"John wants to work till midnight cause I just found out that the summer flounder fishing grounds will open in four days and I'll be leaving for awhile. He'd work all night if he could but his neighbors will get pissed off if he does. They're from out of state and they don't mind a little boat building going on because they think it's cool to have a quaint old man building a quaint wooden boat next door, but they got their limits."

"So can't he hire anybody else to take your place?"

"No money. He's more than broke. The guy he's building this for is paying in stages. The next check comes when the entire hull is planked. The last one came when all the ribs were in place. Even the next check probably won't be enough to keep John out of trouble."

Skip wanted to ask what kind of trouble his grandfather might be getting into but knew better. If Gramps needed help he would stay and give him that help if he could figure out some way to be invited to. His earnest concern for Gramps was surprisingly deep. Yes, despite the emotional risks he would stick around for a while and find out what was going on there. At the very least he would be paying his grandfather dockage money and maybe he could even make up some pretext for paying him more in advance.

Skip's rapidly processing brain was interrupted by the slamming of the screen door. Gramps had three bottles of beer on a beat up old tray and a half bag of pretzels. The three men sat on variously sized wooden blocks near the table saw while drinking and munching pretzels.

"Think we can finish the planking in a couple of days?"

"Nope."

"What would it take to do that"

Ed looked at the mostly naked ribs and the pile of un-planed planks. He then looked out over the water for a moment before replying.

"We need two more men who know what they are doing or we need four days just like this one."

"I'd like to get it done in two days. Mr. Harrison will be driving up from New York and I'd like to show him some real progress. I just heard a weather report and a lit-tle rain might be coming in next week. Without you and with rain I'll be way behind schedule and I don't want to upset Mr. Harrison."

Gramps didn't mention anything about Mr. Harrison's money, but Ed and now Skip, knew that was the real concern.

"You know, I always wanted to work on a wooden boat. I've built some fiberglass ones but this is the real thing. I can hang around for a few days and help out if you'd like. I know my way around tools and boats pretty well."

Gramps didn't reply for a moment and he appeared to be weighing various aspects of the proposal.

"Can't pay you right away."

Now it was Skip's turn to be quiet. He knew his grand-father would not do anything that might make him be-holding to anyone. He paused a moment longer for effect.

"Well could you give me a break on the dock-age, at least?"

Again Gramps was silent.

"Yeah . . . yeah. We can work something out."

"We'll still need another guy and a good one," said Ed,"or it won't get done."

Skip heard the sharp crack of breaking quahog shells which "paved" the driveway as they were run over by something. Then a red, mud splattered open Jeep pulled up to the old garage and parked. The driver bent over to the passenger side for an instant and emerged with a wide brimmed khaki hat, sunglasses and a large canvas sailing bag. Walking straight up to Gramps the newcomer gave him a big hug.

"Miss me?"

Gramps smiled the kind of smile that didn't require an answer

"Hey, Ed!" Ed just sort of nodded.

The newcomer's attention turned to Skip.

"I could stand here all afternoon and I bet you these two would never introduce us."

A hand was extended and Skip took it. "My name is Janice Bruno.....but my friends just call me 'Daisy.'"

CHAPTER TWELVE

JANICE BRUNO WAS ABOUT AS PRETTY AS THEY CAME. Women, some reluctantly, referred to her as being strikingly beautiful. She could easily have been a model for a variety of health and beauty products, since all aspects of her body were absolutely perfect. Her deep red, straight hair was usually worn in a ponytail, which usually protruded from a baseball cap. Her skin, of course, was freckled, a consequence of spending summers out on a boat or at the beach. Daisy had long, athletic legs, and carried not an ounce of loose skin. She moved with a kind of regal grace and it was not unusual to see every head turn as she walked past the field of view of a group of people. Conversations would halt for a perceptible instant and then pick up again with people trying to pretend that they hadn't. A few snide women would remark to one another that Daisy's bosoms could stand to be a little bigger, but guys, if they overheard this, unanimously took that statement for what it was worth—nothing—as they tried hard not to crack a smile.

The big mystery in town was why Daisy wasn't married. She was well known in the town that she had come to as an eight year old. She attended local schools, was a standout gymnast, cheerleader and sailor, made every honor roll and was elected homecoming queen at least once. There had been enough visible short-term romances for all who were interested in the "big mystery" to know that she wasn't gay. If marriage were something Daisy wanted, it would probably take her all of a week to wrap up the most eligible bachelor in Rhode Island; the lucky guy would move the nuptial plans along as fast as he could, too, being afraid that Daisy might for any number of reasons change her mind before the ceremony took place.

One man in Wickford knew exactly why Daisy wasn't married and not caring a rat's rump about being politically correct, he mentioned the reason to her about once a month.

"Daisy, for a woman you are just too damned independent for your own good. You scare guys away like a Great White would a seal in a swimming pool. Can't you just pretend that you are not perfect long enough to have a half decent relationship that lasts more than two weeks? You ain't getting any younger you know."

Actually Daisy did know and for all her apparent lack of interest in men she actually had been thinking about her future. She did want a family and she knew that it was about time for her to settle down. But there really was nobody who held her interest. It had occurred to Daisy during episodes of sleepless nights that perhaps she really had a psychological problem that only made it seem to her that she hadn't met the right man, in which case she knew that she would never meet him. That possibility might have to be looked into pretty soon she had finally admitted to herself.

Daisy lived alone right in the village in an old fisherman's cottage which was literally only marginally smaller than the lot it was on. It was a well kept, picture perfect home surrounded by bright flowers during any season that flowers would grow. And when flowers didn't grow outside they flourished in the attached greenhouse that took up the entire back south wall of the house. Daisy would like to have her morning coffee in the greenhouse amid bougainvillea, assorted geraniums, bright hibiscus flowers and an old codger's fig tree for which she winter sat.

Daisy had built a successful little business in town that could in time become an institution. Her clients were largely locals, who if they were males, didn't care what Daisy was selling. She also attracted a growing number of young professionals who came from quite a distance to sample her artistically prepared pastries, gourmet coffees and the ambiance of her little European chic cafe.

The bakery kind of fell into Daisy's hands. She had worked there for old Mrs. Turner in high school on Sunday mornings when people liked to stop by after church for fresh bread and "sweets." If you were dating Daisy at the time, you might find a little something extra that she knew you liked in a bag on top of the order you were picking up for your parents.

While in college Daisy worked summers, not only behind the counter, but also in the prep room. Mrs. Turner was slowing down and increasingly depended on Daisy to prepare and bake the old fashioned treats whose recipes and trade secrets she once thought she would never divulge. Although it cut into her sailing time, Daisy was glad to put in many hours at the bakery. Her father's death from cancer at the end of her sophomore year had saddled her mother with debts, which if not serviced, would cause the house to be taken from them. A combination of most of the debt being forgiven, and some being paid off by Daisy's extra effort, prevented that from happening.

After graduating from college with a degree in a major that was interesting to study, but provided no immediately marketable skills, Daisy made the Grand Tour of Europe which stretched out for almost two years until she returned home for the funeral of her mother. Daisy once again found herself working at the bakery but only until "something better came along." After a few months, Mrs. Turner proposed that Daisy take over the business, a possibility that Daisy at first rejected out of hand. But she agreed to run things while Mrs. Turner recouped from bouts with the usual infirmities of old age.

Mrs. Turner had always liked the effusive and energetic Daisy who she knew had never cheated her and who had always treated her as a kind, elderly relative. It had not escaped the still sharp old lady's notice, either, that business always increased substantially when Daisy was behind the counter. So slyly, she taught Daisy most of what she knew.

During Mrs. Turner's two-month period of convalescence at an assisted living center Daisy discovered something. She liked running the bakery! It turned out that her schooling and travels gave her a certain *savoir faire* which she brought to the business. She incorporated some new items into the offerings that she had first sampled abroad, put the business ledger and inventory on computer, did a little creative marketing and discovered that she could actually make some serious money if the business were her own.

Daisy had been dutifully visiting Mrs. Turner a few times a week, keeping her abreast of the changes and progress she had made and dropping off the bank deposit slips. She had made up her mind to broach the subject of coming up with some mutually satisfactory financial terms for acquiring the business. Finally she did. Unfortunately, Mrs. Turner had expired, as unexpectedly as people could expire at 79 years of age, before terms could be explored.

The executor of Mrs. Turner's will asked Daisy to stay on until it was determined how the assets of the estate were to be distributed, to which she sadly agreed. The lawyer knew of the discussions between Mrs. Turner and Daisy and nodded sadly when Daisy told him that she wished she had accepted Mrs. Turner' offer for the bakery when it had first been made.

And so it was altogether a surprise when attorney Meegan formally informed Daisy in his office a few weeks later that she had been left the property and business, free and clear, by Mrs. Turner. He also handed her a note from Mrs. Turner that she read silently while she sat in a chair opposite him and which brought tears streaming from her eyes.

"She really was quite fond of you, you know, Daisy." Daisy left the office in a fog after receiving a set of wrapped legal documents and an avuncular hug.

"She'll do quite well, I'm sure." Daisy heard Mr. Meegan say to his receptionist as she walked out the door.

And so she did. Mrs. Turner's Bakery business increased to the point where Daisy had six people on her payroll in six months. The outdoor umbrella tables on a newly built deck with a view of the harbor were a big hit, as well as the expanded upscale offerings. But the best part, Daisy realized, was that work she enjoyed provided her with a means of living where she really wanted to live. She could still sail and do the many things she grew up doing in the area.

After a couple of years of settling in, Daisy rewarded herself with the purchase of a Herreshoff "Twelve and a Half," a classic wooden rig with deep Rhode Island roots. Though the hull that was nearly 60 years old had been re-built several times, it needed to be rebuilt again. And so it was that former neighbor and family friend, John Wil-cox, came back into her life. There was nobody better at such a restoration and John was glad to do it. He was even glad to have her help out with the work at nights and on weekends. John was surprised at how much she remem-bered about wood, tools and sailing from another time, so long ago. The old man with gray-white hair and a weath-er beaten face and the beautiful woman with flaming red hair looked forward to the work and each other's compa-ny. During the winter before the boat was to be launched, John would fire up the old little pot bellied stove with driftwood, about an hour before Daisy would arrive. That would keep the shed at a good temperature for working until ten o'clock when they would usually knock off.

As time went on the relationship became familial. Daisy would never fail to bring over bread or pastry, and John would do maintenance and repairs at Daisy's shop, and later at the house she purchased. Neither would accept payment from the other. John came to regard Daisy as the daughter he had once had, loved and lost. Though she never would say it, Daisy was glad to once again have a father in her life. She missed both her parents greatly and in her reflective moments, Daisy wished she had been able to spend a lot more time with her parents than she did.

John feared that Daisy's cheering presence would evaporate once the boat work was completed. And though in fact she could have kept the little boat closer to her home, Daisy arranged to keep it at John's dock on the pretense that he could "keep an eye on it." The artifice worked for both and ensured that the paths of the odd couple crossed several times a week.

Over time Daisy noticed that an inspector of some sort would skulk around John's property with a clipboard. If John were around he would keep his eyes drilled on him every minute, though he would never say anything to Daisy about why that was. Daisy never asked. For some reason the man reminded her of a kid who was always in trouble in grade school. When he was around and John wasn't Daisy eyed him, too, but not so obviously that he would detect her attention.

Daisy soon got to know all the fishermen and small boat owners who frequented John's little boatyard. And she got to appreciate the complex little network by which all would help one another out. A sawmill owner in Exeter would drop off some lumber, and leave with a sack of softshell clams, left to John by a fisherman whose boat was tied up at one of John's docks, and who might on occasion drop off a slightly undersized bass (which was already dead by the time it was determined to be undersized) to Mrs. Scott who occasionally would serve such a thing as the "fish special of the day" in her restaurant. If the fisherman and "the wife" showed up for dinner at the restaurant the waitresses were all instructed that for them dinner was on the house. Eventually, Daisy was drawn into the network and would now and then provide "left over bread" or an "unclaimed birthday cake" for a needy family of the watermen. Strictly by coincidence, styrofoam shipping containers stuffed with prime live lobsters, iced and packed in rockweed, would subsequently find their way to the back door of the bakery. Or maybe a half cord of firewood would be neatly stacked in Daisy's wood rack, stacker's identity unknown.

Life was good and improving Daisy mused. She had John, who had again become an important person in her life. Her business provided rewarding challenges and more than ample remuneration. She had several nice women friends to kayak or sail with (who were always trying to fix her up with their husband's brothers). And she lived in a quaint New England seaside town that she loved along with all its interesting characters.

On a particularly nice June day Daisy prepared to go sailing after closing up shop. The red Jeep was packed with a few items she wanted to put on board the as yet un-named boat, which looked so good after all the work done over the winter that it could win a prize at a boat show. It might, she thought to herself. As Daisy put the key in the Jeep's ignition she heard the honking of a horn. Linda, one of members of the facetiously named and officially non-existent Women's Kayaking Association of Wickford pulled alongside in a minivan.

"Guess what? I'm pregnant again."

Before congratulatory words came out of Daisy's mouth, other words ran through her head.

"I wonder how long it takes to get an appointment with a counselor," she thought.

CHAPTER THIRTEEN

SKIP COULD NOT KEEP HIS EYES OFF DAISY. IF HE RAN into her on the street he would have recognized her without an introduction, for sure. It made him wonder about his own supposed "invisibility" in Wickford.

Daisy mentioned to John that someone named Linda was pregnant again. John gave Daisy a shrug and a funny look. Daisy gave him a shrug and funny look back; then she mentioned that she would be sailing with the little Cordeiro girl.

"Could you send her down to the dock when she comes? I want to get the sail cover off and tighten up those turnbuckles before she gets here."

"Will do." said John.

Daisy gave the boys a bright smile.

"See you all later."

All too quickly, for Skip at least, she made her way towards the dock.

Without any explanation John darted after her. "Daisy, do you think..." was all Skip heard before Ed asked: "Want to help me get one more plank in place?"

As Ed and Skip finished up the riveting, John slipped behind them.

"Ed, Daisy is going to have Ruth take care of the bakery crew for the next couple of days and she is going to give us a hand with this." A sweep of his hand indicated that he meant the boat.

"Can she do that?" asked Skip, immediately regretting the question.

John and Ed laughed a real hearty laugh.

"Son, if you know what's good for you, you best not let Daisy hear you ask a question like that or that sweet young thing will tear out your baby blues."

Skip felt sheepish as he suddenly recalled the day that he and Daisy met and how she had flipped his rowboat over and smashed a dozen eggs on his head in a fit of anger. It was hard for him to not laugh at the thought of the two of them, looking like a pair of drowned rats, making their way to the dock. But, "Thanks for the tip." was all he said, as off-handedly as he could muster.

"What time you want us here, boss?" asked Ed.

"Seven should be fine. Any earlier and we'll disturb the neighbors and we don't want to do that.

Skip HAD TROUBLE SLEEPING ABOARD *Spray.* HE WAS like the little boy he once was with his first crush on a girl. Actually, the same girl. He remembered the days of sailing *Swamp Yankee,* swimming with the old Black Lab, building sand castles at Scarborough Beach and Sand Hill Cove and a dozen other things-all with Daisy. And he painfully recalled the letters he had written her from California. Sometimes he rewrote them three times because he smudged the ink on a single letter, or misspelled a word in the last sentence. He would check the mailbox for a response from her every day for weeks afterwards. But there never was one. He wondered why. Incredibly, it still hurt to think about this and he was surprised that he could be affected by such a long dormant memory. Again, he wondered if it was wise to stick around Rhode Island. Was he up to it?

But the genie was out of the bottle, he knew. It wouldn't matter where he went now. He knew too much already. He was going have to tough it out mentally, right there and then. Maybe he needed the exorcism. It would probably do him good in the long run. Maybe he would even find out why Daisy never wrote him back. Come to think of it, nobody ever wrote Skip back, not even Gramps or his teacher.

While tossing around in the bunk, Skip alternated between thinking about the past and thinking about the following day when he would be working with Daisy. That would be weird! But exciting. God, was she good looking!! She made his heart beat faster, as corny and stupid as it sounded.

"Is she married? Was she married? Does she have a boyfriend? Of course she is hooked up with someone," and related thoughts all ran through his mind, which was in some sort of very restless dream state. Strangely, despite that state, Skip was acutely aware of the fact that he looked forward to the dawn, waking up, and getting to work with Gramps and Daisy.

When dim daylight did actually arrive, Skip anxiously tumbled out of the bunk and put on some coffee. Then he attended to personal hygiene in a way which would have been ludicrous, even to him, the day before. He made a mental note to buy some dental floss. He should pick up some new pants, shirts and shoes, as well. Skip even took a shower, though the water was at best, tepid. Without shore power, though, it would have to do. Maybe he could rig up a solar heating circulator, or something, if he stuck around.

Sipping his coffee at the teak salon table, Skip wished that the hands on the Chelsea nautical clock would move faster. At ten of seven he simply could no longer fight the compulsion to get into his inflatable and row ashore.

As he walked up the ramp he saw Ed Northup coming down the driveway in a beat up, rusted out, old pickup truck. He walked towards the truck as Ed got out. A dog, which must have been lying down on the truck bed, popped up and looked as surprised to see Skip as Skip was to see him.

"Hey, Ed."

"Mornin' there, Skip.'"

Ed reached over the side of the truck and gathered up the dog around the legs, like a shepherd might pick up a lamb, and placed him on the ground. The dog, which looked like some sort of husky half-breed, steadied himself and then took a few steps. He walked off balance, like he was injured.

"What's his name?"

"Coyote."

"Interesting name."

Ed pursed his lips and nodded his head a few times.

"He does sort of look like a coyote," said Skip, trying to ignite a conversation with Ed, whom he had already learned was not the talking type.

"That's cause he is a coyote. When he was a pup I accidentally hit him with this here truck. He ran out in front of it one night from one of them turf farms out there in Exeter. I was moving too fast to swerve past him and he wasn't moving fast enough for me not to push in that back leg of his a bit."

Coyote stood with his right rear foot about an inch off the ground, as if to verify the story.

"People say I should have just shot him and collected the bounty, but when I stopped the truck and looked him over, I thought of him just like he was any old hurt puppy. I could never have done nothing bad to him. It wasn't his fault that I maybe had one too many to drink. I took him home and he healed up, but it took some time and he's not quite right. He's a good dog, though, aren't you now, Coyote?"

With that Ed reached over and scratched Coyote's head. Coyote closed his eyes and made a funny little yappy sound. It definitely wasn't a bark.

John came out of the house. He had two coffee mugs in each hand and was walking carefully towards them, so as to not spill anything.

"Mornin', boys...mornin', Coyote."

An engine sound called the attention of the three men to Daisy's arrival. She parked and joined them.

"Good morning, guys! What a great day it is!" she said breathlessly, like it was the best day of her life.

"It hadn't even begun yet," thought Rick.

Daisy had stopped by the bakery and picked up a small plastic tray of assorted muffins and donuts which she set on a large block of wood. She mentioned that she also brought some rolls for sandwiches which she said she would make later, for lunch.

Everyone selected something to eat from the tray and sipped coffee. Gramps held his mug in one hand and looked at the boat bow on, perhaps checking the symmetry of the ribs. Skip stared out at the harbor towards Dunn's Market, near where he had been yesterday. Ed idly ran a hand over one of the planks he had fastened the day before. Daisy, who had eaten a big powdered donut, which had left her with a white chin, appraised Skip from head to toe without moving her own head a single bit.

Ed threw a hunk of blueberry muffin in Coyote's direction. Coyote seemed to appreciate it and looked to Ed for more, which he got. It was obvious to Skip that Ed had grown quite fond of his damaged little coyote dog.

The quiet spell was broken when Gramps laid out the way the work would go for the day. A pile of good and true planks would be planed, cut and stacked. Gramps would inspect each. Then they would split into pairs and simultaneously fasten the planks to the port and starboard side. Periodically, Gramps would check that the planks amidship were at precisely the same height. Theoretically, they should be, if the plank widths were the same. But practically, usually due to slight differences in port and starboard ribs, there could be some creeping ahead of one side which would have to be compensated for by making a board here and there a bit less wide. The way we'll check is to use the hose. Gramps explained that he had a 30' length of garden hose, the ends of which were stuffed with 6" pieces of clear plastic tubing of smaller diameter. The hose was filled with water and the height of the water could be seen through the clear plastic. Basically, the water level would be set at the top of a plank on one side of the hull and you would then check to make sure that the water level was the same at the top of the corresponding plank on the other side. Skip noticed by the way that Ed and Daisy nodded and looked at one another that they had heard this at least once before. Skip realized that Gramps was summarizing the technique for his benefit.

Skip wondered if the nifty laser levelers of modern day boatbuilders went on the blink, whether the technology dependent workers would know about the old hose method for finding level. Probably not.

"You and Daisy will work port," said Gramps looking Skip right in the eyes.

Four hours later, and much to the amazement of all of them, the skeleton had morphed into a partial hull and reasonable facsimile of a boat. The four worked smoothly together, like they had been doing so for years. To some extent, Skip observed, they had.

As they worked, they talked. Some conversations were between port and starboard sides, others were between port and port, or starboard and starboard. The conversation on the port side was entirely Daisy driven and laden with questions. Skip was on the defensive from the very first moment, but he was determined not to say anything stupid or revealing. Talking to Daisy was mentally exhausting, since even an innocent question of hers such as: "So what is your real name, Skip?" could be taken a couple ways.

But after awhile Skip realized that Daisy wasn't suspicious about him at all. She was just asking the kinds of questions that most people would ask to make conversation with someone that they had just met. Skip relaxed a bit and asked a few questions himself-about her work, sailing in the area, her boat, etc. He kept the verbal flow simple and superficial. Skip was good at keeping things simple and superficial.

At noon there was a siren, apparently from the closest fire station, so that people could set their watches and know that it was time to knock off work for lunch. Skip thought the sound was superfluous, but it sort of contributed to the "Norman Rockwell" flavor of the area. He didn't say anything, though.

"Lunch time!" said Gramps.

Ed walked took a few steps and turned on the garage's outside faucet. He took a thin bar of soap which was in a chromed wire mesh soap holder screwed into the side of the garage and washed his hands. Skip followed suit while Daisy and Gramps went in the house. They emerged ten minutes later with a pitcher of homemade iced tea complete with floating lemons, glasses, napkins and a plate full of assorted sandwiches. All four sat at a weather beaten and obviously well used wooden picnic table. The table had Swamp Yankee written all over it. The replacement board used for the seat that Skip was sitting on had blue paint residue which was the same color blue as the paint used on the docks at the marina a couple of hundred feet away. No doubt it had drifted up on Gramps' shore after some storm damaged the docks. The planks on the table surface itself were of oak, pine and some wood Skip could not identify. They had been run through a planer so that they would be the same thickness. Naturally they were fastened down with screws which all had different heads and were made out of galvanized steel, stainless steel, or bronze. To remove them you would need a flat head screwdriver, Phillips head screwdriver and an Allen wrench set.

The sandwiches were very good, as attested to by the fact that there were none left; the three men thanked Daisy for her effort. John then thanked the other three for their help and praised the quality of the morning work. "If we keep working at this pace we'll easily be finished before Mr. Harrison shows up from New York."

They finished more than half of the total work by 4:30 when they had to stop because they ran out of caps for the rivets. Gramps thought he had an extra box squirreled away somewhere, but he couldn't find it.

"Why don't we meet tomorrow at the same time. Ed, could you pick up two boxes of caps at Lanni's Hardware on your way home, so we'll be set for morning?" "Sure," said Ed as he made his way to the faucet.

"I'll sleep well tonight. Nice job, boys." With that Daisy pecked Gramps on the cheek and was gone.

Her sudden departure took Skip by surprise. As they worked and talked during the afternoon he had been also thinking about ways to broach the subject of going sailing or out for a sandwich with Daisy that evening. But it was just as well she left, decided Skip. Asking her out today, even for a casual outing, would be premature. Besides, Daisy probably already had something planned and would have to reject his invitation which would have a negative consequence for him. "Don't be impatient," he reminded himself.

"What's the hurry?"

As Ed pulled a clean sweatshirt over his head Skip asked him if he would mind it if he hitched a ride to Lanni's with him. "I need some things for the boat."

Actually, he didn't need anything for the boat. But he would go along for the ride and see a bit more of his old town. Maybe he would pick up a shackle or two. You couldn't have too many shackles on a boat.

Though the distance to Lanni's was only a mile and a half there was quite a bit of traffic. Skip noticed that the cars were all newer and more expensive than what you would see in St. Thomas. It hit Skip that it was the first time in a week that he had thought about St. Thomas and that led to other thoughts about how the investigation might be proceeding and how that might apply to him. He would have to see if he could find a computer and go on-line to check things out. There might be some internet cafes around or perhaps the town library would have computers for public use. Skip also wondered how JJ was making out. Had he put St. Thomas behind him this quickly, as well?

"Here we are." Skip didn't remember Lanni's clearly, but it looked like it must have looked back when he lived in town. The store was in an older building which had been added on to several times over the years and which had been well kept. Ed and Skip walked in and Skip could see that it was an old style hardware store in that there were barrels and bins of screws, nails, cracked corn and grass seed. If you wanted 7 screws you got 7 screws and not 20 in a pre-packaged monster pak. He liked that.

Skip wandered around and did pick up a shackle, small stainless carabiner, and a couple of rugged plastic spring clamps. He glanced at an impressive collection of old tools which were for sale and he knew he would be back soon to rummage through them. He saw Ed making his way to checkout and fell in behind him.

"These are for John Wilcox. Can you put them on his charge?" "Sure." The high school kid at the computer register typed in "Wilcox" and was about to enter in the stock number when he frowned.

"No can do," he said looking at Ed. "There is a freeze on Mr. Wilcox's store charge account. You'll have to pay cash or see Mr. Lanni."

"OK. How much is it?"

"It comes to $38.56 with tax."

Ed pulled out a well-worn leather wallet and flipped through the bills.

"No can do, either. Guess I'll have to come back tomorrow morning to pick them up."

"Wait a minute," said Skip. "I think I have it." Skip plunked two twenties down on the counter and half expected the kid to hold them up to the light.

With his change came a receipt and on the receipt was the notation: "Balance overdue: $763.14"

The two men got back in the car and as soon as they shut their doors Coyote dropped prone on the truck bed.

"I can drop you back in town, if you want."

"Sure. Think I'll grab the meatloaf special at the diner and walk back to John's. I'm going to turn in early tonight. I'm not used to this manual labor!" Ed smiled.

"Skip. You might not get your money back from John right away."

"No problem. I'm not going anywhere for a few days."

"Well...it might take more than a few days....like I told you yesterday, John is having some financial problems."

"Don't mean to pry, but John doesn't look like a big spender. Usually guys like him have saved up a bundle."

"Yeah, well if he did, he lost it somehow. Lot's of old timers like him are getting killed by property taxes, what with being on the water like he is and what with this town being overrun by rich New Yorkers driving the land values up and up. Most of the old families that lived on the water have already sold out. They end up with a pile of cash and move inland. But John would rather die than move to Exeter. He really would. The rumor is that Mr. Stilwell offered him a million dollars for the property and John told him to go screw himself. All John knows is boats and the water. He'll leave his place in a pine box. I just hope he don't get boxed up early cause of all the pressure on him."

Skip didn't say anything. But it hurt him to hear that Gramps was having so much trouble. At that moment he decided he would stay the summer in Wickford. He would concoct some story for Gramps. Pretend he really needed a job. Whatever it took.

Once the decision was made Skip felt good. It was just too bad he couldn't tell Gramps who he was and give him a great big hug. He really wanted to hug him! And it was too bad he couldn't tell the redhead who he was, either.

Life was funny. Here he was, a man wanted by the law for the proverbial crime he didn't commit. Yet if he had not become a wanted man, he would never have sailed to Wickford, discovered that Gramps was alive and found Daisy. The gods were continuing to toy with him, like they had all his life. Skip was living proof of the current relevance of studying Greek and Shakespearean tragedies. The gods had placed him inches away from a man he loved and a woman he could love; but they prevented him from revealing his true identity to either of them.

Skip's train of thought was broken by the lurching of the truck as it braked. They were in the center of town and Ed had stopped for an older woman in a cross walk.

"Hey, thanks Ed for the lift. I'll get out right here. See you tomorrow!"

"No problem. Say "Hi" to Billy for me. A little advice, though. Have the fish and chips or the chicken pot pie. Billy's meatloaf is only fair and it will give you gas."

Skip did have the meatloaf, and it did give him gas.

CHAPTER FOURTEEN

BACK ABOARD *Spray*, SKIP DECIDED TO SETTLE IN early for the night. He thought about exploring the harbor in his inflatable, since there would be a long, lingering and beautiful sunset, but he really was tired from both the manual labor and the lack of quality sleep the night before.

Before climbing into the bunk he had one thing to do, though. Skip decided he would take a roll of cash from behind the fuse panel and use it the following day to pay off the balance due at Lanni's. He would not tell Gramps. If Gramps didn't have supplies, then he couldn't finish building the boat. If he couldn't finish building the boat, he wouldn't get paid by Mr. Harrison. And sooner or later, he knew, if you were low on money, something real bad would happen.

A transient thought irritated Skip. If he ever had to pay back the money he "found" with Jimmy's things, and didn't have it to pay back, that would add to his problems. Logic told him that there was no connection that could be made between him and the money, so he was safe. But the little voice in his head also told him that if he were a suspect in Dean's death, and a theory was developed that he raped and beat Sandy, too, then it would take only a few moments for the creative minded detectives on St. Thomas to come up with a story linking the money and the other two crimes. Jimmy would have been the only one who could tell the police what really happened to Dean and Sandy. Rick was now convinced that Jimmy had to have been Dean's murderer or, at the very least, have been involved in a plot with the murderer. He didn't hurt Sandy, though. That was Dean's doing without a doubt. Upon a little more reflection it was apparent to Skip, even if it wouldn't be to anyone else, except maybe JJ, that Jimmy didn't premeditate the murder. He definitely would lift cash, if he thought he could get away with it, but he would not murder to get it. Something must have gone wrong.

Skip selected $1000 worth of mixed bills. Too many $100s would be noticed and remembered by the clerk at Lanni's. He used only three of them and the rest of his wad was made up of $20s and $50s. He realized that he had too many big bills in his cache and that he was going to have to break them into smaller ones that would attract less notice or it was going to be hard to spend the money. Jimmy used to talk about how he and one of his "associates" made casino trips for this purpose. Big bills didn't attract any attention at all in a casino. They would buy a stick of gum with a $100 bill if they wanted small bills. Other times they would use small bills to buy chips, then cash out the chips asking for 100s. "Screw banks, casinos are the way to go," Jimmy used to say. There must be one around here, somewhere, Skip thought.

After neatening up the boat and cleaning himself up Skip rolled into the bunk. This time the lapping of wavelets on the hull put him to sleep quite quickly.

WHEN SKIP AWAKENED AT 5:30 HE FELT THAT HE HAD slept pretty well. Until events of the last several weeks he always associated sleeping on a boat with a good night's sleep, with or without a bedmate. That train of thought caused him to wonder how old *Thor* had fared in the storm. He hoped that the Norse god had taken care of his namesake.

In ten minutes Skip had shaved, showered and shampooed. Dressing quickly in his only other pair of decent work clothes Skip made his way into the inflatable. Before sitting on the pontoon he carefully mopped the heavy dew off it with a rag that he repeatedly squeezed dry. The little outboard engine started on the second pull and sounded noisier than it was in the early morning quiet.

Skip tied up at the town dinghy dock and was in the diner at five minutes of six. It was fairly crowded with an assortment of commercial fishermen, sports fishermen, blue-collar workers and casually dressed businessmen. They all seemed to know one another and you could hear a lot of "helloes" and "goodbyes" followed by first names.

Skip picked up a courtesy newspaper, took a stool at the counter and ordered the Fisherman's Morning Special which included two eggs any style, toast, homefries, bacon, ham and sausage. The menu stated that for an extra dollar you could get two golden brown Johnnycakes which were made of Rhode Island grown cornmeal. Judging by the plates around him, Johnnycakes were somewhat favored by the locals. On the wall was a framed magazine article. Skip could read most of it from his seat and evidently, though Billy made a lousy meatloaf, he won a major Johnnycake cookoff for the tenth year in a row.

"I'll have the Johnnycakes, too," he said to an efficient and cheerful waitress.

After breakfast Skip walked briskly up the hill to Lanni's which was already filled with contractors picking up supplies for the day. Going to the marine section Skip picked up more copper rivets, a quart of polyester resin and a square yard of fiberglass mat. The latter two items would replace what he used to create the hidden compartments aboard *Spray* that he made to hold and hide the money. Skip was a firm believer in having a well maintained and properly provisioned boat. At the Constellation yard in St. Thomas he was considered obsessed about this. He would carefully inspect each returning chartered boat, using several checklists. As fast as something could be replaced or repaired it was.

"Better to have it and not need it than need it and not have it," Skip always said.

Skip would sneak the rivets into the garage somehow where Gramps would be sure to find them. They probably would be needed and having them might save a trip and some time.

The line at the register moved quickly. A different clerk from the one there the previous day didn't even look up when Skip said: "And Mr. Wilcox also wants me to pay off the balance he owes." He put down $800 and told the clerk to keep the change on account. A moment later Skip was given a receipt and then the next customer was being serviced.

It took a little scurrying, but Skip made it back to the Wilcox place just as, once again, Ed pulled up and parked.

"Morning, Coyote. Hey, Ed!"

Basically it was dejas vu; by 7:30 there were the sounds of sawing, planing, jointing and hammering coming from the yard and again the progress was remarkable.

When they took a short break at about 10:30 for more coffee and some of Daisy's treats, Ed almost mentioned to John that he had a problem buying things at Lanni's the previous afternoon. Skip made hand and face motions which stopped Ed in mid-sentence from doing so.

"At Lanni's yesterday they... uh, they... had a neat old Craftsman table saw that I'm going back to look at."

This performance did not escape the notice of Daisy who didn't say anything but whose right eyebrow was raised up in a way that seemed to demand an explanation.

"So what was that all about?" she asked when they resumed working. Rick explained, without telling her exactly how much the entire bill came to.

"He can pay me back after Mr. Harrison squares with him," he told her, though he had no intention of ever bringing up the subject with Gramps.

Then Daisy told him how she had offered to give, or lend John some money because she knew that he was falling behind with paying several bills and though everybody liked John and extended him more credit than would be the norm, they would not do so forever. She even related that when she saw an electric bill on the table that was two months overdue, she just took it and paid it without ever telling him.

John never seemed to pick up on it. That almost prompted Skip to tell Daisy about the $800, but he figured the fewer who knew about that the better. If she knew she might also start wondering where his money came from and that would not be good.

"How did John lose his money?"

Daisy pretty much reiterated what Ed had said the day before about taxes but then she dropped a bombshell on him.

"And then, he spent all his savings years ago looking for his daughter and grandson."

Skip gulped and could feel the heat suddenly radiating from his face when he heard this. He felt like he could faint or throw up.

While the saw and planer sounds masked their conversation, Daisy told Skip things that she had apparently only found out recently. John had alienated his daughter who evidently was a closet alcoholic. The daughter had a rough life in that she had a child, who Daisy used to play with, born of a father killed in Vietnam before marriage could take place. One day, the daughter and John had a confrontation and the next thing John knew, she was driving away. He expected her to come back with the grandson who he was very fond of, but she never did. There was never even a post card from her. John didn't know if the fact that she had not returned home was due to her stubborn nature or foul play. "He beat himself up pretty badly for years, regretting whatever he said or did to cause her to run away."

John went to the police and eventually hired several detective agencies. He even paid to send a detective out to California because somebody in town swore that she saw John's daughter at Disneyland. Nothing ever came of it. They figured, if it were her at Disneyland, she could have been visiting from anywhere. Finally, the money ran out and John just seemed to have lost the will to search any longer. He had been riding an emotional roller coaster too long and could not take having his hopes of finding his daughter and grandson repeatedly dashed.

"He still wonders if the boy is alive or dead. A detective eventually found the death certificate for the daughter but the son apparently fell off the face of the earth. John told me that if the boy who is my age is alive, he'll know where to find him."

Exactly where to find him. 41°34.12 N, 71°26.75 W. Once again Skip's knees were shaking as a result of all that had been revealed to him so quickly by Daisy. Could she see what the information was doing to him, he wondered. Apparently, she was absorbed enough in their work that she couldn't.

Skip remembered the day in Disneyland. What kid wouldn't? He was being a pain in the ass and moping around to irritate his mother, but he enjoyed the day in spite of himself. In fact, it was one of the best days he and his mother ever had in California. It would haunt him that there were not many more. He could see, only then, that his mother had been trying to create a new life with new memories. He wished that he had not been so stubborn. It suddenly occurred to him that he had played a role in the death of his mother. He had never seen that before. There would be many "If onlys" in Skip's future.

The part about his mother not being married, that he was literally a bastard, was news to him. He knew his father had been killed in Vietnam. He assumed that any medals, and photos had been left in Rhode Island and disposed of after Gramps had "died."

He knew when and where his father, Gerald Thornton, had been killed. His mom had told him and he had confirmed it a few years ago when he found an online database of soldiers killed in Vietnam.

Skip was so nauseated and bewildered that when John called for a lunch break he had to come up with a lame excuse about having eaten some bad meatloaf and needing to go back to *Spray* to get some Pepto Bismol and close his eyes for awhile. His co-workers looked at him a bit strangely, but in fact he did exactly what he said he would do. Once in his bunk he started breathing deeply and was soon in a sleep of sorts, but not a restful one. Images of the past and echoes of recent conversations assaulted him. Waking up an hour later to the sounds of hammering in the yard, Skip was surprised that he was drenched in sweat. He was hungry though. He grabbed and ate a handful of canned cashews and chugged a small bottle of water before making his way back to the crew.

"Feel better?" asked Daisy with real concern on her face. "I do. I should have listened to Ed and not ordered Billy's meatloaf."

Ed laughed from the other side of the boat where he was working alone. Skip joined him and together they re-established the plank fastening routine. They were going to be finished today just like John said they would, and early too, even with Skip's leave of absence.

About three o'clock, after lemonade and a few of Daisy's cookies, including an anise flavored one for Skip which Daisy said would "settle his stomach a little more," John abruptly said he had to take a little trip to town hall and would be back soon.

The three of them shifted over to the side Ed had worked on alone earlier. The port side was already finished and starboard would be soon.

"Bet he is promising Rita that he'll have the money from Mr. Harrison now that this boat is planked and be in to pay a tax installment next week."

"Rita has been good to John, but she has pressure on her," said Daisy.

Daisy went on to mention how Rita, a customer of hers, had mentioned that she had heard "scuttlebutt" that unnamed people wanted to get John to sell his property to them. They wanted to pressure him by serving him with fines relating to expensive-to-fix septic violations and they wanted her to make sure John would get on the tax sale list the moment that he was in tax arrears long enough.

"That sick puppy, Ian, has been skulking around here for months. He flushed a dye tablet down the toilet and hasn't been able to find any trace of color by the shore, but he'll be back to look for something else. I wouldn't put it past him to pour a few buckets of port-a-john waste by the docks here at night and by coincidence come checking water quality the next day."

Skip made a mental note to be more alert while aboard *Spray*. He would investigate how to make an anonymous tax payment, too. Ian must have been the guy in the house the day he arrived in Wickford.

"I told John I would help him out with the taxes but he got real angry with me," said Daisy. "He told me that it was his problem and that he would work his way out of it on his own.

"Ian's no good. Never has been," said Ed. "When we were kids he used to catch a fish, cut off a fin and throw it back in the water just to watch it swim in circles. He saw Coyote over here one day and offhanded mentioned that his friend the dog officer might be interested in hearing about me keeping a wild animal."

Daisy and Skip waited for him to say more but were interrupted by John, who came out of the garage proclaiming with a smile, "Better to have it and not need it than need it and not have it! I must have hidden these away." He had just found the rivets "hidden" by Skip.

The rest of the planking was finished up as easily as could be wished. The four surveyed their handiwork and were very pleased. John's fleeting smile made the satisfaction more valuable to the other three. He thanked them like this was one of the most important things that had ever happened to him. It was. Now he would get the next payment from his well-healed customer and he could take care of the far too many bills that had accumulated and threatened to embarrass this proud old man.

"Got to go call Mr. Harrison. He'll be sure to come over for an inspection in a few days and he's going to like what he sees. Ed, we are even. Good work! Daisy and Skip, there is still time for a nice harbor sail in the Twelve. You guys earned it. Bet it will be a pretty sunset later."

Skip had been thinking of how he could approach Daisy in a non-threatening way. John had just done it for him. Looking at Daisy he said as nonchalantly as he could muster, "I'd like that." And with just the slightest hesitation she replied, "I'd like that, too. Let me just grab a few things."

CHAPTER FIFTEEN

As John predicted, the sunset was pretty. Lots of wispy pink and even purple clouds hung in the western sky, silhouetting the landmark St. Paul's Church steeple.

The gentle sail through familiar waters was delightful for Skip because of the quaintness of the seaside town, pleasant because the Herreshoff 12 1/2 was such a perfect little boat, and heart thumpingly exciting because Daisy was no more than four feet away from Skip in the compact classic cockpit.

Daisy played the role of local guide, assuming that the somewhat tight-lipped and slightly mysterious man, who apparently grew up in California, didn't know much about Little Rhody or its watercraft. "The "H-12," was designed by the legendary Nat Herreshoff of Bristol, Rhode Island, who knew a thing or two about boats." Skip was careful with his questions, observations and replies which made him look a bit awkward, if not actually somewhat slow. But he did not want to spill the beans as far as his background was concerned. "Oh, I think I knew that." He actually knew quite a bit about the "Wizard of Bristol," his many sail and power boat designs, and his well regarded shipyard.

Skip tried to be as truthful as possible with Daisy as they chatted but he was certain that Daisy conversations were going to get very complicated and that sooner or later he was going to make a mistake with consequences that he preferred not to contemplate on such a beautiful evening.

Sailing with Daisy was like it had once been. When Skip took the tiller, he knew just how close to shore he could go before he had to tack. After tacking they both shifted their weight to leeward almost on cue to get the right "heel" for efficient sailing. If Daisy thought that this apparently well choreographed maneuvering was odd she didn't let on at all. For Skip it was all so magical. For Daisy, just very comfortable.

On the way back from the breakwater, apropos of nothing, Daisy blurted out that there was "a lot more going on here with John than you know." She proceeded to tell him about more money problems and more incidents involving Stilwell and his stable of stooges. Bottom line was that there was a plan afoot to get John off his land by financial default. If he had a stroke while dealing with his aggravating problems then so much the better. Daisy wondered aloud how far Stilwell would go. Would he actually cause physical harm to be inflicted if matters were not brought to a head quickly enough for his development plans?

Apparently much was at stake for Stilwell and associates. John's property had water rights out to the channel. Many old Wickford homes did, since throughout the past there had been scores of small yards in town building assorted boats for shipping, fishing, pleasure and even smuggling. Stilwell wanted those rights so he could link two small boatyards into one large, modern one with all the usual resort amenities. His planned waterfront condos

would fetch a fortune because they could offer the expected comforts and the unbeatable convenience of seeing
from a deck or patio one's very own yacht at a slip barely a
hundred yards away. The key was John. If he had access to
the channel, Stilwell's development didn't and he and the
associates did not have time to wait for a natural solution
to their problem.

Recognizing that she may have gone on a bit too far
with this revelation, especially with a virtual stranger, Daisy
apologized. "Not necessary. John seems like a real nice guy and
I wish I could help him out in some way. If you figure out
how I could do that just let me know." Daisy promised
she would and then as they slowly came up the narrow
channel in the diminishing night breeze they just made small
talk. Skip dropped that his "real" name was James Fox, but
that nobody ever called him that. Daisy countered without
any apparent reason that she wasn't currently seeing
anyone and elaborated, perhaps in response to Skip's wide-
eyed stare, that she had never been married either. As she
looked out at a sinking crescent moon she said with just a
tinge of regret that because of all her business responsibilities
and time spent looking after John she was just too busy for a
real relationship. In response to her query about his sailing
skills, Skip said he was taught by his mother and grandfather,
but he guiltily neglected to mention that that had occurred
in the very same waters they had just sailed over.

It had been a long day and a good one but the conversation
had played out. Both felt that there would be time for
more at some point but that to continue that evening
would be to invite a faux-pas that might have permanent negative effects.

"Let's get the sails down. We can row in from here."
Skip dropped, detached and bagged the jib. He then let
down the main halyard slowly, while expertly flaking the
sail over the boom. Daisy joined him in putting on the sail
cover and their hands entangled briefly. Both pulled back

from each other like they had been jolted by 50,000 volts of electricity. They may as well have been. Awkwardly they apologized to each other and pretended that they didn't react as they had, but even a casual observer would know and note that something just happened that may have some special significance.

Without a word, Skip removed the oars from their brackets, set them and positioned himself to row. The first few strokes took them nowhere because the H-12 has a 900 pound lead keel and is slow to pick up speed. But in a few minutes they were tied up at the dock where they quickly coiled lines, snugged cleats, and stowed gear the way sailors do wherever they are. Skip extended a hand to help Daisy out onto the non-skid decking which Daisy would normally not take.

That she did so, murmuring a soft "thank you" as she deftly joined him in walking up the ramp, would have amused John.

Only a single dim light was on in John's house. He had long been asleep after what to him was an important day. Daisy and Skip quietly walked up to her Jeep so as not to disturb him. Skip thanked her for a nice sail and she said that it was an enjoyable night for her and that they would have to do it again. At that Skip's heart skipped a beat; in an instant she jumped into the Jeep's driver's seat and was gone.

THE AIR HAD COOLED DOWN CONSIDERABLY BUT IT WAS still a beautiful evening. Rick decided to sit down by the flagpole and have a smoke. He wanted to savor the evening and going back to *Spray* would mean that it was officially over which he did not want to yet admit. He was exactly where he wanted to be and with whom he wanted to be there but he was conflicted by all the deception. A little voice told him that these new relationships with Grampa or Daisy were time bombs. When the bombs went off he would lose what he had never expected to regain and then he could be sure that he would never, never ever get those relationships back. But what could he do? Once again he felt that he was a hapless character in a Greek Tragedy and that he would always be one. He had been cursed.

Something else popped into his mind and it was very disturbing that it had not popped into his mind earlier. Did he have any other living relatives? His mom had told him that John had died and that his other grandparents were dead too. If she lied about John, had she lied about them as well? Did he have any uncles and aunts that might still be in the area? Cousins? If Leah had lived would she have ever told him the truth about all of this?

As he mulled over this latest taunting torment Skip shook his head. He was going to be a psychiatrist's dream patient someday. Though he could be suffering from Olympic-class self-deception it was remarkable, at least to him, that he was as normal as he was given the rapidly occurring revelations. He should be a raving lunatic right now. Maybe he would be when this all unraveled and he hoped he wouldn't drag others into the abyss with him.

Mercifully Skip was distracted by a slight noise before he could go down other mental paths with likely poor outcomes. It sounded like some raccoon or possum had bumped into a can of rivets. He hoped it wasn't a skunk. He peered carefully in the direction of the sound and let his eyes adjust. He saw nothing. Then he heard something he could not identify very close to where he had been working on the boat earlier in the day. Flash! Woooosh! Crackle! The bright light of what he was certain was igniting gasoline blinded him like the discharge of those old-fashioned flash bulbs you see in vintage movies. In that instant he clearly saw the man who was with Gramps when he first found him only days ago.

As if frozen by a strobe light Ian was holding a small gas can like you would have for a lawnmower and he was backing away. "Hey, you!" Skip yelled. This startled Ian who dropped the can and ran off into the darkness. Skip took off like a hound after a nearby fox but then he stopped abruptly. Even in his heightened adrenaline-fueled state, either because of his nature or Marine training, Skip calmly but quickly weighed the options. He could catch Ian, of that he was certain, but what then? Call the police? Wouldn't the police want to know who he was? Or he could beat Ian to a pulp and may very well do so at another time, but that probably wouldn't work out for him or John either. Clearly the best course of action was to put out the fire immediately. Fortunately the flames were right by the garden hose which was only a few feet away. He turned on the faucet and set about aiming a stream then a spray at the base of the flames, then all over the bow area of the boat. In truly a matter of seconds there was no more fire, only the strong smell of unburned gasoline.

The porch light came on and John peered through the screen door. He saw Rick. "What happened? I saw a flash and then saw you running up here in the firelight. How badly is she damaged? Who did this?" John, working to catch his breath, was by Skip's side trying to see the hull but the light was not good enough. He went to get a flashlight in the kitchen and was back very quickly. Skip noticed that he was walking unsteadily and it was obvious that John was very anxious to look over his unfinished creation.

As the white halogen beam played over the surface of the newly fastened planks both men could not believe what they saw. Almost nothing but wet wood! The gas vapor had burned brilliantly but the heavy hard wood had not reached a high enough temperature to ignite. It had browned up slightly almost like suntanned skin but that was it. The normal sanding for hull prep would remove all traces of the blemish. "I guess someone does not want me to finish this boat," was all that John could say with resignation in his voice. "John....this boat will be finished. And we're going to finish it together very soon. You and me. I promise." This voice was filled with confidence and determination and something else that John could not put his finger on.

Skip guided John back to the porch. "Try to get some sleep, John. Nothing else is going to happen tonight. We'll find out who did this and deal with him later." Skip made his way back to his boat. "And nothing like this is ever going to happen to you again, Gramps, that I swear to God," he whispered to himself.

SKIP WAS UP EARLY THE NEXT MORNING. HE DID NOT sleep well at all and imagined it would have been the same for Gramps.

Skip walked around the picnic boat and admired her fine lines. No transom was on her yet because John thought it would be easier to slip in the twin diesels and generator without one. When he got to where the fire had been the smell of gas was much less than it had been the previous night. A few hours of hot July sun and strong prevailing south westerlies would remove all traces of odor in short order. Apparently nobody was aware of the fire except for three people. Skip tried to estimate how much time had elapsed between ignition and extinguishing the fire. It could have been 45 seconds or three minutes. The mind was funny about evaluating time in incidents like this.

The screen door slammed and John's extended arm held out a full coffee mug for Skip. "Thanks for saving this boat...and me. I don't know what would happen to me if this here boat were lost Skip. I wish you had caught the bastard who did this red handed. I wish I had caught the bastard red handed! I have a pretty good idea who it was, though."

Skip mumbled something about guys who do this sort of thing always eventually making a mistake that causes them to get caught. Before falling into the half sleep the previous night he had decided that the Ian info had to be kept to himself or someone he could absolutely trust. This was need-to-know-only information. John could not ever be told, so that when Ian got his due John could deny any knowledge of the situation. And Ian would be getting his due very soon.

John seemed a bit tentative. He was not who he was a few days before. He was missing a certain snappiness. "I want to finish this project as soon as I can, Skip. Wash my hands of it. I agreed to provide a finished hull with mounted engines, shafts and fuel tanks. I also have to deck it over and install ports, hatches and whatever glass Mr. Harrison decides on. After launching and trials the boat will steam under its own power to a fancy Long Island outfitter for interior finish work. Not much more than an interior decorator, I bet. I don't do that sort of stuff."

Though John would sooner die than admit it, he was scared quite a bit by the fire. He was down to his final resources which really consisted almost entirely of his own skills; there were no more cushions for him to fall back upon. The boat needed to be finished, he needed to get paid, and then he could take stock and decide on his next step. "I am going over to Sonder & Nugent to order the wood I need for the aft cockpit and deck. I'll be back ear-ly afternoon."

Skip said he would meet him later and then he took a bike into town for breakfast. The diner was busy and as Skip scanned the booths and counter he saw Ed sitting alone. He eased himself into the seat across from him with a "Mind if I join you?" Ed said he could, then proceeded to tell him that it was always nice working with John on a project; he always learned a little bit more from "The Master."

Skip cranked his neck one way and then the other. Then he stretched his back, bringing clenched fists up by his head. This was merely a screen for surveying his surroundings. When he was satisfied that there was no one in earshot he proceeded to recapitulate the events of the previous night. Ed listened without interruption. He didn't appear to be surprised and he didn't stop eating. Skip or dered his second coffee and related how John just wanted to finish up the boat before something else happened. Of course, Skip would stay around until launch time.

Ed plunked eight dollars down on the table and the two men got up to leave. When they were outside Ed led the way to the duck feeding bridge on Brown Street. He looked due east at John's property about a half mile away. Then he looked into Skip's eyes. "You got to fight fire with fire, Skip. Stilwell is not going to give this up. Not a chance. He needs to be sent a message that will make him back off forever. It has to be a real strong message if you catch my meaning."

Ed never picked fights but he had been in a few. He won substantially more than he lost and some of the rougher fishermen who misjudged his mettle wished that they had never messed with his traps or tried to stop him from dragging in some transiently productive open fishing grounds. When someone who did not know Ed mentioned to someone who did about encroaching on something Ed was doing the reply was a terse, "Best leave that one alone."

John had been very good to Ed over the years. Ed was old school. If somebody took care of him, he took care of them. If somebody screwed him, they got way screwed. "Let me think this over, Skip. I think we can settle this for John once and for all. In fact we might even have some fun." Skip wasn't sure, but as Ed headed for the docks, he thought he heard him chuckle.

*B*OOBY *TRAP* WAS THE NAME OF STILWELL'S REASON-ABLY impressive motor yacht. The connotation was unambiguous given that as painted on the transom, the two "Os" bore more than a passing resemblance to ample and fetching bosoms. Stilwell fancied himself a version of Hugh Heffner, certainly a stretch by any measure, but in a small town you could sometimes get away with a projection like that.

Booby Trap often was found at a mooring in a quiet corner of Newport Harbor. Not only was it quiet, but it was a spot that could not be easily surveyed from land to any great degree. The New York Yacht Club was close by

and the famous Beacon Rock mansion, once home to the sculptor of the Iwo Jima Memorial, towered above the several tethered vessels in the area. It was a spot calculated to impress young, sexy and usually very unsophisticated women. And it did. A typical *Booby* cruise would involve a tour around the harbor that was always packed with mega-yachts from around the world. Of course, strong drinks were continuously dispensed from the moment the little mermaids came aboard. Sometimes the guests went for a dip off the teak swim platform and often the girls skinny dipped in the clear water or sunned topless on the fore-deck. A catered lobster dinner on the fantail at sunset would follow and then a few post-prandial drinks would prime all aboard for an evening of fun.

On this day, a couple of weeks after the attempted destruction of John's boat, Stilwell and Ian had some items to discuss before two sweet young things were brought out by one of the Newport launches. "I am sure he saw me. I saw him!" "Well then why didn't he come after you either immediately or later?" "I don't know and it is weirding me out." Stilwell was certain that the one called "Skip" either had been blinded by the bright light of the igniting gasoline or had been looking in the wrong direction at that instant. Either way he was not concerned.

While the two men sat on the flying bridge with their mojitos they did not take notice of a lobster boat picking up a mooring a couple of hundred yards away. It was that kind of location. Powerboats, fishing boats and sailboats of all sizes and designs moored there but were coming and going with no discernible schedule.

Ed and Skip had picked the day for their little operation after checking the astronomical calendar. There would be no moon that night when they went about their business. An added bonus was that there might be a little fog as there often was in Newport when the rest of Narragansett Bay was clear. That would obscure their approach later in the evening and muffle sound to a degree.

Casually Skip used binoculars to observe Stilwell and the *Booby Trap*. Such equipment attracted no attention on the water. Skip could have been looking at Bonniecrest mansion, a sleek 100' Med style boat flyng an Aussie flag, or a couple of nearby cuties on paddleboards.

Technically what he was doing was recon, for which he had been well trained by the Marine Corps. But this was much more fun. He paid very close attention as two very attractive women in slinky outfits were dropped off by the launch, *ALERT*. That they were not outfitted in

J. Crew apparel or wearing Topsiders was not worthy of contemplation by any of the males in a position to notice. Even the smirking launch captain did not mind waiting awhile as the giggling little darlings removed their high heels and more or less crawled aboard *Booby Trap* where they were greeted by the two trappers themselves. He had witnessed this scenario many times before, and not just aboard this boat.

Sticking to the official *Booby Trap* schedule, the two girls changed out of their tight, white Capri pants into some nice thong-like bathing suits. With surprisingly good diving form they both took the plunge off the yacht's high bow, quickly followed by their much less graceful, though quite enthusiastic hosts. Skip made a mental note that all four of those aboard the yacht swam well.

Ed made some ham and cheese sandwiches. As the sun set they finished them off in the small wheelhouse of *Coyote*. Neither man was a big drinker but it was agreed that they would have only one beer each that night. Even when you are perfectly in control of your faculties, sometimes a glitch calls for fast thinking and action. Dulling your senses to any degree lessens the chance of success in any mission and this was now an active mission in the minds of both men.

At 10:00 pm Skip took a last look over at the *Trap*. Stilwell adjourned to his private cabin early and Ian was dancing to music, just a hair too loud, in the main salon with his bare breasted mate.

"It's a go," said Skip. The men opened the wide transom door and dangled their legs from the shallow swim platform. The water was warm and they decided not to use wetsuits. Besides, if they were seen in them it might be a harder thing to explain if anyone asked. They slipped on fins, rinsed out their masks then spit in them to prevent fogging, and then adjusted the snorkels that they might not actually use because they could attract attention with them on a quiet night like it was when the men exhaled.

Ed tied a mesh bag to his dive belt in which there was one item that was annoyingly buoyant. It would only annoy him for a few minutes though. Both men slipped into the water soundlessly and made their way towards the "target." When they were only a hundred feet away they heard the putt putt sound of a small engine on an inflatable boat running without lights. They made their way to a large mooring float that they hid behind until the teenagers passed them. Proceeding to *Booby Trap* they hung onto its swim platform. Ed removed the large plastic peanut butter jar from the bag. In it were stuffed about ten heavy cotton rags saturated with gas and diesel oil. The diesel oil wouldn't ignite easily but once the burning gas fumes ignited the diesel fuel it would keep the fire going. Both men dried their hands as best they could on the swim platform's dry teak. Then they took out the rags, wadding them up into little balls that they lightly tossed into the cockpit. A couple hung up on the ladder going to the bridge but that was OK. Finally they put three outstretched rags on the right, left and center of the swim platform. The occupants would smell nothing unless they came out for some night air since the bow of the boat was pointing into a nice five knot breeze. A vapor shadow developed aft and the men quickly swam away by pre-arrangement. They did not want the gas fumes to dissipate or they would not be able to start a fire when they wanted to. Once back at *Coyote* they climbed aboard and toweled off, slipping the towels overboard with their residual diesel and gas smell. Ed fired up the well-muffled engine and let it idle. Skip let the mooring line slip back into the water while Ed put the boat in gear. It moved so quietly that one could not be sure that the engine was actually running except for the fact that the boat was in motion. A hundred feet directly behind *Booby Trap* the smell of gas and diesel was distinct. Almost too strong. Ed spun the boat 180 degrees and then put her in neutral. He reached for his loaded flare gun and slowly walked to his transom.

Taking careful aim and adjusting his angle of fire, Ed gently squeezed the trigger. A red trace showed the path of the projectile as it gracefully arced to the cockpit of its target. But even before the flare exploded against the rear bulkhead the vapor shadow brilliantly ignited. Flash! Wooosh! Crackle! Ed was back at the wheel in an instant with a big smile on his face and *Coyote* swiftly glided into the shadows behind Beacon Rock and then headed out of the harbor towards Castle Hill Light at the entrance to the Narragansett Bay. If Skip had to guess, he would say that there was a pretty good chance that Ed had done something like this more than once before.

Back at the Booby Trap, four naked and scared people hurriedly climbed up to the foredeck through the forward hatches; without any attention to form or concern about immodesty they abandoned ship and swiftly swam to the nearby shore.

Message sent. Message received.

CHAPTER SIXTEEN

*C*OYOTE MADE HER "ESCAPE" FROM BRENTON COVE
without attracting any attention at all. That was because all attention in the vicinity was focused on
the burning *Booby Trap* which lit up the area like a pile
of very dry Christmas trees set ablaze around the Vernal
Equinox. Boats moored close by moved if anyone was
aboard to move them and distant sirens could be heard as
Skip and Ed rounded the north end of Fort Adams. Running south up the shore towards Castle Hill, past Jackie
Kennedy's Hammersmith Farm, the sounds and lights of
Newport soon disappeared.

Ed reached into a small six-pack cooler and pulled
out the two cans of Narragansett beer that had not been
cracked open when they had their sandwiches a little
while earlier. Each man took a good long pull and then,
as if part of a script, they toasted each other; Ed then held
his can high and said, "To John! May his worries be over."

There was no wild recapping of events. Skip hoped
that nobody was hurt and was anxious that maybe some

one might have been. The unanticipated consequences of even well thought out, praise worthy actions are frequently regrettable. He would have to listen to the news first thing in the morning. "We'll round Beavertail and run up the West Passage to Wickford. Should be tied up in a couple of hours," said Ed. Skip spelled him at the wheel when the Jamestown-Verrazzano Bridge was clearly visible to the north. Both men were tired, mostly from mental strain rather than physical activity but true to Ed's prediction they were back at *Coyote's* berth in two hours. "See you at the diner tomorrow?" "I'll be there."

S KIP DIDN'T KNOW HOW ED SLEPT BUT HE DIDN'T FEEL he had slept at all. There was too much racing around in his head. Irrationally, he actually felt as he entered the diner that someone was going to yell out: "Hey everybody! There's the dude that torched *Booby Trap* last night!" But of course nobody did. Ed was in his favorite booth, back to Skip, reading the Providence Journal. "Morning, Ed." "Morning, Skip." The pretty little waitress rushed over with coffee for Skip, she being a bit more attentive to his habits since he arrived in town, than Skip had noticed.

Ed folded over a section of the ProJo and slid it across the table to Skip.

Newport – Newport police and fire departments responded to a request for assistance by the Newport harbormaster around 11:00 pm last night. A luxury yacht caught fire at its mooring in the southwest section of the harbor and was fully engulfed in flames by the time the recently acquired fireboat arrived at the scene. The fireboat directed one stream of water at adjacent vessels that were at risk for heat damage and with another stream put out the flames aboard the apparently unoccupied vessel. "The yacht is unsalvageable but fortunately no fuel was detected leaking into the harbor waters," said Capt. T. A. Quinn, a veteran of the NFD. "Fire

damage was so significant that the yacht could
not be immediately identified." A precautionary
fuel spill containment boom was deployed
around the vessel which will be towed to an
undisclosed site. An investigation surrounding
the circumstances of the blaze is ongoing."

Skip pushed the newspaper back across the table to Ed.
"Interesting," was all he could say. He was still concerned
about the safety of the four occupants of *Booby Trap*
though he was pretty sure he saw splashes as Stillwell and
guests jumped into the harbor waters. He reminded himself they were only about a hundred yards from shore. Still.

THE two men left the diner, Ed to get ready for fishing and
Skip to go back to help John. THE necessary engine gear and
lumber had been delivered and the project was wrapping up
quickly, much to John's relief. With a little luck the vessel
commissioned by Mr. Harrison would be handed over to his
finishing yard before Labor Day. But that also presented a
new problem for Skip. What would he do then? He didn't want
to leave Gramps and he didn't want to leave Daisy. Would John
have additional work for him? Unlikely. John was emotionally
exhausted. He would be taking on no big projects soon. THere
was work to done around the yard, of course. THE docks needed
considerable replanking. Some pilings needed to be reset after
apparent ice damage the previous winter. John's roof should
probably be replaced, too. But all that could easily be completed
in a few weeks. John would balk at doing anything but Skip
could probably talk him into it as advance payment for future
dockage. And then what? Would it be possible to find a real
job? It would probably have to be an "under the table"
arrangement like on a fishing boat. Skip did not want to use his
IDs from Jimmy unless he really had to. He didn't think they
could stand any simple, not to mention serious, scrutiny.

His relationship with Daisy was going surprisingly
well. Perhaps "relationship" was not quite the right word
but they both seemed to be over their initial tentativeness

and genuinely enjoyed each other's company. Skip wanted to take the next step but was afraid to "spook" her; instead, at least at first, he joined the ranks of young men for whom the price of a donut or a loaf of bread was a small expense for the simple opportunity to see a bright smile, have a good laugh or participate in a short exchange about nothing in particular. Often they met at the bakery at closing time after which they would go to John's for a light dinner and then either a sail or a walk by the Town Beach. Skip was becoming a bit uncomfortable with the dinner part though because lately John seemed to be giving him a "look" like he knew something that Skip didn't. But what could he know? It was probably something to do with Daisy, her being his *de facto* daughter and all and Skip being an unknown quantity to a great extent. Neither one of them seemed to ask a lot of questions about his past which was a bit worrisome, but given the scale of things he had to worry about he mostly put that out of his mind.

Daisy kept John's place presentable, often tidying it up when he was away. The flowers in the window boxes and around the flagpole were her doing; her meticulous gardens around her meticulously kept little house furnished an abundance of extra plants and plenty of the usual summer vegetables.

Increasingly *Spray* became the boat for sailing when the two had more time together, like on weekends. The first couple of outings were daysails on the Bay to Bristol and Potter's Cove on Prudence Island. It was immediately apparent that as comfortable as Skip felt sailing Daisy's Herreshoff, Daisy felt sailing "his" Pearson. Obviously she had done a lot of big boat cruising over the years. She knew which panel switches to switch to start the engine, use the instruments, and turn on the cabin or running lights. She didn't have to read a manual to use the GPS. Skip revealed as much about his former life as he dared during these excursions where they would stop for a swim off the boat or have a drink in the cockpit and Daisy mentioned more than once with mischievous eyes that it might be fun to sail down in the Caribbean some winter.

Daisy was slowly admitting to herself that she really liked Skip. He did seem reserved but she knew she sometimes had that effect on men. He worked hard, was polite and smart and he was genuinely protective of John. He liked to do the things that she liked to do and it wasn't an act just to get her in bed. In fact, for the first time in quite awhile she thought that making love with Skip was probably going to happen and she realized as she thought this that she was smiling. She decided, though, that she might have to drop a few hints and use her womanly wiles because Skip really seemed to be the skittish type and she didn't want to "spook" him. Whether he was that way because of her or John she would have to find out.

Ed and Skip became as good friends as it was possible to become in the short time that they had known one another. They fished recreationally together when Daisy was busy. Sometimes they went for little skipjacks off John's docks at sunset and occasionally they would land a monster bluefish that could take a finger off if you were not careful removing the hook. Ed showed him some good places for striper fishing like off the Hazard Avenue rocks in Narragansett. A couple of times Skip helped out on *Coyote*, dragging for scup but catching a variety of things like black sea bass and even lobsters. On the last trip Ed gave an update on the great *Booby Trap* conflagration. In published reports it seems that the police did catch up with Stilwell. Apparently he stated that he went ashore the night of the fire with a client for dinner. They finished late and he decided to stay at his friend's apartment overnight. When he came out to his boat by launch the next morning, he was shocked to find that *Windsong* was nothing more than a smelly, charred hulk. He reported to fire marshals and the Newport harbormaster that he had not owned her long and that he did not even have time to have the new name painted on the transom. He speculated that the fire might have been caused by a generator that had been giving him problems for a few weeks.

"You can't make this up," said Rick. "Oh yes you can! And he did! And how about that touch of changing the name of his boat to *Windsong* so as not to arouse speculation about what may really have been going on aboard her? Evil genius! God, only a real scum bag would come up with a trick like changing a boat's name to hide the truth."

It took a couple of seconds for that to register on Skip. But it brought home to him how close he himself could be to becoming a scum bag in the eyes of his new and old friends if his true situation became known and his story, brief as he tried to keep it, unraveled. He was going to have to tackle that elephant sooner or later and he did not look forward to it.

Daisy usually took the second week of August off for vacation. She had planned to go hiking and camping with her friends, Sophie and Isla, in the Pacific Northwest. Both young women were transplants out there from Rhode Island and they were supposed to do a few days at Crater Lake and then a few days at Mt. Ranier. But the plans fell through only a week before they were all supposed to meet. Sophie found out she was pregnant and was having a tough time, and Isla just got her first "real" job with a software company and couldn't even think of asking for time off.

Daisy was sort of relieved at this sudden change. And it only took her a moment to come up with "Plan B" which would be to see if Skip would consider an offshore cruise. They could do Block Island or go out towards the Vineyard and Nantucket. It would depend on the wind, of course. *Spray* would be very comfortable for two and it wouldn't take any time at all for her to provision the boat. She even had all the local charts and guidebooks that she knew Skip didn't.

Skip hesitated briefly when Daisy made the suggestion. As excited as he was by the prospect he tried not to reveal it. She was a bit taken aback by this but did not show it and attributed it to Skip's reserved nature. But one reason for faltering was that a still somewhat paranoid Skip thought that he might be stopped by the Coast Guard and asked for the usual documentation, which he knew could get messy. The second reason which he could freely share with Daisy and which satisfied her was that John might need him. Deep down he hoped John wouldn't and when John was asked after work that day he said he didn't. John said that he could handle bunging the new transom now that the engines, shafts and fuel tanks were installed. Then he would have several wood sealing coats to apply with a lot of waiting in between them until the were dry enough to sand. He assured them that two men would be wasting a lot of time on this phase of the operation.

Neither one knew that John would not for any reason throw a monkey wrench into the plans that he saw unfolding. If he felt a heart attack coming on he would will it away until after they left the dock. He wanted the two of them to go on this cruise and act the way two people their age should act in summer if they had time and a good boat. "God Almighty, just what the hell was wrong with these two anyway?" he thought to himself.

True to her promise, Daisy provisioned the boat on Thursday for a scheduled departure on Friday after she closed down the bakery at noon. Skip double-checked the rigging, sails, engine fluids, fuel, refrigeration system, solar panels and money supply. $10,000 in loose cash - that ought to do it for a week he quipped to himself. And though he tried to keep his anticipation in check, the upcoming week was looking very good indeed. Cautiously he asked himself, "Can my luck finally be changing for the better?"

Spray was ready to go. Since Skip ran a yacht charter service for so long he was used to making sure that all systems were checked. He never lost a client because one of the boats in his stable was unfit to go out for charter. As soon as a client came back from a cruise the vessel was inspected and put in "Bristol-fashion," if that weren't already the case.

John and Daisy introduced Skip to some of their Wickford friends who were exceptional marine craftsmen. The storm damage to the Pearson 365 on the trip up from the Caribbean was not severe, but the dodger and bimini had been shredded, some stainless support tubing was lost and some bent, quite a bit of teak trim was cracked or missing and inexplicably a chunk of stainless steel bow anchor mount had what looked like a barracuda "bite" in it about 2" diameter. More strange was that the bite edges showed no deflection as Skip would have expected from the kind of impact that could cause such a gap.

In between John's projects *Spray* was gradually restored by "George the Boatright" and his son, Dom, who never wore shoes, "Young Robby the Welder," who could cut a steel offshore dragger in half by himself and then weld in a section that would make it 12' longer, and "Frank the Fireman," who stitched a good tight canvas as well as anybody Skip had ever seen. And "Metal Man," aka "Don," took one look at the anchor mount, and pronounced it worthless. He scribbled down a few measurements in his notepad and came back in two hours with a perfect replacement that he machined out of a piece of stainless scrap from an offshore oil rig. His machine shop had seen a lot of restoration work for America's Cup and high-end vintage yachts and John chuckled when he saw the new piece saying that you could be pretty sure that Skip's broken mount would be reincarnated as another piece of marine hardware in the near future. If any of these men had surnames, they had not yet been revealed to Skip. It appeared, though, that if anyone asked about the men by their actual names, nobody would know who they were talking about.

SPRAY'S LINES WERE THROWN OFF AT A BIT PAST NOON and a nice, dry 10 knot northerly filled in and looked like it would hold. "The Block would be an easy sail. No tacking and we could be on a hook or mooring by 5:30 to have cocktails and watch a great sunset. I have some nice beef ribs, cornbread baked this morning, and roasted potatoes. All I have to do is heat everything up in the oven. The moon is pretty bright and would be low enough when it rises in the east to guide us right into Cuttyhunk, but it is a bit farther and with the yacht club cruises likely to have this as a stop we will have trouble finding a good spot for the night." "Then the Block it is," said Skip in a voice that clearly revealed that he was excited to be setting sail on such a beautiful day with such a beautiful woman.

Neither looked at a chart or the GPS. Daisy had done these legs many times before and Skip had pored over several charts so often the last few nights that if eyes could wear paper out the NOAA publications would look like Swiss cheese. On they sailed, past Dutch Island, past Whale Rock, under Bonnet Shores, making a slight turn west after Point Judith, then deviating a bit to let one of the island ferries go by before picking up the turning point "1BI" in the glow of a lowering sun. The North Light illuminated by a golden-yellow sun looked spectacular as they cruised past and Daisy slipped out her fancy camera to get a few great shots. Skip asked if he could take one of her with the lighthouse in the background. Actually he was only interested in Daisy, but the pictures of both could be in a travel brochure for the island. Her flowing red hair and beautiful tan, freckles and all were a sight to behold and he would have to ask for a copy of those pictures later on.

THEy took the sails down and furled them OFF the en-trance to Great Salt Pond where several other boats com-ing from Long Island Sound were doing the same thing. THEn *Spray* motored up the narrow channel past the little breakwater where youngsters were still swimming, their parents either sitting in nearby beach chairs with their feet in the water or casting for whatever fish were biting at the moment.

And then they both caught the heady scent of coastal Rhode Island – the unbelievably fragrant sea roses which were all the more intoxicating since the sail out over open water had purged their nostrils of any competing essences.

Of course Daisy had a contact out on "The Block" who had a mooring for them. He was an itinerant funeral director and since the island had no immediate need of his services he was off sailing. Daisy said his boat name was "*Wake*" but Skip was pretty sure that she made that up. The two got *Spray* tied up and surveyed the harbor that was packed with hundreds of boats of all description. Both felt exactly the same thing: "I love boats and I love sailing in them whenever I can."

"Last one in has to make cocktails!" With that Daisy was down the hatch. Skip took the loss and neatened the lines in the cockpit before heading down to change himself. Though the sun partially blinded him he was almost certain that he got what would have been a quite decent glimpse in the darkened salon of an almost impossibly white bum and the bonus glimpse of two spectacularly creamy bosoms offset by as rich a tan as a redhead can get. The view, such as it was, was transient as Daisy came storming up the companionway in an American flag patterned bikini. She was laughing as she undid the pelican latch on the safety line and then dove into the New Harbor waters.

Skip needed no more encouragement; he donned his suit and was soon swimming by her side. He was laughing like a fool but it felt so good to be truly feeling the way that he did. Daisy took a couple of strokes towards him and threw her arms around his neck. They both felt the rush but this time instead of a cautionary recoil they clasped each other so strongly that they began to sink. Sputtering as they broke the surface they laughed some more. And then suddenly they kissed.

Very passionately. "Guess the womanly wiles still work OK," she thought. "Wow, OMG what was that?" thought he.

Skip's drinks would be delayed until the sun was below the horizon and the afterglow in the western sky reached its peak. Their own afterglow after intense love making was more delightful than the celestial one. Once they made it up into the cabin after abandoning their swimming they practically ripped each other's suits off and both had a feeling that something very special was unfolding. That there was passion was no surprise to either but deep down Skip and Daisy both felt that this might be something else, too.

As they sat in the cockpit sipping Dark 'n' and Stormys they touched, not awkwardly, but comfortably and tenderly. Daisy stroked his arm which was draped around her like it was the most natural thing; he lightly caressed her hair. Neither wanted to move and break the spell.

But the spell was broken when Daisy's stomach growled rather loudly. They both laughed. "I guess its time for dinner!" "I'll set the dinette," said Skip. The beef ribs, baked cornbread and roasted potatoes would have been the highlight of any other day.

THE NEXT MORNING WAS BLOCK ISLAND PERFECT. THE rising sun shimmered over a calm and quiet harbor where the only sign of humans was a couple of kayakers gliding close by the shore leaving only a quiet ripple as they weaved between moored boats. The two new lovers were entwined and uncovered in their berth, feeling at once very happy, sated and refreshed. After dinner and before turning in the previous night they went skinny-dipping in the moonlight and were like two playful otters, diving, and swimming into each other. Despite the lunar brightness each could see a halo around the other in the warm water which occasionally showed even brighter flashes of bioluminescence where the water was disturbed by a moving

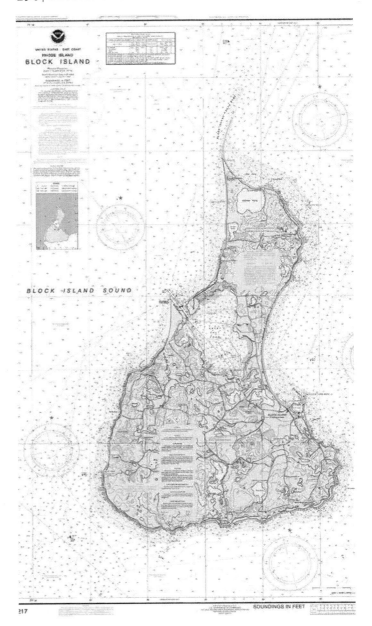

foot, hand or other appendage, stimulating a small jelly-fish or another light emitting marine organism.

The solar shower bag hanging from the boom was still warm so they took turns rinsing themselves well in the cockpit. "Don't want to get "salt ass" early in the trip," laughed Daisy. Skip laughed too. The last time he had heard that expression was many years ago when Gramps hosed him off at the dock with cold water, sticking the nozzle right down the back of his bathing suit. Skip had probably been swimming with Daisy at that time too.

The two patted each other dry in the moonlight with a towel and it seemed as natural as if they had done it before a hundred times. Then they made love again, stifling what would elsewhere have been very pleasurable and certainly audible moans because they knew that the way sound traveled over water they would surely be the subject of much titillating speculation the following day. Both fell quickly into the deepest of sleeps as if they were drugged.

By the height of the sun, Skip knew it was not really early morning anymore. But he did not want to separate himself from Daisy yet. As he thought about this a distant call got Skip's attention but he could not make it out. It was repeated at irregular intervals. Daisy stirred, "That's Aldo coming out with our breakfast." "Who's Aldo, and how does he know what I want?" Daisy just laughed.

Sure enough, a small Boston Whaler with a fellow named Aldo in command made its way to *Spray* after several stops at nearby boats. He called out, "*Andiamo, Andiamo!*" which meant "Let's go! Let's go!" and nobody seemed to mind that he was making a lot of noise in the quiet harbor. When Skip looked down at the assortment of surprisingly fancy pastries he could see why. He ordered a blueberry Danish, Daisy got an old fashioned Bear Claw and they both got coffee. As Aldo went on to the next boat the two toasted one another with their drinks. "To the Block!" "I make better Bear Claws, but Aldo is not far behind me," she said a little boastfully but with a bright smile.

Topping the previous night would be tough but they had a perfect day on the island. Daisy knew the place well but Skip's single visit in the past was hazy. He sort of recalled a zoo of sorts with camels and ostriches at one of the old Victorian hotels but caught himself from mentioning it. Riding rented bikes up and down the hilly landscape, often reminiscent of the English countryside, they came upon that same zoo with its expanded odd assortment of animals including a Sicilian donkey, a yak, a big tortoise and even a kangaroo. Continuing on a little past Southeast Light they took a rugged staircase down the two hundred foot cliffs at Mohegan Bluffs where there was a spectacular beach. The water was crystal clear, and as the waves slowly broke on the sand and flat, polished granite stones, for a moment you could see right through them as if they were windows at an aquarium which in a sense they were. Skip and Daisy body-surfed and laughed a lot as they got smacked around by the breaking waves; the latter repositioned Daisy's bikini top which she then had to reposition again very quickly before she washed up on shore. Tiring a bit they sunned above the high tide line at the base of beautifully colored clay cliffs that were tan, orange, gray and black, transforming in intensity as the sun's angle to them changed. Daisy had packed a picnic lunch that fortified them enough to make it back up the stairs and bike some more around the Block.

They rode all the way to the far end of the island, leaving their wheels at Sachem Pond and then hiking to the rugged North Light which looked out over a very strong and frothy rip current reaching more than a mile offshore. Many small boats flanked both sides of the rip in the annual quest there for large bluefish.

On the way back to Old Harbor they stopped to buy lemonade at a tree shaded stand from a couple of eight year olds who reminded Skip of another time. He wondered if Daisy still had that memory. Skip folded up a five-dollar bill into a nub without drawing Daisy's attention. She mounted her bike and he turned to the kids. "Here's a little tip, best lemonade I ever had," he said as he pedaled off.

A couple of miles later they pulled over at Mansion Beach. The seas were gentle and the water clear. Hundreds of people were enjoying the quintessential day at the beach with brightly colored umbrellas and coolers to be seen everywhere. Daisy may have had many of these family outings, perhaps some right there, but Skip had not. It was time to catch up. They spent hours walking the beach, sunning, swimming and talking. Both were at ease in a way that they had not been until that afternoon. As the sun dropped they made their way to the showers at the adjacent State Beach and changed up so that they would be restaurant presentable, at least by Block Island standards.

Daisy knew a nearby establishment that had a good view of Old Harbor. As they followed the hostess to the best table they looked like "a nice young couple" the kind that all parents would like to see in their families some day. The two enjoyed a refreshing prosecco while waiting for the grilled Block Island yellowfin tuna, a house specialty. Coffee and Island blueberry pie completed the meal but the latter demanded a walk through town to burn off a few calories. For the first time in his life Skip actually enjoyed visiting the kind of shops you find at all beach resorts and amazingly for him, he purchased a nice, heavy "BLOCK ISLAND" sweatshirt like the tourists that he good naturedly mocked all of his adult life. He also managed to deflect Daisy's hand as she tried to pass a credit card to a clerk to pay for a pretty little sundress. "You'll look great in that," he said with a smile. And she would.

Returning to *Spray* by launch both felt that all was well with the world. After a pleasurable interlude they snuggled in their berth, fanned by a nice breeze that funneled over them from the forward hatch. The main hatch cover was slid forward so that they could see the stars dancing back and forth as the boat was swayed by a gentle night breeze. Suddenly there was a staccato sound which sounded like an underwater woodpecker, pecking on the hull directly below them. Skip sat bolt upright. "What is that?" He reached for his shorts but Daisy, who was choking with laughter, snatched them away and threw them to the cabin sole. "Skip, that's just the Block Island Cusk Eel. It only comes out of its burrow at night. It's calling for its mate, listen." Sure enough there was an identical but more distant repetition and then another and another. Skip fell back on his pillow. "Calling for its mate, eh?" and with smiles on their faces Skip and Daisy were down for the night.

CHAPTER SEVENTEEN

T HE FOLLOWING MORNING SKIP AND DAISY WERE awakened again by Aldo who was only a couple of hundred yards away from *Spray* as he made his pastry delivery rounds. With her hands, Daisy pushed back and smoothed her slightly tousled hair and quickly made her way up the companionway steps after grabbing an air horn and donning one of Skip's T-shirts that draped over her like a sheet over a statue of the Venus de Milo. She signaled the Boston Whaler with two short horn blasts and Aldo changed course instantly, no doubt recalling the beautiful redhead from the previous morning.

Skip joined Daisy in the cockpit where she gave him a nice little peck on the cheek. They enjoyed cranberry scones, banana bread and coffee. After draining their cups, Skip reached for a waterproof chartbook of southern New England waters that he had been perusing the night before. "Where to today?" Without hesitation came the reply "Hadley Harbor." "Can we make it?" Then she reached for the Eldridge, and studied the current charts while glancing often at her watch. "Easily, if the usual wind pattern holds."

THEY stowed gear and secured the usual things that needed securing. Slipping their mooring at 8:15 they ex-ited Great Salt Pond then turned south for a few miles before veering east. THIS course brought them by the spectacular cliffs they had climbed down together on the island's south shore. The wind was light so Daisy suggested firing up the "iron jib" after they put Southeast Light behind them. By the time they were abeam of the Sakonnet River entrance there was breeze enough to hoist the main and set the roller furling jib. The two alternated at the wheel for about an hour each. Skip used his free time to play with the auto helm that he eventually got working to his satisfaction. They used it sparingly, mostly to build faith in it, but the boat traffic of commercial tugs, barges and draggers out of Buzzards Bay along with the assorted yachts coming from the Vineyard and Elizabeth Islands, required human vigilance.

Daisy watched the lobster pot floats that they came upon that told her the direction of the current and gave her a rough estimate of its magnitude. Though a quick look at the electronics provided this information, as well, it was always good to practice for that inevitable time when they would fail. Based on her observations Daisy decided to sail between the old leper colony island of Penikese, and quaint Cuttyhunk where in 1602 Bartholomew Gosnold of Jamestown fame harvested sassafras, making himself a small fortune. On they sailed eastward along the scenic north shore of Nashawena, so reminiscent of coastal Scotland, until they were looking down Quicks Hole, a usually fast flowing channel separating Nashawena from the neighboring island of Pasque. "How about a swim and lunch, Skip? We're making great time?" "Fine by me. Will you take her in?"

The beach at Quicks Hole reminded Skip of so many in the Caribbean. Impossibly white sand lapped by impossibly clear water. Expertly, Daisy took *Spray* within a hundred feet of the shore where there was still ten feet of water. As soon as forward motion stopped, Skip dropped the anchor via the electric windlass, paying out about 60 feet of chain as they drifted back towards the channel. Sitting in the shade of the Bimini they enjoyed sandwiches and beer before donning their suits and diving in. "Could life get any better than this?" both thought. Swimming to shore they walked along the deserted beach avoiding the areas roped off by naturalists to protect the nesting Piping Plovers. Out of the blue a worrisome thought penetrated Skip's consciousness. Daisy was so familiar with the surrounding waters. How many times had she been to Quicks Hole? With how many guys did she stroll past these annoying little chirping birds? As he was about to take these questions to the next level in his head, which would really be a mood killer, an angel of mercy interceded, persuading Daisy to share a thought. "John took me here the first time with my parents. I bet I've stopped here ten times with him and them, and then with just him, on the way out to or back from some interesting place. I've been so lucky, Skip!" "You sure have!" quipped a relieved Skip with a big wide grin. He then, pulled her towards him and gently kissed her. They separated from the embrace slowly and strolled back up the beach hand in hand to near where *Spray* was a riding at anchor.

A NICE BROAD REACH BROUGHT THEM TO THE ENTRANCE to the well-protected Hadley Harbor, directly across from Woods Hole.

The currents were favorable because Daisy picked the right approach earlier using her Eldridge charts. Had she chosen the other approach from Vineyard Sound they could have battled a five-knot current which often would put even heavy duty navigation aids on their sides or even under water; they would not have been able to make it in to the Hadley Harbor sheltered waters under such conditions easily or even at all by nightfall. Sails secured, *Spray* powered the last half mile into the anchorage which still had plenty of room for them. After making sure the CQR had dug itself in, they rigged up the inflatable to do a bit of exploring. The nearby boats hailed from all over, but mostly New York and New England. *Spray* was on the small side of what Skip saw bobbing around the cove.

The island of Naushon, which surrounds much of the tree fringed harbor, is owned by the Forbes family, as are all the other larger Elizabeth Islands except for Cuttyhunk. Daisy mentioned that Bill and Hilary Clinton once sneaked over to Hadley from their summer White House on Martha's Vineyard for some respite there from the press and ran into James Taylor who was known to frequent the area.

Making their way back to the boat, they watched as a large ocean going trimaran expertly maneuvered into a space just ahead of *Spray*. As it was very slowly approaching the shore an attractive, bikini clad woman threw a large Danforth off the stern. From somewhere in the cockpit, line that was obviously neatly coiled paid out on its own. Then the agile anchor thrower strode briskly forward to the center pontoon where she grabbed another neatly coiled line hanging from a little stainless bow rail. She stepped onto a stubby bowsprit, waited a few seconds until the tri gently grounded and then hopped onto the shore. In a minute she secured the line to a strong looking shore-side oak and hopped right back onto the boat where she then paid out line at the same rate as the fellow at the stern pulled in the line attached to the stern anchor. The two exchanged hand signals, then made lines fast. Daisy, Skip and a few others who witnessed the neat little operation were filled with admiration. It was obvious that the trimaran couple had done this sort of thing a few times before and yachtsmen appreciate such accomplishments, especially in light of the much larger number of poorly executed events that they have all observed. "Well done!" shouted Skip. "Thank you," they replied in unison.

The unexpected unfolding relationship with Daisy, the sailing adventure with her, and his insertion into his grandfather's daily life had almost made Skip feel normal again. He had nearly forgotten that he was an innocent but wanted man because of the death of a scumbag, that he was in possession of a stolen boat, and that he had a pile of cash which could be explained to no law enforcement person's satisfaction. None of the credentials he had obtained from Jimmy really fit him and even his idea of renewing them and getting his photos on the replacements could be dangerous because it was not out of the question that Jimmy was also wanted for something or other somewhere. So when Skip looked at the transom of the trimaran and saw: "*La Sirenetta*, ST. THOMAS USVI" his good mood of the moment vaporized in a flash; the undeniable reality of his precarious situation was brought home to him once again.

Skip sat himself down in the cockpit before he fell into it. Of course Daisy was oblivious to his private little hell but the guardian angel put her up to asking if he wanted a Dark 'n' Stormy. "A nice tall one," he croaked while contemplating how to sneak a good bit more rum into it. Daisy appeared a few minutes later with a tray of drinks and some chips and salsa. In Daisy fashion she gushed on about what a great sail they had had and how the marine forecast was for four more perfect days. Skip was dimly aware of what she was saying and fortunately nothing she did say required an answer, which in any case she would not have received. Had Daisy been able to see Skip's glass she would have noticed that it was already half empty. Vacantly he stared out at the boats in the harbor.

Motion on *La Sirenetta* caught his eye. The couple aboard launched their inflatable using a davit system. Then while still tethered to the tri they fired up the outboard. They gave a wave in the direction of *Spray*, and then HEADED RIGHT TOWARD HER. "This can't be happening! Do they somehow recognize me or the old *Pleiades*?" thought a truly panicked Skip. The couple pulled up along side *Spray* and introduced themselves as

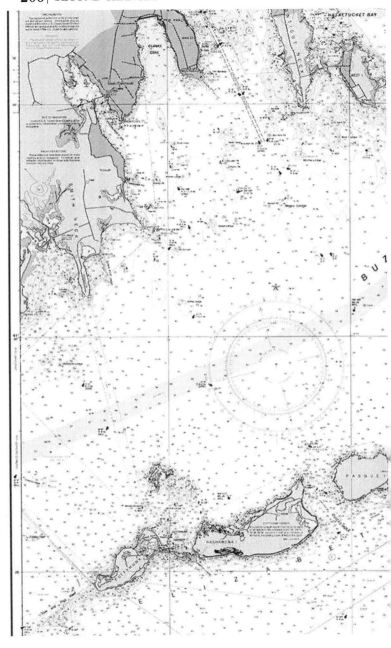

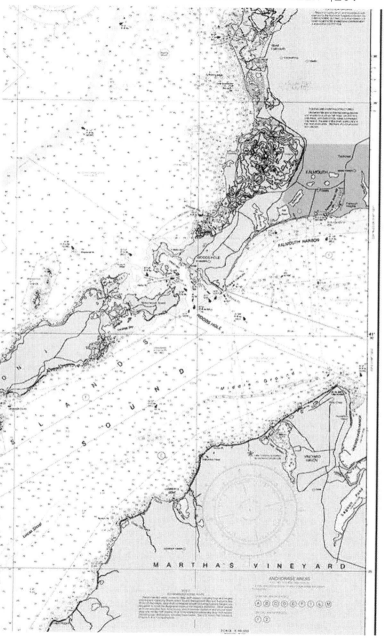

Greg and Abby something or other. "Hi! I'm Janice, but everyone calls me 'Daisy.' Skip and I were so impressed with your boat handling skills. You made it look so easy!!" Greg and Abby modestly attributed their smooth tie-up to vessel design though anyone could see that it wasn't that.

"We wondered if you could lend us a large pot to cook up some lobsters we bought off a boat this morning." Daisy asked a suddenly flustered Skip if they had one big enough. He couldn't get down into the cabin fast enough as me mumbled, "Sure, let me look." He didn't dare let Daisy look because he suddenly had a recollection of stashing a small, neat stack of wrapped cash in a pot recently to use to pay off some more of John's bills. He was right. Not thinking clearly he removed the stack and stuffed it in a pocket of his cargo shorts while he simultaneously almost leaped up into the cockpit. He wanted to present the large enameled steel pot ASAP and get rid of the two pests who had descended on him out of nowhere. To his surprise, this Greg and Abby were now seated in the cockpit having been invited aboard for drinks and apps by Daisy. "Sweet Jesus, how does this crap happen to me?" he thought. "Make yourselves comfortable, I'll have your drinks up in a moment and we've got some nice cheeses to go along with some crackers and smoked oysters." Skip figured this offer would buy him more time to think things through and though Daisy eyed him a bit suspiciously she became quickly absorbed in a discussion about the merits of sailing in the area.

Returning to the cockpit, Skip feared hearing something like "Hey, aren't you the guy who…" He didn't ask any questions of the guests for fear of stumbling over something but Daisy did. Fortunately the conversation was along the lines of where they had been cruising and where they might go and had not gotten down to personal information sharing. With luck it wouldn't and the visitors would be off to cook their damned crustaceans. But of course this is not the way things work for Skip. Their newfound iends, Gregarious Greg and Amiable Abby, had several extra lobsters and "Won't you please join us aboard tonight for very fresh seafood?" was answered with, "We'd be delighted to!" when one guest truly would not be delighted to at all.

After the tri people had retreated with the pot, Daisy, asked Rick if he were feeling OK. "A bit too much sun," was the best he could manage. But Daisy was still exuberant about the day and whole trip, actually. She was so innocently excited to share the evening with another couple about their own age that Skip decided that he just had to suck it up and make the best night of it he could, avoiding the land mines that he knew were there, and if need be, lie as skillfully as he had learned how to over the last few months. It was all getting rather tedious but there was no way around it.

When they boarded *La Sirenetta* it was obvious that the owners were experienced sailors. There was a neatness that spoke both of personality traits and of concern for safety. A quick glance around at life rafts, man overboard slings, radar, EPIRBS, self-steering rig, neatly coiled lines, color coded halyards, and labeled cleats informed Skip and Daisy that they would enjoy coastal or blue water sailing with Greg and Abby. Inside the cavernous main salon was a comfortable home at sea. Greg and Abby gave a nice tour of "The Little Mermaid" which was the translation of the Italian name of the boat.

Over a fabulous dinner of seawater steamed lobsters, mussels, corn on the cob and potatoes, sailing experiences were exchanged. To Skip's consternation Daisy volunteered that he had spent much time sailing in the Virgin Islands and Caribbean. But the dreaded questions never came that would trip Skip up. It turned out that their hosts had never been to St. Thomas but had recently purchased the boat at deep discount because it had been destined to be delivered to a charter company in the Virgin Islands that had gone out of business. Apparently a freak early season tropical storm down there, named *Abby* of all things, had wiped out the assets of the charter business. A Baltimore non-sailing doctor had actually owned the boat which he was going to use as a tax write off, but with no immediate prospect of cash flow his accountant advised that he quickly "divest." They had picked up *La Sirenetta* in Annapolis where they lived and learned to sail as kids. The two met while crewing on an Annapolis to Bermuda class winner and married shortly after. That was ten years ago and this cruise and new boat constituted their 10th wedding anniversary celebration. Over the years the couple had cruised and raced scores of top mono and multihulls, most fairly new but some old classics, too. That explained their apparently choreographed arrival to Hadley Harbor.

The evening dinner was very pleasant as it so often is for boaters in these circumstances. The men adjourned to the stern for cigars and talk while the women enjoyed coffee and conversation accompanied by Daisy's signature oatmeal raisin cookies. Abby was fascinated by Daisy's business and Greg asked for contact info in the event that they wanted to cruise to the Virgins someday. As they said their goodbyes under a brilliant canopy of stars overhead they all honestly hoped that their courses would intersect someday. Early next morning *La Sirenetta* would flush through the Cape Cod Canal to Boston then Maine while later in the day *Spray* would be flushed through Woods Hole into Vineyard Sound.

THE DISTANCE ACROSS VINEYARD SOUND TO MARTHA'S Vineyard was not very great. But as it turned out there was no place to anchor or moor in Oak Bluffs or Vineyard Haven according to the harbormasters who had been hailed at both places, the height of the summer cruising season being upon them. Daisy even got on the VHF to some friends who were live-aboards in Edgartown who described the crowding there, too, as "zoo like." Nantucket was out of sailing range for the day. But Daisy said she had an idea. She disappeared below where she was occasionally glimpsed at the nav station with a rolled chart and large scale chartbook. "Are you positive you only draw four and a half feet, Skip?" "Positive" "Then here is our new heading to West Chop."

From West Chop you could round into Vineyard Haven but Daisy instructed Skip to run up the shore of Martha's Vineyard in the opposite direction. In her own fetching bikini, Daisy made her way up to the bow with binoculars. "We're going to have to take in sails and motor up a very narrow channel about a half mile up ahead." "I see nothing!" "Have a little faith, Skip," she said with a smile. Two low breakwaters materialized which were preceded by lots of white submerged sand with a greenish cast. That meant one thing to Skip: shoaling. He zoomed in on the cockpit GPS to get more info and what he got disturbed him. "Hey, Daisy! It says five feet of water at the entrance!!" "So you said you draw four and a half. What's the problem? Once you get over the shoal it quickly goes to ten feet. Tide's about half and coming in." A large lobster boat, whose skipper obviously had local knowledge, inserted itself in line with the channel just ahead of *Spray*. It did not slow down at all. "Follow that boat, Skip!" He did, but at a crawl, just in case. It was disconcerting for Skip to see people quahogging on either side of the channel, only yards away from *Spray*, with water only up to their waists. But just as it appeared that the boat would ground, the water turned darker, the depth sounder registered 10 feet, and then they were in the protective confines of Lake Tashmoo. From that point on there were no worries about the depth of the water and Daisy directed Skip to an anchorage close by a dinghy dock.

In a few minutes they had smoothly dropped anchor and backed down on it. Not as impressive a job as they had seen with the tri the day before, but not bad, either. Daisy returned from the bow with a big grin on her face. Entering the cockpit she raised her hand to a "High Five" position. Their palms cracked loudly. "We make a pretty good team, don't we, Skip?" "Yes, we certainly do!!

A STRAIGHT ROAD RAN FROM THE DINGHY DOCK RIGHT into Vineyard Haven. The two sailors enjoyed the 20 minute walk as most boaters do when ambulation has been restricted to the confines of a vessel. The first order of business was finding a good lunch spot. A clam shack on the water with a great view filled the bill. Both ordered BLT's and chowder. The latter was ordered somewhat reluctantly, the waitress informing them that it was not a clear chowder as they had hoped, and quipping that, "Y'all must be from Rhode Island to ask!" They laughed and said they would give the Vineyard version of Boston chowder a try, though neither thought they would be much impressed. Real Rhode Islanders preferred what others referred to as "dishwater with potatoes" which devotees knew allowed you to savor the real taste of clams. They might try a good red chowder for a change of pace but the tasteless white glue, thickened with flour enough to stand up a knife in and passed off by Bostonians as the "real thing" was usually to be avoided. To their surprise, Skip and Daisy found that the house version wasn't bad, being of the very thin white variety.

As they were paying their bill, Daisy heard her name being called. She looked around to see and old college friend sitting at a table by the door with her significant other. Introductions were made and the two women did a quick catch up since they apparently saw each other several times a year. As luck would have it the couple was going off island for their vacation. They lived on the Vineyard, but for a few weeks each summer they rented their cottage out for "big bucks" to defray the smaller bucks they earned living on the island year round. Generously, Walt and Deb offered the use of their pickup truck for as many days as Daisy and Skip would need it. All they had to do was drop them off at the ferry, and leave the truck in the long-term lot when they were done with it.

After bringing them to the ferry and thanking their benefactors, the couple took a late afternoon drive with Daisy at the wheel, first stopping in Oak Bluffs at a little stand for an ice cream. It was very corny, but they then took a spin on the nearby "Flying Horses Carousel," an island favorite, mounting adjacent steeds. Daisy reached out for and got two brass rings and no five-year-old little girl would have looked happier. An observer would have seen two young adults laughing and having a good time, perhaps on their honeymoon. From there they stopped for penny candy which they ate from their small, brown paper bags as they made their way up a path to the Methodist Campground with its many delightfully quaint gingerbread style homes. "I think I could live in something simple like that with you," observed Daisy. She was looking at a little gem by the Tabernacle. It had a wraparound porch with old wicker rocking chairs, window boxes full of several varieties of flowers in the height of bloom, beautiful old stained glass windows by the entryway, and a bedroom balcony from which hung from a bracket a brand new American flag that still had creases from being packed in its box. "I don't think that I could." Daisy shot him a look that showed that she was very hurt by the reply.

Catching this unexpected emotion, Skip added quickly, "But we could live in that one," pointing to the one next door that was equally cute but primarily blue in color. Daisy looked it over. She laughed, realizing that he was definitely not the type of guy that would choose to live in a hot pink house, no matter how adorable it may be to her. Placing her hand in his, she then turned toward him, stood on her toes and kissed him very tenderly. He pulled her tightly to his chest and kissed her back till he almost fainted. "Daisy, if that is the only way I could have you, in that house, then I think I could come to like the color very much." Both now knew that they were playing a new game.

BEFORE LEAVING OAK BLUFFS, DAISY SUGGESTED that they call John. She thought that he might even be a little upset that they had not. The fact was that John was glad that he had not heard from them. He wanted them to become absorbed in each other, figured that they probably would be, but was cautious with that hope since Daisy's track record with men to date had not been all that good. He had been busy while they were away, getting the painting and varnish done on Mr. Harrison's boat which now looked pretty sharp. Pretty sharp indeed! He felt the pride he always felt when he nearly finished a project like this. But he was also, as usual, a bit sad that his work was nearly over, though of course that was the goal. He never could explain this contradiction to himself.

On the call Daisy brought John up to date with what they had been doing and she used the words, "And you remember..." a lot. She told him that Skip was a very good sailor, they were having a lot of fun, that the vacation was doing her a lot of good, concluding with, "I miss you and will see you in a few days!" "That Skip is quite a guy, isn't he?" was the last thing John said to her, which seemed a bit strange to Daisy.

TAKING ADVANTAGE OF HAVING THE TRUCK, THE CREW of *Spray* took a leisurely drive up Lamberts Cove Road, eventually coming to the quaint fishing village of Menemsha. Walking around the venerable docks they watched a good-sized swordfish being unloaded from a well-used, old wooden boat about 35' long. The catch was placed in a bed of crushed ice and then covered with more. "Can we buy some swordfish today?" "Yes you can, pretty lady, but not cut from this one. It's promised to the Pier restaurant in Edgartown for the catch of the day. But Pete in the market over there will cut you a steak or two from a smaller one we just brought in, too." Daisy thanked the burly Old Salt who was a fair facsimile of the Gloucester Fisherman. The choice cuts were iced down in a battered cooler that had been bouncing around the truck bed. Once the evening dinner was secured Daisy and Skip drove up to Aquinnah, the former Gay Head, and took in the beautiful view of the Atlantic Ocean, Vineyard Sound and Buzzards Bay in the distance. All the waters were plied by a variety of watercraft, large and small, commercial and pleasure. The cliffs, still considered sacred ground by the Wampanoag tribe members who still live in the area, were spectacular though Daisy remarked how she thought Block Island's were a tad more impressive. Skip wasn't so sure about that but for the usual manly reasons agreed that certainly that was so. On the beach and in the waves below he noticed and mentioned that all of the people seemed to be naked. "A native custom," quipped Daisy with a grin.

YOU CAN'T BEAT FRESH SWORDFISH PREPARED ON A stern rail mounted charcoal grill. It was accompanied by assorted fresh vegetables bought at a roadside stand they found on the way back to Tashmoo. Delicious local oysters had preceded the all-island feast, their shells then ceremoniously committed to the harbor waters to continue the circle of life. Just another beautiful day and night of cruising in New England thought Skip.

The relaxed crew of *Spray* slept much later than usual owing to the fact that the boat was tucked in under a tree-topped rise that effectively eliminated any view of the rising sun. But also the fact that both felt safe, and free from the usual concerns of daily life had quite a bit to do with the pleasant extra hour of bunk time. Fleetingly it occurred to both that they would have to get back to reality soon. But neither gave words to that thought for fear of tainting the remaining days afloat. After a tasty breakfast of canned Hungarian bacon and toasted Portuguese Sweet Bread, *Spray* was made ready for the sail to the mystical Cuttyhunk. The name itself conjured up indescribable anticipation.

JOHN TURNED IN TO BED EARLY AFTER THE CALL FROM "the kids." He had not been feeling his best since his two helpers had departed but he couldn't quite put his finger on the cause. Stress, of course had something to do with it. "God damn that Stilwell and the horses he hangs around with." He would see about moving up his annual physical and maybe get a handle on why he had been feeling so tired. He was thinking that maybe he wouldn't jump into another project too quickly. Just puttering around the house and catching up on some repairs and remodeling might do him some good. Yes, that sounded like a good plan. When Daisy and Skip got back, he might talk it over with them. Mr. Harrison's boat was just about finished since Ed had had some extra down time and helped out more than he thought he would be able to with the rest of John's crew gone.

THe next morning John felt the worst he had ever felt. At least the worst he had felt in a couple of decades. His breathing was labored. He felt nauseous. He thought that if he could just get up and move around a bit he would certainly feel better. But he was wrong. As he sat on the edge of the bed to catch his breath he fainted. He came to with hot sun shining on his face. Struggling to open his eyes he almost fainted again with the intense brightness. For the sun to be reaching him at that place on the fLoor, it had to be about noon. THat meant he had been there for about six hours. Maybe thirty. No it was just six, his barely functioning mind told him.

Despite being a thick-headed Swamp Yankee, it was clear to John that he could not drive to the hospital but he was sure that he had to go. As foggy as his mind was he also was thinking that he didn't want anyone to find out about this episode until he had it figured out himself. Human nature being what it was he knew that when you had a spell like this, well-meaning people would always begin any future conversation with a conspiratorial, "Well how are you really feeling now, John." And not so well meaning people would start scheming about how one's weakness could be turned into an advantage for themselves.

He had the private number of a new young doc in town whose "S" class boat had sprung a plank. A few days before he begged John to see what he could do with it so that he wouldn't miss a classic boat regatta that he wanted to race in. John was very busy (When wasn't he?) but he slipped in a couple of short sister ribs to get the new-comer through the season. Doc Crouse paid him well and said that he still owed John "big time" for making time to do the repair. "If you ever need a favor, Mr. Wilcox, just give me a call."

John had not been in a hospital except for a few emer-gency room calls usual for men who worked with their hands. He didn't like being there overnight but he knew he was dealing with something serious. He made Doc Crouse swear not to tell anybody anything yet. It wasn't a sure thing and a few more specialists had to be consulted, but it looked like John had some heart blockages that could not be taken care of the easy ways. They were thinking a by-pass operation may be needed. Not a good time for that but then again, was there ever a good time? John would have to take it easy until the diagnosis was complete and a plan was formulated. But he did not want to let the cat out of the bag yet, especially with respect to the kids. Daisy would zoom home if she heard anything about this and that was the last thing John wanted. She belonged where she was right then, having fun with a decent guy of her own age, despite what she had said to him about this sort of thing a dozen times in the past.

Of course it was Daisy's life, and on the one hand she had a right to live it the way she wanted. On the other hand, young people were stupid in general. Most smartened up on their own sooner or later but a few could profit from listening to sometimes cranky old-timers who loved them. At the very least they could shorten their stupid phase of life. It was time for Daisy to settle down. She had everything going for her. She had her health, a good education, a good business, she lived in one of God's nicest little places. She should be enjoying all that with somebody. He was a pretty good judge of character and though John still had some questions about Skip, actually quite a few, he felt that he would be satisfied with the answers if he knew them. Yes, Daisy could do a lot worse than hooking Skip. And Skip couldn't do any better than netting Daisy.

As John turned a few more of these thoughts over in his mind he felt himself getting very tired. He felt himself drifting off into a pleasant sleep. He didn't remember taking any medication that might cause drowsiness but maybe there was something in those clear tubes that connected him to those bags of liquid hanging above his head. "Maybe I'll feel a lot better when I wake up," he thought as he started to nod off. He dimly heard some annoying sounds in the background. And he sensed, more than saw, a blinking light or two. If only these little aggravations would stop, he could be dead asleep in a heartbeat.

WHY CANAPITSET?" SKIP POKED HIS HEAD OUT THE companionway after perusing the troublesome looking chart data while Daisy was at the helm. Daisy explained that the current on the Buzzard Bay approach to Cuttyhunk would have been hard against them, they were motoring through a glassy sea with no wind ripples in sight and no wind in the forecast for hours, and the Eldridge current charts showed slackness in the channel when they would arrive at its Vineyard Sound entrance. "But it still looks a bit shallow and there seems to be quite a few rocks flanking the channel." Skip looked dubious. "The tide will be at maximum or I wouldn't even suggest going through, Skip, and I know the area well."

The passage was "interesting" for Skip, peak tide and slack current notwithstanding. He let Daisy take *Spray* through slowly and went up to the bow to act as lookout, getting a very firm grasp of the forestay, just in case. To the east was Nashawena's scrubby shore with a couple of black cows incongruously strolling towards the water's edge. To the west was an appendage of Cuttyhunk with what looked like an abandoned or at least a very seldom used airstrip. All around were rocks that could ruin your day. But before Skip could dwell on this uncomfortable thought they were clear through the gauntlet, with Penikese Island straight ahead and the entrance to Cuttyhunk Pond to port. Rounding up to the entry bell, *Spray* passed close by the anchored *Tabor Boy*, off which were diving and around which were swimming a score of pleasantly noisy teenagers enjoying their summer school cruise. The gaff-rigged schooner was a bit too large to enter the inner harbor.

Spray continued up the narrow channel past an old red-roofed Coast Guard station to port. After securing a mooring on the northern edge of the mooring field, sails were furled and the decks and cockpit were splashed down with seawater. They had accumulated a layer of salt over the past few days that had made them quite dull looking; even a saltwater rinse down made for an improvement. A brief swim was followed by a nice solar shower and then the crew settled back to have Dark 'n' Stormies while watching the parade of yachts fill in the empty area around them. The island rose up about 150' and the topography reminded Skip of many of the Caribbean islands he had visited. Skip and Daisy were feeling kind of mellow. It had been a wonderful week afloat and soon it would be over. A well-padded launch almost noiselessly pulled up to the starboard side of *Spray,* forestalling any more end-of-cruise thoughts. To Skip's surprise it was a raw-bar boat with trays of iced oysters and littlenecks ready for shucking. They took a dozen of each along with cocktail sauce, some extra horseradish and lemon wedges, enjoying the last of the bi-valves as the reddening sun made its way down to the horizon. Skip noticed that Daisy was grinning like a chimp. "What are you smiling about?" Skip challenged good-naturedly. "Oh, nothing!" She giggled again, then gave a cute little snort. That made her giggle some more, prompting another inquiry as to the source of her amusement. "Well, if it is true that libido is increased by eating raw shellfish, then I'd say we're in trouble. Now it was Skip's turn to grin like a chimp. "Real trouble!" was all Skip could manage as he reached for her hand and led the way down into the cabin.

They would leave the exploration of Cuttyhunk until the following day.

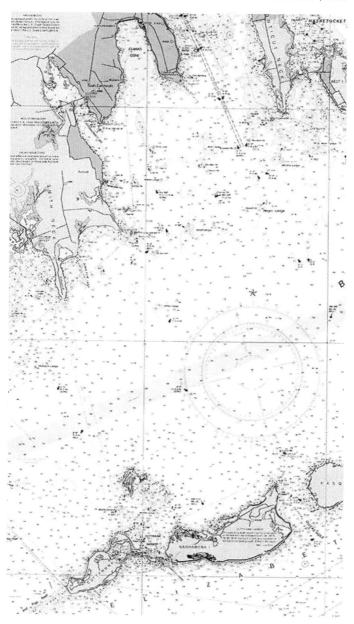

CHAPTER EIGHTEEN

After securing the inflatable at the dinghy dock Skip and Daisy found a coffee shack on the little fishing pier nearby. They then made their way upward to the old phone booth that in relatively recent times still had a crank phone, probably one of the last in America. Passing the Methodist church to the right and Historical Association to the left they had to pause as a half dozen deer before them gracefully leapt over the low stone wall flanking the road to Lookout Hill. The view from the top was gorgeous and the range exceptional. They could easily make out the spires of Newport's Pell Bridge, perhaps 30 miles away.

The charm in Cuttyhunk was in how remote it seemed and how far back it was frozen in time. No Starbucks, no cars, no traffc lights, no CVS. No nothing! Well actually there were a few gift shops and a restaurant or two but the island doesn't attract the kind of people lured to Las Vegas' bright lights or Fifth Avenue's glitzy stores. The soldiers stationed on Cutty during WW II to watch for enemy subs would not notice that a whole lot had changed over the years.

Turning to stroll back, Skip stopped and scanned the view for 360 degrees. He took it all in. At a glance he could see the point at which he entered Rhode Island waters from Long Island Sound, what seemed like forever ago. So much happened to him since then! As he shielded his eyes from the sun he was pretty sure he could make out the smudge of Block Island and then he could clearly see the entire route sailed by *Spray* in the last few days. Daisy found herself doing the same thing. "We've come a long way, haven't we?"

THey looked into each other's eyes for several moments. "I love you Daisy!" "And I love you, too, Skip!" The kiss was tender and long, the embrace longer and warm. Slowly they separated and walked down the hill, hand in hand, both a little weak kneed. Both lost in thought, trying to figure how this was all going to play out. Their relationship was way different from what it had been when they left Wickford.

The rest of the afternoon was spent beach combing. Daisy found a good handful of white, brown and green sea glass in the sand where small waves were breaking and then she picked a large bouquet of very blue chicory flowers that were obviously quite tolerant of the saltwater. Skip salvaged several expensive looking lures and a half buried piece of rotten wood all hidden just above the high tide line, along with crinkly, dry seaweed, well worn and bleached shells, as well as the occasional Mermaid's Purse. Attached to the board was a six-inch cleat that was in good shape. Scratching the bottom of the base he confirmed that it was a bronze casting. He pried it free of the splintering wood and showed it to Daisy. She laughed as she watched him caress it and then slip it in his pocket. "Guess you share that Swamp Yankee gene with John!" Skip laughed, as well. It took a minute, though, before it hit him that John may actually have been the source of that gene.

Returning to the boat Daisy went below. Both she and Skip got a tad too much sun for one day. The boat was a

little stuffy so Skip opened the forward hatch to drive a
little cool air through the cabin while Daisy turned a Ma-
son jar into a nice vase for the chicory flowers which she
then set on the table. "That sea air feels so good! Mind if
I take a little nap?" Skip didn't mind at all. He needed to
think about a few things, anyway, and decided that a good
way to do it was while fishing with the new lures he had
found. He grabbed a rod and five gallon pail out of the
lazarette, said goodbye, and took the inflatable to a beach
a couple of hundred yards away near the base of the channel breakwater.

What occupied Skip's mind again was no longer
whether he should tell the truth to Daisy about his sor-
did sounding past, but rather when and how he would do
it. However he envisioned the confession it always had a
messy ending. But it had to be done. And he had to do it
for his grandfather's sake as well. John should know that
he still has a grandson, one who loves him dearly. Both
John and Rick needed closure. "Rick!" That was the first
time that he referred to himself by his real name since
leaving New York.

He took a few casts with the Rebel lure into some
disturbed water in the middle of the channel. There was
something there, but not on the surface. Reeling in he
made up his mind about what he was going to do. The day
after they returned to Wickford he would lay out everything to Gramps and Daisy together. He could only hope
that they would understand. Maybe it was time to start
praying again that everything would turn out all right. But
he knew it wouldn't turn out all right immediately. Besides
possible problems with Daisy and Gramps there were
other complex issues to be addressed. What should he do
with the money? What should he do with the boat? And
were the police back in St. Thomas going to believe him?

He took a few more casts. There was something out
there interested in his little plastic fish. He flicked the
lure up high above his targeted area and let it come down
with a smack to get the attention of whatever was swirling
around. Then he let the lure just sink to the bottom. Wham!

Wham, wham!! The line stretched tight and started to dance around. He gave a tug to set the hook, keeping the line taut, reeling in steadily. With the rod tip up, he let the fish take a little line now and then to tire itself out. The water was very clear so that he could soon see his quarry a few feet below the surface. And his quarry could see him, too, reacting to that frightening sight with a last ditch, urgent and forceful effort to escape. The fish came to the surface, splashing mightily and then he just quit. Skip reeled him in gently onto a flat rock and deftly grabbed him. It was a beautiful Black Sea Bass that would make a nice island-style ceviche. Skip looked the bass in the eye and the bass seemed, as much as a fish could, to be looking back. His gills were slowly opening and closing the way they do just before a fish gives it up. Gently Skip removed the hook and as he was about to consign the fish to the plastic pail he changed his mind, carefully releasing it in the water by his foot. "Live another day, fish!" The bass wobbled away slowly for a few moments then in a blur darted to the deep water, perhaps with the thought that it was best to get far away from the strange air dweller fast, before it changed its mind.

Skip made his way back across the uneven stones of the breakwater to the inflatable, his mind returning to his quandary. He felt that he had as much resolve as he was ever going to be able to muster to carry out his plan to reveal the truth to Daisy and John.

By the time Skip boarded *Spray*, Daisy was up and about. "So where is dinner?"

"Looks like it got away. I was in the mood for that canned ham and some beans tonight, anyway!" Skip smiled as he thought about the liberated fish. Maybe it would return the favor of its freedom by putting in a good word for its liberator with someone on high.

THE RETURN TO NARRAGANSETT BAY THE FOLLOWING morning was a pleasant one. The water in Cuttyhunk harbor was flat calm as they departed and the low, yellow rays of the sun illuminated everything in a flattering way. The mirrored reflection of the boats in the water could not be visually differentiated from the actual image except that it was upside down.

By the time they were abeam of Sow and Pigs Reef the wind was stirring enough to rest the iron jib. But the light seas and chop were such that one could still see more sea life than was usually the case. A sunfish was lolling around on the surface. It looked like a shark that another shark ate the back half of, its large dorsal fin flip-flopping from side to side. Miles after that sighting a pod of large turtles was sunning and could easily be mistaken for rocks exposed by a low tide. And as they approached R "6" off Newport's Brenton Reef a school of small bluefin tuna exuberantly exploded into the air around *Spray*.

The waters around Fort Adams were teeming with boats. Opti dinghys, 12 Meters, mega yachts, schooners, lobster boats were all well represented. As they motored up to a mooring near Beacon Rock that Daisy had a standing invitation to use, Skip thought of his recent escapade in the area with Ed and again was thankful that nobody was hurt. Apparently all had worked out fine as a result of the duo's efforts, at least for John. The grapevine reported that Stilwell had rather suddenly dropped his marina plans. He went to some lengths to make sure that the grapevine widely distributed this message, perhaps to let the nameless boat torching perpetrators know that he did not need further inducements to stop hassling a certain old man. Skip also heard that *Booby Trap* was not covered by insurance because the marine surveyor hired by Stilwell had let his license expire. That was good news because it would have been a shame if Stilwell ended up with a better boat as a result of the fire. Guys like him would take that as a sign that being bad always pays off.

Daisy noticed a grin on Skip's face as he went forward with the boat hook to pick up the mooring lines. "What are you smiling about?" she asked mischievously. "Can't a guy smile just because it's a beautiful day and he's with a beautiful girl?"

The following day they would be heading home. After *Spray* was secured Daisy suggested that they quickly clean up, put on their best "outfts" and go ashore to one of Newport's acclaimed restaurants to celebrate the end of their very successful cruise.

Those already aboard the launch that came to pick them up could not help but remark to themselves that an extremely good-looking couple was about to join them. The man and woman had perfect tans, wore stylish sunglasses, were slim and trim, and their windblown, sun lightened hair looked like it had been coiffed by a very good salon. One of the women in the launch discreetly leaned over to tell another that she was pretty sure that these two were famous movie stars trying not to attract attention to themselves. "Good luck with that," was the instant whispered reply.

The launch disgorged its passengers on a dock close by Thames Street which was crowded, as it usually was in the summer, perhaps a bit more so because a cruise ship was moored offshore. Skip and Daisy joined the sidewalk throng and enjoyed a bit of people watching and window shopping. They were surrounded by yachting types, smartly dressed New Yorkers, and the expected family vacationers, all enjoying a perfect end of summer day. Skip felt good to be part of that crowd.

But Skip's comfortable moment dissipated in an instant. A short way ahead of him was a man he knew well from St. Thomas, purposefully striding in his direction. Had Skip already been recognized? He reached for Daisy's hand, hoping to guide her across the street and out of the way but the traffic would not allow it. In desperation he pulled her towards the closest souvenir shop, but could not get through the door and off the sidewalk because of a line of people exiting. As Daisy was about to ask what they were doing, a deep voice boomed out, "Well I'll be damned! If it isn't Rick Thornton! I thought that was you! What are you doing here? And who is this sweet young lady? You always had an eye for the good ones, Rick, Old Buddy."

The ambush was complete. There was no place to run or hide. Skip's throat went dry, his knees shook, and his face flushed so that he must have looked like a beet. For an uncomfortable moment for all three of them, no words came out of his mouth. "Woody" Coughlin picked up the slack though, introducing himself to Daisy and then without taking a breath explaining that he was picking up a boat in Newport to deliver to St. Thomas. "That damn storm wiped out our fleet, yours too from what I hear. I didn't see you or any of your crew afterwards and wondered what happened to you, JJ and that snake, Jimmy Fox who still owes me a couple of hundred bucks."

While wondering what it would take to shut Woody up, Skip realized it didn't matter any more. The damage was done. At the mention of the name "Jimmy Fox" Daisy's hand slipped from Skip's and he was aware of her drifting away behind him. "What's up with her?" Skip found his voice and managed to reply flatly, "Long day, she's just tired out."

"What a nightmare this is going to be," thought Skip. The nightmare resulting from the chance meeting would materialize a bit later, but there was much good news from Woody, too. In fifteen minutes Skip found out that he was not a wanted man, Mean Dean was dead and buried and everybody seemed happy, and the cute girl who smacked him in the head as Dean beat and raped her had recovered from her injuries and was safely back home somewhere. Coughlin even asked if Rick wanted to help him with the boat delivery back to St. Thomas. Rick declined.

"Well, say bye to your cute little friend," and then somewhat abruptlyWoody was on his way to meet his partial crew at a nearby watering hole.

Clearly the post tropical storm chaos on St. THomas had beneficially obscured a lot of issues relating to Skip, JJ and Jimmy. One thing that was becoming apparent was that a connection involving Jimmy, Mean Dean and a lot of money had existed. Something told Skip to be very careful about looking into that matter, though. And he would have to decide later whether or not to tie up loose ends with his former employer. Of more immediate concern was smoothing things over with Daisy. Again Skip felt the frustration that had haunted him all his life…as one of his problem gets solved, another immediately emerges to take its place.

SKIP LOOKED ALL AROUND THE AREA WHERE HE LAST saw Daisy but there was no sign of her. He went down side streets, into nearby stores and down by the waterfront. THen he did it all again. And again. After two hours he went back to the water taxi dock and caught a launch back to the mooring, dreading every moment of the upcoming encounter. Boarding *Spray*, he called her name nervously First, then frantically. No answer. He went below and on the chart table he saw the note, weighed down in place by a pair of parallel rulers. He read it three times.

"You are a bastard! I don't know what game you are playing with me Skip, Jimmy, Rick or whoever you are but I quit. I feel so stupid that I actually trusted you and I hate to admit it but I thought I was in love with you. You made a fool of me! Damn you!!! Was it funny to you to be back here like some kind of ghost? Why were you hiding from John all these years? What is wrong with you? You are truly very sick. I NEVER want to see you again. NEVER. Do not try to contact me. Disappear. I won't tell John about any of this because it would kill him. Just leave now before you hurt him, too."

Skip scooted up the companionway hoping to make it to the ladder gap in the stern rail. But he only just made it to the cockpit when he vomited and then dry heaved for several minutes. His eyes were filled with tears, bile burned his throat and he felt like screaming and crying. He knew it would come to something like this. It always did for him. The Greek Tragedy thing. He was almost there in resolving things with Daisy and John. If only he told them the truth earlier. But a little voice told him that that was not so. Whenever he revealed the whole story the fireworks would have been ignited. He was just doomed.

But having just found out that he never even had to leave St. Thomas after all, nobody was looking for him, and he didn't need to hide behind so many lies made his fall out with Daisy unbearable. Even the money would bring him no pleasure. It was his free and clear. Jimmy was gone. Mean Dean was dead. It wasn't as if Mean Dean was going to leave ill gotten gains in a will to anyone. Who would Skip return the money to anyway?

THere was no getting around it. Skip's life sucked and always would. THere was only one thing to do. Sail back to Wickford, try to tell Gramps his story and hope for his understanding, say goodbye, and then maybe go back to St. Thomas. Daisy was lost forever and Skip's presence in Rhode Island would only ruin the relationship that Gramps had with Daisy.

SPRAY GLIDED INTO DOCK SPACE BEHIND JOHN'S HOUSE, coming to a gentle stop as she grounded on some soft silt. Skip had noticed that the tide was extra low when he passed the breakwater at the entrance to the harbor. Securing the boat, Skip surveyed the area. He did not need to have a scene with Daisy. And he admitted to himself that trying to explain himself to this fiery redhead had no chance of working. Hard as it would be, he would not even try to and he was going to have to move on for everybody's sake.

He walked up to the door and called for John. He then yanked the lanyard of the bronze bell a few times but nobody responded. One last check of the garage with no result and he returned to the boat. It was early evening and it was not as if John was expecting them back. John probably went out for dinner, hopefully not with Daisy. Skip wanted to tell his story first, express his sorrow at the way things turned out, thank him, and be on his way.

The evening slipped into night. Skip opened another can of beans to go with the leftover canned ham. He had the last beer aboard with his dinner and then mixed an especially strong Dark 'N Stormy which he sipped slowly in the cockpit while he relived his first day in Wickford when he learned that he still had a grandfather. "So much has happened to me," he thought, "So much." Another Dark 'N Stormy made him melancholy. He dozed, waking up to see if there were any lights on in the house. There weren't but there might have been while he had drifted off. He made his way to his bunk thinking that he would get a good night's sleep and deal with things with a fresh mind the following day. But sleep he did not, for lots of reasons, not the least of which was the faint scent of Daisy in the sheets.

Awakened in the morning by the sound of a truck, Skip slipped on some clothes and poked his head up the hatch. It was Ed and Coyote and they were coming down to the dock. "Oh, you're back. Saw Daisy yesterday afternoon. She's holding up pretty well, considering." "Great," thought Rick, now the whole town thinks I'm a son of a bitch. "Ed, there is a lot more to the story than you heard." There was a pause. "Actually Skip, I didn't hear anything from Daisy. I was the one who told her." A bit slow to catch on Skip only managed, "I guess we're not talking about the same thing."

And they weren't. But Ed filled him in about John being hospitalized a few days before and then suffering a massive heart attack in the hospital that was so bad they rushed him up to the cardiac center in Providence where he had an emergency by-pass operation. Of course John didn't want to tell anybody, least of all Skip and Daisy. "That stubborn old Swamper probably thought he would just sneak back down here in a few days and we wouldn't notice that he had what looks like a zipper on his chest from those 32 staples they closed him up with."

After telling Skip that John's prognosis was decent, Ed told him to take his truck up to Providence.

J OHN WAS ALERT AND SEEMED VERY GLAD TO SEE SKIP who was more than a little intimidated by all the tubes and wires hooked up to his grandfather. He asked about the trip and Skip danced around that for a bit. "More important, how are you feeling, John?" "Better than I was. Doctors say I'll be good as new in a few weeks." John recounted the story for Skip in a way that made it sound that he just sprained his ankle. "That's great......John I, ahh, have something important I must tell you but it can wait a day or two. It's…" Without warning Daisy bounded into the room and stopped short like a cat would that suddenly saw a hated dog sniffing around its food bowl. Two pairs of eyes instantly locked on to each other and though impossible, there was a feeling on the part of Skip that smoke was rising out of the redhead's hair. "What are you doing here? I told you to just disappear. John, don't listen to a word that man says….he is a liar. He lies about everything."

Rick hung his head and then avoided looking at either of them while an unbroken torrent of angry words ricocheted around the room. A nurse popped in from the hallway and asked brightly if everything was all right in the room." They all gave her the look. "Well, OK then. Just keep it light. John really does not need any excitement today."

Need it or not he was about to get some, anyway. Daisy took a deep breath and looked directly at Skip while speaking loudly to John. "Do you know who this really is?" She paused for effect. In a calm and surprisingly clear voice, John replied. "Of course I do, Daisy. It's my grandson...Ricky Thornton." Then he paused for effect. It would be hard to say which of the two young ones was more shocked by the news delivered so matter-of-factly. "I knew it was him the moment I saw him. And when he didn't let on who he was I figured that something truly awful must have happened to him, to make him hide who he was." This last thought had not occurred to Daisy as she analyzed the apparent depravity of Skip's actions over the last couple of days. "I didn't want to scare him away so I just played dumb and hoped I could coax him into sticking around to help me with odd jobs and such until he felt like talking. I didn't even give my own grandson free dockage because I was afraid it would make him suspicious and maybe run beyond my reach. I wasn't about to let that happen." On hearing this Skip fought to maintain his composure. He had thought that he had been the one controlling the situation since he arrived, when all along it was his grandfather.

With emotions barely held in check Skip raised his head to look at Daisy. "I'm going to tell you both everything." Of course it would not be that easy. "Well I don't want to hear anything and neither does John!" With that Daisy took two strides towards the door. She was stopped dead in her tracks by a stern voice. "No, Daisy . . . . You will stay right here and we will both listen to what he has to say and be done with this little drama one way or another before this day is over!" He motioned for her to take a seat.

In a monotone Rick began his story, starting with when he and his mom left Wampanoag Point. When he got to the part about writing so many letters to Daisy, John and his teachers, and never getting a single reply, tears flowed freely down all three faces. John sobbed at hearing about his daughter's death and from both sides of the bed a hand reached out to pat or stroke his shoulder and arms. On and on it went. Rick mentioned how he joined the

Marines because he had no other place to go and how in fact the Corps and those he served with became his family. But he saw things during his time in service that he wished he had never seen and did things he wished he could undo.

After mustering out he stumbled on a yacht delivery job that would take him to St. Thomas, and the tropics became his salvation. For him it was all so magical. It was a place where clear waters, swaying palm trees and warm breezes helped him forget about the past and start his life anew. The work with boats at Constellation Yacht Charters gave him purpose and he enjoyed friendships like he never had growing up in California. The only omissions in Rick's "confession" involved his relationships with women, particularly Sandy in the Mean Dean affair. But he told everything about the encounter with the near hurricane, the loss of Jimmy, the discovery of the money, JJ's dropoff, and Woody Coughlin's revelations at their chance meeting in Newport. When he finished the only sound was the clicking of medical machines and distant hushed and indistinguishable voices in the hallway.

"Well that's it. All of it. I guess I'll be going now Gramps. I didn't intend to trifle with you and I wanted to tell you my story many times and just hug you some days. I do love you and I'm sorry it didn't work out better." Rick slowly stood up to leave.

"You're going no place you damn young fool!" With that John motioned Rick to come to his bedside, his arms stretched out very awkwardly. They hugged gently and tearfully; then John waved the other young fool over to his bedside too. She almost flew out of her chair to join them and the three just carried on sobbing and hugging. The cathartic episode, lasting several minutes, left them all quite exhausted, but each knew without any doubt that from that moment forth their lives would be forever changed for the better.

Poking her head into the room unseen and sensing that what she saw was not bad, the nurse quietly withdrew. As she walked down the hall she heard all three laughing loudly. She wondered what they had suddenly found so funny.

EPILOGUE

J OHN RECOVERED QUICKLY AND WELL FROM HIS SUR-
GERY. AT least it appeared that way to everyone. Truth
was he was skittish about every twinge in his chest
and every little cough because he didn't really believe that
he was back one hundred percent. But eventually he did
and in fact it was true.

Daisy and Skip healed up their wounds of a different
kind, too. Daisy must have apologized a hundred times
for not recognizing "Rick." And when she did unexpectedly discover who he was, she regretted never considering,
like John did, that Skip must have been in a predicament
which though it could not be easily explained, was not due
to any maliciousness or fault in his character.

Daisy would always refer to Rick as "Skip," and when
the priest asked one year after John's release from the hospital, "Do you, Skip, take...." some church attendees swore
that she actually glowed.

After the honeymoon in St. Thomas they returned to Wickford to live happily ever after. About the only ones in town who weren't happy about the way things turned out were quite a few bakery customers of the single male variety.

Rick returned to St. Thomas several times that first year after the wedding to make some things right. But he could not return or make restitution for the old *Pleiades* no matter how hard he tried. The owners of the regrouped Constellation Yacht Charters had already settled with the insurance companies for yacht and facility losses. Rick's *Spray* was a fly in the ointment that they felt should not be removed. And to Skip's surprise and consternation the insurance company also had no interest in repossessing *Spray*. She had been already written off. "So you found this boat just drifting in the ocean after the tropical storm, right?"

"No, I borrowed it and was going to return it..." "So you found this boat just drifting in the ocean after the tropical storm, right?"

"No, I'm telling you, I borrowed it and was going to return it when..."

"So you found this boat just drifting in the ocean after the tropical storm, right?" said the exasperated insurance company lawyer one more time in a theatrically loud voice.

Skip finally got it and said "Right." The company then assisted him in processing a salvage claim to the vessel, resulting in *Pleiades/Spray* legally becoming the property of one Richard Thornton.

A few months after the wedding the Thorntons took up residence at 41°34.12 N, 71°26.75 W. John could not have been happier, the house being too big and too much work for him. He knew that Skip and Daisy would turn it into the seaside "Doll House" that it once had been. When the young couple told him that they would be joined by another tiny one in six months, John cried. He never thought that his later years would turn out to be that good.

A short time after the revelation you could find him on any given night in the old garage, building from memory a cradle that was shaped like a dory he once had as a boy.

IF YOU ARE EVER IN THE HAITIAN SECTION OF FLAT-BUSH IN Brooklyn, you may come across a family run restaurant serving genuine Haitian cuisine that goes by the unlikely name of Thor's Kitchen. Try the *riz colle´aux pois* accompanied by bouillon. And if you ask the always cheerful owner, one Jean Jacques Dessalines, aka "JJ," where the restaurant name came from he will only say, "That's a very long story!" but you'll never get an actual answer. However you will get the deepest, most joyous, laugh you ever heard and then a big smile that will brighten your day.

ACKNOWLEDGEMENTS

Thanks to the "boys" at Points East Publications, especially Nim Marsh and Bob Muggleston, who subtly made me aware that I wasn't getting any younger and that if I wanted to transition from magazine and newspaper article writing to a novel, I should do it right away. Tim Murphy of Portsmouth, Rhode Island made this project real for me by stitching together and formatting what I had written over an extended period of time. And Stillwater River Publication's Steven and Dawn Porter patiently held my hand through the formerly intimidating process of actually producing a book and bringing it to market.

But most of all I would like to thank my wonderful wife, Abigail, for encouraging me to write over the years. Without her counsel and commentary, much material would still be rattling around my head with no outlet.

ABOUT THE AUTHOR

Greg Coppa is the author of hundreds of published works on a very wide range of subjects. The acclaimed Hallmark Hall of Fame movie, *November Christmas*, starring Sam Elliott and John Corbett was based on one of his prize-winning short stories. A lifelong sailor, Greg has extensively cruised the waters of Narragansett Bay, Cape Cod and Long Island Sound. *Second Chances* is his first novel.

Made in the USA
Lexington, KY
14 July 2018